LIEUTENANT HORNBLOWER

Books by C. S. Forester

Novels
PAYMENT DEFERRED
BROWN ON RESOLUTION
PLAIN MURDER
DEATH TO THE FRENCH
THE GUN
THE AFRICAN QUEEN
THE GENERAL
THE EARTHLY PARADISE
THE CAPTAIN FROM CONNECTICUT
THE SHIP
THE SKY AND THE FOREST
RANDALL AND THE RIVER OF TIME
THE NIGHTMARE
THE GOOD SHEPHERD

The ·Hornblower' novels in chronological order
MR. MIDSHIPMAN HORNBLOWER
LIEUTENANT HORNBLOWER
HORNBLOWER AND THE 'ATROPOS'
HORNBLOWER AND THE 'HOTSPUR'
THE HAPPY RETURN
A SHIP OF THE LINE
FLYING COLOURS
THE COMMODORE
LORD HORNBLOWER
HORNBLOWER IN THE WEST INDIES

Omnibus Volumes
THE YOUNG HORNBLOWER
CAPTAIN HORNBLOWER, R.N.
HORATIO HORNBLOWER

History
THE NAVAL WAR OF 1812
HUNTING THE BISMARCK

Travel
THE VOYAGE OF THE 'ANNIE MARBLE'
THE 'ANNIE MARBLE' IN GERMANY

Biography
NELSON

Plays
U 97
NURSE CAVELL
(with C. E. Bechofer Roberts)
Miscellaneous
THE HORNBLOWER COMPANION
MARIONETTES AT HOME

For Children
POO-POO AND THE DRAGONS

C. S. FORESTER

Lieutenant Hornblower

London

MICHAEL JOSEPH

First published by
MICHAEL JOSEPH LTD
26 *Bloomsbury Street*
London W.C.1
FEBRUARY 1952
SECOND IMPRESSION FEBRUARY 1952
THIRD IMPRESSION FEBRUARY 1952
FIRST PUBLISHED IN COLLECTORS' GREENWICH EDITION 1953
REPRINTED APRIL 1957
REPRINTED OCTOBER 1958
REPRINTED JANUARY 1961
REPRINTED MARCH 1966
REPRINTED AUGUST 1968

0718102177

I

LIEUTENANT William Bush came on board H.M.S. *Renown* as she lay at anchor in the Hamoaze and reported himself to the officer of the watch, who was a tall and rather gangling individual with hollow cheeks and a melancholy cast of countenance, whose uniform looked as if it had been put on in the dark and not readjusted since.

"Glad to have you aboard, sir" said the officer of the watch. "My name's Hornblower. The captain's ashore. First lieutenant went for'ard with the bosun ten minutes ago."

"Thank you" said Bush.

He looked keenly round him at the infinity of activities which were making the ship ready for a long period of service in distant waters.

"Hey there! You at the stay tackles! Handsomely! Handsomely! Belay!" Hornblower was bellowing this over Bush's shoulder. "Mr. Hobbs! Keep an eye on what your men are doing there!"

"Aye aye, sir" came a sulky reply.

"Mr. Hobbs! Lay aft here!"

A paunchy individual with a thick grey pigtail came rolling aft to where Hornblower stood with Bush at the gangway. He blinked up at Hornblower with the sun in his eyes; the sunlight lit up the sprouting grey beard on his tiers of chins.

"Mr. Hobbs!" said Hornblower. He spoke quietly, but there was an intensity of spirit underlying his words that surprised Bush. "That powder's got to come aboard before nightfall and you know it. So don't use that tone of voice when replying to an order. Answer cheerfully another time. How are you going to get the men to work if you sulk? Get for'ard and see to it."

Hornblower was leaning a little forward as he spoke; the hands which he clasped behind him served apparently to balance the jutting chin, but his attitude was negligent compared with the fierce intensity with which he spoke, even though he was speaking in an undertone inaudible to all except the three of them.

"Aye aye, sir" said Hobbs, turning to go forward again.

Bush was making a mental note that this Hornblower was a firebrand when he met his glance and saw to his surprise a ghost of a twinkle in their melancholy depths. In a flash of insight he realised that this fierce young lieutenant was not fierce at all, and that the intensity with which he spoke was entirely assumed—it was almost as if Hornblower had been exercising himself in a foreign language.

"If they once start sulking you can't do anything with 'em" explained Hornblower, "and Hobbs is the worst of 'em—acting-gunner, and no good. Lazy as they make 'em."

"I see" said Bush.

The duplicity—play acting—of the young lieutenant aroused a momentary suspicion in Bush's mind. A man who could assume an appearance of wrath and abandon it again with so much facility was not to be trusted. Then, with an inevitable reaction, the twinkle in the brown eyes called up a responsive twinkle in Bush's frank blue eyes, and he felt a friendly impulse towards Hornblower, but Bush was innately cautious and checked the impulse at once, for there was a long voyage ahead of them and plenty of time for a more considered judgment. Meanwhile he was conscious of a keen scrutiny, and he could see that a question was imminent—and even Bush could guess what it would be. The next moment proved him right.

"What's the date of your commission?" asked Hornblower.

"July '96" said Bush.

"Thank you" said Hornblower in a flat tone that conveyed so little information that Bush had to ask the question in his turn.

"What's the date of yours?"

"August '97" said Hornblower. "You're senior to me. You're senior to Smith, too—January '97."

"Are you the junior lieutenant, then?"

"Yes" said Hornblower.

His tone did not reveal any disappointment tnat the newcomer had proved to be senior to him, but Bush could guess at it. Bush knew by very recent experience what it was to be the junior lieutenant in a ship of the line.

"You'll be third" went on Hornblower. "Smith fourth, and I'm fifth."

"I'll be third?" mused Bush, more to himself than to anyone else.

Every lieutenant could at least dream, even lieutenants like Bush with no imagination at all. Promotion was at least theoretically possible; from the caterpillar stage of lieutenant one might progress to the butterfly stage of captain, sometimes even without a chrysalis period as commander. Lieutenants undoubtedly were promoted on occasions; most of them, as was to be expected, being men who had friends at Court, or in Parliament, or who had been fortunate enough to attract the attention of an admiral and then lucky enough to be under that admiral's command at the moment when a vacancy occurred. Most of the captains on the list owed their promotion to one or other of such causes. But sometimes a lieutenant won his promotion through merit—through a combination of merit and good fortune, at least—and sometimes sheer blind chance brought it about. If a ship distinguished herself superlatively in some historic action the first lieutenant might be promoted (oddly enough, that promotion was considered a compliment to her captain) or if the captain should be killed in the action even a moderate success might result in a step for the senior surviving lieutenant who took his place. On the other hand some brilliant boat-action, some dashing exploit on shore, might win promotion for the lieutenant in command—the senior, of course. The chances were few enough in all conscience, but there were at least chances.

But of those few chances the great majority went to the senior lieutenant, to the first lieutenant; the chances of the junior lieutenant were doubly few. So that whenever a lieutenant dreamed of attaining the rank of captain, with its dignity and security and prize money, he soon found himself harking back to the consideration of his seniority as lieutenant. If this next commission of the *Renown's* took her away to some place where other lieutenants could not be sent on board by an admiral with favourites, there were only two lives between Bush and the position of first lieutenant with all its added chances of promotion. Naturally he thought about that; equally naturally he did not spare a thought for the fact that the man with whom he was conversing was divided by four lives from that same position.

"But still, it's the West Indies for us, anyway" said Hornblower philosophically. "Yellow fever. Ague. Hurricanes. Poisonous serpents. Bad water. Tropical heat. Putrid fever. And ten times more chances of action than with the Channel fleet."

"That's so" agreed Bush, appreciatively.

With only three and four years' seniority as lieutenants, respectively, the two young men (and with young men's confidence in their own immortality) could face the dangers of West Indian service with some complacence.

"Captain's coming off, sir" reported the midshipman of the watch hurriedly.

Hornblower whipped his telescope to eye and trained it on the approaching shore boat.

"Quite right" he said. "Run for'ard and tell Mr. Buckland. Bosun's mates! Sideboys! Lively, now!"

Captain Sawyer came up through the entry port, touched his hat to the quarterdeck, and looked suspiciously around him. The ship was in the condition of confusion to be expected when she was completing for foreign service, but that hardly justified the sidelong, shifty glances which Sawyer darted about him. He had a big face and a prominent hawk nose which he turned this way and that as he stood on the quarterdeck. He caught sight of Bush, who came forward and reported himself.

"You came aboard in my absence, did you?" asked Sawyer.

"Yes, sir" said Bush, a little surprised.

"Who told you I was on shore?"

"No one, sir."

"How did you guess it, then?"

"I didn't guess it, sir. I didn't know you were on shore until Mr. Hornblower told me."

"Mr. Hornblower? So you know each other already?"

"No, sir. I reported to him when I came on board."

"So that you could have a few private words without my knowledge?"

"No, sir."

Bush bit off the "of course not" which he was about to add. Brought up in a hard school, Bush had learned to utter no unnecessary words when dealing with a superior officer indulging in the touchiness superior officers might be expected to indulge in. Yet this particular touchiness seemed more unwarranted even than usual.

"I'll have you know I allow no one to conspire behind my back. Mr.—ah—Bush" said the captain.

"Aye aye, sir."

Bush met the captain's searching stare with the composure of innocence, but he was doing his best to keep his surprise out of his expression, too, and as he was no actor the struggle may have been evident.

"You wear your guilt on your face, Mr. Bush" said the captain. "I'll remember this."

With that he turned away and went below, and Bush, relaxing from his attitude of attention, turned to express his surprise to Hornblower. He was eager to ask questions about this extraordinary behaviour, but they died away on his lips when he saw that Hornblower's face was set in a wooden unresponsiveness. Puzzled and a little hurt, Bush was about to note Hornblower down as one of the captain's toadies—or as a madman as well—when he caught sight out of the tail of his eye of the captain's head reappearing above the deck. Sawyer must have swung round when at the foot of the companion and come up again simply for the purpose of catching his officers off their guard discussing him—and Hornblower knew more about his captain's habits than Bush did. Bush made an enormous effort to appear natural.

"Can I have a couple of hands to carry my sea-chest down?" he asked, hoping that the words did not sound nearly as stifled to the captain as they did to his own ears.

"Of course, Mr. Bush" said Hornblower, with a formidable formality. "See to it, if you please, Mr. James."

"Ha!" snorted the captain, and disappeared once more down the companion.

Hornblower flickered one eyebrow at Bush, but that was the only indication he gave, even then, of any recognition that the captain's actions were at all unusual, and Bush, as he followed his sea-chest down to his cabin, realised with dismay that this was a ship where no one ventured on any decisive expression of opinion. But the *Renown* was completing for sea, amid all the attendant bustle and confusion, and Bush was on board, legally one of her officers, and there was nothing he could do except reconcile himself philosophically to his fate. He would have to live through this commission, unless any of the possibilities catalogued by Hornblower in their first conversation should save him the trouble.

II

H.M.S. *Renown* was clawing her way southward under reefed topsails, a westerly wind laying her over as she thrashed along, heading for those latitudes where she would pick up the north-east trade wind and be able to run direct to her destination in the West Indies. The wind sang in the taut weather-rigging, and blustered round Bush's ears as he stood on the starboard side of the quarterdeck, balancing to the roll as the roaring wind sent one massive grey wave after another hurrying at the ship; the starboard bow received the wave first, beginning a leisurely climb, heaving the bowsprit up towards the sky, but before the pitch was in any way completed the ship began her roll, heaving slowly over, slowly, slowly, while the bowsprit rose still more steeply. And then as she still rolled the bows shook themselves free and began to slide down the far side of the wave, with the foam creaming round them; the bowsprit began the downward portion of its arc as the ship rose ponderously to an even heel again, and as she heeled a trifle into the wind with the send of the sea under her keel her stern rose while the last of the wave passed under it, her bows dipped, and she completed the corkscrew roll with the massive dignity to be expected of a ponderous fabric that carried five hundred tons of artillery on her decks. Pitch—roll—heave—roll; it was magnificent, rhythmic, majestic, and Bush, balancing on the deck with the practised ease of ten years' experience, would have felt almost happy if the freshening of the wind did not bring with it the approaching necessity for another reef, which meant, in accordance with the ship's standing orders, that the captain should be informed.

Yet there were some minutes of grace left him, during which he could stand balancing on the deck and allow his mind to wander free. Not that Bush was conscious of any need for meditation—he would have smiled at such a suggestion were anyone to make it to him. But the last few days had passed in a whirl, from the moment when his orders had arrived and he had said good-bye to his mother and sisters (he had had three weeks with them after the *Conqueror* had paid off) and hurried to Plymouth, counting the money he had left in his pockets to make sure he could pay the post-chaise charges. The *Renown* had been in all the flurry of completing for the West Indian station, and during the thirty-six hours that elapsed before she sailed Bush had hardly had time to sit down, let alone sleep—his first good night's rest had come while the *Renown* clawed her way across the bay. Yet almost from the moment of his first arrival on board he had been harassed by the fantastic moods of the captain, now madly suspicious and again stupidly easygoing. Bush was not a man sensitive to atmosphere—he was a sturdy soul philosophically prepared to do his duty in any of the difficult conditions to be expected at sea—but he could not help but be conscious of the tenseness and fear that pervaded life in the *Renown*. He knew that he felt dissatisfied and worried, but he did not know that these were his own forms of tenseness and fear. In three days at sea he had hardly come to know a thing about his colleagues: he could vaguely guess that Buckland, the first lieutenant, was capable and steady, and that Roberts, the second, was kindly and easygoing; Hornblower seemed active and intelligent, Smith a trifle weak; but these deductions were really guesses. The wardroom officers—the lieutenants and

the master and the surgeon and the purser—seemed to be
secretive and very much inclined to maintain a strict reserve
about themselves. Within wide limits this was right and
proper—Bush was no frivolous chatterer himself—but the
silence was carried to excess when conversation was limited
to half a dozen words, all strictly professional. There was
much that Bush could have learned speedily about the ship
and her crew if the other officers had been prepared to
share with him the results of their experience and observations during the year they had been on board, but except
for the single hint Bush had received from Hornblower
when he came on board no one had uttered a word. If
Bush had been given to Gothic flights of imagination he
might have thought of himself as a ghost at sea with a
company of ghosts, cut off from the world and from each
other, ploughing across an endless sea to an unknown
destination. As it was he could guess that the secretiveness
of the wardroom was the result of the moods of the captain;
and that brought him back abruptly to the thought that
the wind was still freshening and a second reef was now
necessary. He listened to the harping of the rigging, felt
the heave of the deck under his feet, and shook his head
regretfully. There was nothing for it.

"Mr. Wellard" he said to the volunteer beside him. "Go
and tell the captain that I think another reef is necessary."

"Aye aye, sir."

It was only a few seconds before Wellard was back on
deck again.

"Cap'n's coming himself, sir."

"Very good" said Bush.

He did not meet Wellard's eyes as he said the meaning-
less words; he did not want Wellard to see how he took
the news, nor did he want to see any expression that
Wellard's face might wear. Here came the captain, his

shaggy long hair whipping in the wind and his hook nose turning this way and that as usual.

"You want to take in another reef, Mr. Bush?"

"Yes, sir" said Bush, and waited for the cutting remark that he expected. It was a pleasant surprise that none was forthcoming. The captain seemed almost genial.

"Very good, Mr. Bush. Call all hands."

The pipes shrilled along the decks.

"All hands! All hands! All hands to reef tops'ls. All hands!"

The men came pouring out; the cry of "All hands" brought out the officers from the wardroom and the cabins and the midshipmen's berths, hastening with their station-bills in their pockets to make sure that the reorganised crew were properly at their stations. The captain's orders pealed against the wind. Halliards and reef tackles were manned; the ship plunged and rolled over the grey sea under the grey sky so that a landsman might have wondered how a man could keep his footing on deck, far less venture aloft. Then in the midst of the evolution a young voice, soaring with excitement to a high treble, cut through the captain's orders.

"'Vast hauling there! 'Vast hauling!"

There was a piercing urgency about the order, and obediently the men ceased to pull. Then the captain bellowed from the poop.

"Who's that countermanding my orders?"

"It's me, sir—Wellard."

The young volunteer faced aft and screamed into the wind to make himself heard. From his station aft Bush saw the captain advance to the poop rail; Bush could see he was shaking with rage, his big nose pointing forward as though seeking a victim.

"You'll be sorry, Mr. Wellard. Oh yes, you'll be sorry."

Hornblower now made his appearance at Wellard's side. He was green with seasickness, as he had been ever since the *Renown* left Plymouth Sound.

"There's a reef point caught in the reef tackle block, sir —weather side," he hailed, and Bush, shifting his position, could see that this was so; if the men had continued to haul on the tackle, damage to the sail might easily have followed.

"What d'you mean by coming between me and a man who disobeys me?" shouted the captain. "It's useless to try to screen him."

"This is my station, sir" replied Hornblower. "Mr. Wellard was doing his duty."

"Conspiracy!" replied the captain. "You two are in collusion!"

In the face of such an impossible statement Hornblower could only stand still, his white face turned towards the captain.

"You go below, Mr. Wellard" roared the captain, when it was apparent that no reply would be forthcoming, "and you too, Mr. Hornblower. I'll deal with you in a few minutes. You hear me? Go below! I'll teach you to conspire."

It was a direct order, and had to be obeyed. Hornblower and Wellard walked slowly aft; it was obvious that Hornblower was rigidly refraining from exchanging a glance with the midshipman, lest a fresh accusation of conspiracy should be hurled at him. They went below while the captain watched them. As they disappeared down the companion the captain raised his big nose again.

"Send a hand to clear that reef tackle!" he ordered, in a tone as nearly normal as the wind permitted. "Haul away!"

The topsails had their second reef, and the men began to lay in off the yards. The captain stood by the poop rail looking over the ship as normal as any man could be expected to be.

"Wind's coming aft" he said to Buckland. "Aloft there! Send a hand to bear those backstays abreast the top-brim. Hands to the weather-braces. After guard! Haul in the weather main brace! Haul together, men! Well with the foreyard! Well with the main yard! Belay every inch of that!"

The orders were given sensibly and sanely, and the hands stood waiting for the watch below to be dismissed.

"Bosun's mate! My compliments to Mr. Lomax and I'll be glad to see him on deck."

Mr. Lomax was the purser, and the officers on the quarterdeck could hardly refrain from exchanging glances; it was hard to imagine any reason why the purser should be wanted on deck at this moment.

"You sent for me, sir?" said the purser, arriving short of breath on the quarterdeck.

"Yes, Mr. Lomax. The hands have been hauling in the weather main brace."

"Yes, sir?"

"Now we'll splice it."

"Sir?"

"You heard me. We'll splice the main brace. A tot of rum to every man. Aye, and to every boy."

"Sir?"

"You heard me. A tot of rum, I said. Do I have to give my orders twice? A tot of rum for every man. I'll give you five minutes, Mr. Lomax, and not a second longer."

The captain pulled out his watch and looked at it significantly.

"Aye aye, sir" said Lomax, which was all he could say. Yet he still stood for a second or two, looking first at the captain and then at the watch, until the big nose began to lift in his direction and the shaggy eyebrows began to come together. Then he turned and fled; if the unbelievable order had to be obeyed five minutes would not be long in which to collect his party together, unlock the spirit room, and bring up the spirits. The conversation between captain and purser could hardly have been overheard by more than half a dozen persons, but every hand had witnessed it, and the men were looking at each other unbelievingly, some with grins on their faces which Bush longed to wipe off.

"Bosun's mate! Run and tell Mr. Lomax two minutes have gone. Mr. Buckland! I'll have the hands aft here, if you please."

The men came trooping along the waist; it may have been merely Bush's overwrought imagination that made him think their manner slack and careless. The captain came forward to the quarterdeck rail, his face beaming in smiles that contrasted wildly with his scowls of a moment before.

"I know where loyalty's to be found, men" he shouted, "I've seen it. I see it now. I see your loyal hearts. I watch your unremitting labours. I've noticed them as I notice everything that goes on in this ship. Everything, I say. The traitors meet their deserts and the loyal hearts their reward. Give a cheer, you men."

The cheer was given, halfheartedly in some cases, with over-exuberance in others. Lomax made his appearance at the main hatchway, four men with him each carrying a two-gallon anker.

"Just in time, Mr. Lomax. It would have gone hard with you if you had been late. See to it that the issue is made with none of the unfairness that goes on in some ships. Mr. Booth! Lay aft here."

The bulky bosun came hurrying on his short legs.

"You have your rattan with you, I hope?"

"Aye aye, sir."

Booth displayed his long silver-mounted cane, ringed at every two inches by a pronounced joint. The dilatory among the crew knew that cane well and not only the dilatory—at moments of excitement Mr. Booth was likely to make play with it on all within reach.

"Pick the two sturdiest of your mates. Justice will be executed."

Now the captain was neither beaming nor scowling. There was a smile on his heavy lips, but it might be a smile without significance as it was not re-echoed in his eyes.

"Follow me" said the captain to Booth and his mates, and he left the deck once more to Bush, who now had leisure to contemplate ruefully the disorganisation of the ship's routine and discipline occasioned by this strange whim.

When the spirits had been issued and drunk he could dismiss the watch below and set himself to drive the watch on deck to their duties again, slashing at their sulkiness and indifference with bitter words. And there was no pleasure now in standing on the heaving deck watching the cork-screw roll of the ship and the hurrying Atlantic waves, the trim of the sails and the handling of the wheel—Bush still was unaware that there was any pleasure to be found in these everyday matters, but he was vaguely aware that something had gone out of his life.

He saw Booth and his mates making their way forward again, and here came Wellard onto the quarterdeck.

"Reporting for duty, sir" he said.

The boy's face was white, set in a strained rigidity, and Bush, looking keenly at him, saw that there was a hint of moisture in his eyes. He was walking stiffly, too, holding himself inflexibly; pride might be holding back his shoulders and holding up his head, but there was some other reason for his not bending at the hips.

"Very good, Mr. Wellard" said Bush.

He remembered those knots on Booth's cane. He had known injustice often enough. Not only boys but grown men were beaten without cause on occasions, and Bush had nodded sagely when it happened, thinking that contact with injustice in a world that was essentially unjust was part of everyone's education. And grown men smiled to each other when boys were beaten, agreeing that it did all parties good; boys had been beaten since history began, and it would be a bad day for the world if ever, inconceivably, boys should cease to be beaten. This was all very true, and yet in spite of it Bush felt sorry for Wellard. Fortunately there was something waiting to be done which might suit Wellard's mood and condition.

"Those sandglasses need to be run against each other, Mr. Wellard" said Bush, nodding over to the binnacle. "Run the minute glass against the half-hour glass as soon as they turn it at seven bells."

"Aye aye, sir."

"Mark off each minute on the slate unless you want to lose your reckoning" added Bush.

"Aye aye, sir."

It would be something to keep Wellard's mind off his troubles without calling for physical effort, watching the sand run out of the minute glass and turning it quickly, marking the slate and watching again. Bush had his doubts about that half-hour glass and it would be convenient to have both checked. Wellard walked stiffly over to the binnacle and made preparation to begin his observations.

Now here was the captain coming back again, the big nose pointing to one side and the other. But now the mood had changed again; the activity, the restlessness, had evaporated. He was like a man who had dined well. As etiquette dictated, Bush moved away from the weather rail when the captain appeared and the captain proceeded to pace slowly up and down the weather side of the quarter-deck, his steps accommodating themselves by long habit to the heave and pitch of the ship. Wellard took one glance and then devoted his whole attention to the matter of the sandglasses; seven bells had just struck and the half-hour glass had just been turned. For a short time the captain paced up and down. When he halted he studied the weather to windward, felt the wind on his cheek, looked attentively at the dogvane and up at the topsails to make sure that the yards were correctly trimmed, and came over and looked into the binnacle to check the course the helms-man was steering. It was all perfectly normal behaviour; any captain in any ship would do the same when he came on deck. Wellard was aware of the nearness of his captain and tried to give no sign of disquiet; he turned the minute glass and made another mark on the slate.

"Mr. Wellard at work?" said the captain.

His voice was thick and a little indistinct, the tone quite different from the anxiety-sharpened voice with which he had previously spoken. Wellard, his eyes on the sand-glasses, paused before replying. Bush could guess that he was wondering what would be the safest, as well as the correct, thing to say.

"Aye aye, sir."

In the navy no one could go far wrong by saying that to a superior officer.

"Aye aye, sir" repeated the captain. "Mr. Wellard has learned better now perhaps than to conspire against his captain, against his lawful superior set in authority over him by the Act of His Most Gracious Majesty King George II?"

That was not an easy suggestion to answer. The last grains of sand were running out of the glass and Wellard waited for them; a "yes" or a "no" might be equally fatal.

"Mr. Wellard is sulky" said the captain. "Perhaps Mr. Wellard's mind is dwelling on what lies behind him. Behind him. 'By the waters of Babylon we sat down and wept.' But proud Mr. Wellard hardly wept. And he did not sit down at all. No, he would be careful not to sit down. The dishonourable part of him has paid the price of his dishonour. The grown man guilty of an honourable offence is flogged upon his back, but a boy, a nasty dirty-minded boy, is treated differently. Is not that so, Mr. Wellard?"

"Yes, sir" murmured Wellard. There was nothing else he could say, and an answer was necessary.

"Mr. Booth's cane was appropriate to the occasion. It did its work well. The malefactor bent over the gun could consider of his misdeeds."

Wellard inverted the glass again while the captain, apparently satisfied, took a couple of turns up and down the deck, to Bush's relief. But the captain checked himself in mid-stride beside Wellard and went on talking; his tone now was higher-pitched.

"So you chose to conspire against me?" he demanded. "You sought to hold me up to derision before the hands?"

"No, sir" said Wellard in sudden new alarm. "No, sir, indeed not, sir."

"You and that cub Hornblower. *Mister* Hornblower. You plotted and you planned, so that my lawful authority should be set at nought."

"No, sir!"

"It is only the hands who are faithful to me in this ship where everyone else conspires against me. And cunningly you seek to undermine my influence over them. To make me a figure of fun in their sight. Confess it!"

"No, sir. I didn't, sir."

"Why attempt to deny it? It is plain, it is logical. Who was it who planned to catch that reef point in the reef tackle block?"

"No one, sir. It——"

"Then who was it that countermanded my orders? Who was it who put me to shame before both watches, with all hands on deck? It was a deep-laid plot. It shows every sign of it."

The captain's hands were behind his back, and he stood easily balancing on the deck with the wind flapping his coat-tails and blowing his hair forward over his cheeks, but Bush could see he was shaking with rage again—if it was not fear. Wellard turned the minute glass again and made a fresh mark on the slate.

"So you hide your face because of the guilt that is written on it?" blared the captain suddenly. "You pretend to be busy so as to deceive me. Hypocrisy!"

"I gave Mr. Wellard orders to test the glasses against each other, sir" said Bush.

He was intervening reluctantly, but to intervene was less painful than to stand by as a witness. The captain looked at him as if this was his first appearance on deck.

"You, Mr. Bush? You're sadly deceived if you believe there is any good in this young fellow. Unless"—the captain's expression was one of sudden suspicious fear—"unless you are part and parcel of this infamous affair. But you are not, are you, Mr. Bush? Not you. I have always thought better of you, Mr. Bush."

The expression of fear changed to one of ingratiating good fellowship.

"Yes, sir" said Bush.

"With the world against me I have always counted on you, Mr. Bush" said the captain, darting restless glances from under his eyebrows. "So you will rejoice when this embodiment of evil meets his deserts. We'll get the truth out of him."

Bush had the feeling that if he were a man of instant quickness of thought and readiness of tongue he would take advantage of this new attitude of the captain's to free Wellard from his peril; by posing as the captain's devoted companion in trouble and at the same time laughing off the thought of danger from any conspiracy, he might modify the captain's fears. So he felt, but he had no confidence in himself.

"He knows nothing, sir" he said, and he forced himself to grin. "He doesn't know the bobstay from the spanker-boom."

"You think so?" said the captain doubtfully, teetering on his heels with the roll of the ship. He seemed almost convinced, and then suddenly a new line of argument presented itself to him.

"No, Mr. Bush. You're too honest. I could see that the first moment I set eyes on you. You are ignorant of the depths of wickedness into which this world can sink. This lout has deceived you. Deceived you!"

The captain's voice rose again to a hoarse scream, and Wellard turned a white face towards Bush, lopsided with terror.

"Really, sir——" began Bush, still forcing a death's-head grin.

"No, no, no!" roared the captain. "Justice must be done! The truth must be brought to light! I'll have it out of him! Quartermaster! Quartermaster! Run for'ard and tell Mr. Booth to lay aft here. And his mates!"

The captain turned away and began to pace the deck as if to offer a safety valve to the pressure within him, but he turned back instantly.

"I'll have it out of him! Or he'll jump overboard! You hear me? Where's that bosun?"

"Mr. Wellard hasn't finished testing the glasses, sir" said Bush in one last feeble attempt to postpone the issue.

"Nor will he" said the captain.

Here came the bos'un hurrying aft on his short legs, his two mates striding behind him.

"Mr. Booth!" said the captain; his mood had changed again and the mirthless smile was back on his lips. "Take that miscreant. Justice demands that he be dealt with further. Another dozen from your cane, properly applied. Another dozen, and he'll coo like a dove."

"Aye aye, sir" said the bosun, but he hesitated.

It was a momentary tableau: the captain with his flapping coat; the bosun looking appealingly at Bush and the burly bosun's mates standing like huge statues behind him; the helmsman apparently imperturbable while all this went on round him, handling the wheel and glancing up at the topsails; and the wretched boy beside the binnacle —all this under the grey sky, with the grey sea tossing about them and stretching as far as the pitiless horizon.

"Take him down to the maindeck, Mr. Booth" said the captain.

It was the utterly inevitable; behind the captain's words lay the authority of Parliament, the weight of ages-old tradition. There was nothing that could be done. Wellard's hands rested on the binnacle as though they would cling to it and as though he would have to be dragged away by force. But he dropped his hands to his sides and followed the bosun while the captain watched him, smiling.

It was a welcome distraction that came to Bush as the quartermaster reported "Ten minutes before eight bells, sir."

"Very good. Pipe the watch below."

Hornblower made his appearance on the quarterdeck and made his way towards Bush.

"You're not my relief" said Bush.

"Yes I am. Captain's orders."

Hornblower spoke without any expression—Bush was used to the ship's officers by now being as guarded as that, and he knew why it was. But his curiosity made him ask the question.

"Why?"

"I'm on watch and watch" said Hornblower stolidly. "Until further orders."

He looked at the horizon as he spoke, showing no sign of emotion.

"Hard luck" said Bush, and for a moment felt a twinge of doubt as to whether he had not ventured too far in offering such an expression of sympathy. But no one was within earshot.

"No wardroom liquor for me" went on Hornblower, "until further orders either. Neither my own nor anyone else's."

For some officers that would be a worse punishment than being put on watch and watch—four hours on duty and four hours off day and night—but Bush did not know enough about Hornblower's habits to judge whether this was the case with him. He was about to say "hard luck" again, when at that moment a wild cry of pain reached their ears, cutting its way through the whistling wind. A moment later it was repeated, with even greater intensity. Hornblower was looking out at the horizon and his expression did not change. Bush watched his face and decided not to pay attention to the cries.

"Hard luck" he said.

"It might be worse" said Hornblower.

III

IT was Sunday morning. The *Renown* had caught the north-east trades and was plunging across the Atlantic at her best speed, with studding sails set on both sides, the roaring trades driving her along with a steady pitch and heave, her bluff bows now and then raising a smother of spray that supported momentary rainbows. The rigging was piping loud and clear, the treble and the tenor to the baritone and bass of the noises of the ship's fabric as she pitched—a symphony of the sea. A few clouds of startling white dotted the blue of the sky, and the sun shone down from among them, revivifying and rejuvenating, reflected in dancing facets from the imperial blue of the sea.

The ship was a thing of exquisite beauty in an exquisite setting, and her bluff bows and her rows of guns added something else to the picture. She was a magnificent fighting machine, the mistress of the waves over which she was sailing in solitary grandeur. Her very solitude told the story; with the fleets of her enemies cooped up in port, blockaded by vigilant squadrons eager to come to grips with them, the *Renown* could sail the seas in utter confidence that she had nothing to fear. No furtive blockade-runner could equal her in strength; nowhere at sea was there a hostile squadron which could face her in battle. She could flout the hostile coasts; with the enemy blockaded and helpless she could bring her ponderous might to bear in a blow struck wherever she might choose. At this moment she was heading to strike such a blow, perhaps, despatched across the ocean at the word of the Lords of the Admiralty.

And drawn up in ranks on her maindeck was the ship's company, the men whose endless task it was to keep this fabric at the highest efficiency, to repair the constant inroads made upon her material by sea and weather and the mere passage of time. The snow-white decks, the bright paintwork, the exact and orderly arrangement of the lines and ropes and spars, were proofs of the diligence of their work; and when the time should come for the *Renown* to deliver the ultimate argument regarding the sovereignty of the seas, it would be they who would man the guns—the *Renown* might be a magnificent fighting machine, but she was so only by virtue of the frail humans who handled her. They, like the *Renown* herself, were only cogs in the greater machine which was the Royal Navy, and most of them, caught up in the time-honoured routine and discipline of the service, were content to be cogs, to wash decks and set up rigging, to point guns or to charge with cutlasses over hostile bulwarks, with little thought as to whether the ship's bows were headed north or south, whether it was Frenchman or Spaniard or Dutchman who received their charge. Today only the captain knew the mission upon which the Lords of the Admiralty—presumably in consultation with the Cabinet—had despatched the *Renown*. There had been the vague knowledge that she was headed for the West Indies, but whereabouts in that area, and what she was intended to do there was known only to one man in the seven hundred and forty on the *Renown's* decks.

Every possible man was drawn up on this Sunday morning on the maindeck, not merely the two watches, but every "idler" who had no place in the watches—the holders, who did their work so far below decks that for some of them it was literally true that they did not see the sun from one week's end to another, the cooper and his mates,

the armourer and his mates, sail-maker and cook and
stewards, all in their best clothes with the officers with
their cocked hats and swords beside their divisions. Only
the officer of the watch and his assistant warrant officer, the
quartermasters at the wheel and the dozen hands necessary
for lookouts and to handle the ship in a very sudden
emergency were not included in the ranks that were drawn
up in the waist at rigid attention, the lines swaying easily
and simultaneously with the motion of the ship.

It was Sunday morning, and every hat was off, every
head was bare as the ship's company listened to the words
of the captain. But it was no church service; these bare-
headed men were not worshipping their Maker. That could
happen on three Sundays in every month, but on those
Sundays there would not be quite such a strict inquisition
throughout the ship to compel the attendance of every
hand—and a tolerant Admiralty had lately decreed that
Catholics and Jews and even Dissenters might be excused
from attending church services. This was the fourth Sunday,
when the worship of God was set aside in favour of a
ceremonial more strict, more solemn, calling for the same
clean shirts and bared heads, but not for the downcast eyes
of the men in the ranks. Instead every man was looking
to his front as he held his hat before him with the wind
ruffling his hair; he was listening to laws as all-embracing
as the Ten Commandments, to a code as rigid as Leviticus,
because on the fourth Sunday of every month it was the
captain's duty to read the Articles of War aloud to the
ship's company, so that not even the illiterates could plead
ignorance of them; a religious captain might squeeze in a
brief church service as well, but the Articles of War had to
be read.

The captain turned a page.

"Nineteenth Article" he read. "If any person in or

belonging to the fleet shall make or endeavour to make any mutinous assembly upon any offence whatsoever, every person offending therein, and being convicted by the sentence of the court-martial, shall suffer death."

Bush, standing by his division, heard these words as he had heard them scores of times before. He had, in fact, heard them so often that he usually listened to them with inattention; the words of the previous eighteen Articles had flowed past him practically without his hearing them. But he heard this Nineteenth Article distinctly; it was possible that the captain read it with special emphasis, and in addition Bush, raising his eyes in the blessed sunshine, caught sight of Hornblower, the officer of the watch, standing at the quarterdeck rail listening as well. And there was that word "death". It struck Bush's ear with special emphasis, as emphatic and as final as the sound of a stone dropped into a well, which was strange, for the other articles which the captain had read had used the word freely—death for holding back from danger, death for sleeping while on duty.

The captain went on reading.

"And if any person shall utter any words of sedition or mutiny he shall suffer death. . . .

"And if any officer, mariner, or soldier shall behave himself with contempt to his superior officer . . ."

Those words had a fuller meaning for Bush now, with Hornblower looking down at him; he felt a strange stirring within him. He looked at the captain, unkempt and seedy in his appearance, and went back in his memory through the events of the past few days; if ever a man had shown himself unfit for duty it was the captain, but he was maintained in his position of unlimited power by these Articles of War which he was reading. Bush glanced up at Hornblower again; he felt that he knew for certain what

Hornblower was thinking about as he stood there by the quarterdeck rail, and it was strange to feel this sympathy with the ungainly angular young lieutenant with whom he had had such little contact.

"And if any officer, mariner, or soldier or other person in the fleet"—the captain had reached the Twenty-Second Article now—"shall presume to quarrel with any of his superior officers, or shall disobey any lawful command, every such person shall suffer death."

Bush had not realised before how the Articles of War harped on this subject. He had served contentedly under discipline, and had always philosophically assured himself that injustice or mismanagement could be lived through. He could see now very special reasons why they should be. And as if to clinch the argument, the captain was now reading the final Article of War, the one which filled in every gap.

"All other crimes committed by any person or persons in the fleet which are not mentioned in this Act . . ."

Bush remembered that article; by its aid an officer could accomplish the ruin of an inferior who was clever enough to escape being pinned down by any of the others.

The captain read the final solemn words and looked up from the page. The big nose turned like a gun being trained round as he looked at each officer in turn; his face with its unshaven cheeks bore an expression of coarse triumph. It was as if he had gained by this reading of the Articles reassurance regarding his fears. He inflated his chest; he seemed to rise on tiptoe to make his concluding speech.

"I'll have you all know that these Articles apply to my officers as much as to anyone else."

Those were words which Bush could hardly believe he had heard. It was incredible that a captain could say such

a thing in his crew's hearing. If ever a speech was subversive of discipline it was this one. But the captain merely
went on with routine.

"Carry on, Mr. Buckland."

"Aye aye, sir." Buckland took a pace forward in the
grip of routine himself.

"On hats!"

Officers and men covered their heads now that the
ceremonial was completed.

"Division officers, dismiss your divisions!"

The musicians of the marine band had been waiting for
this moment. The drum sergeant waved his baton and the
drumsticks crashed down on the side drums in a long roll.
Piercing and sweet the fifes joined in—"The Irish Washer-
woman," jerky and inspiriting. Smack—smack—smack; the
marine soldiers brought their ordered muskets up to their
shoulders. Whiting, the captain of marines, shouted the
orders which sent the scarlet lines marching and counter-
marching in the sunshine over the limited area of the
quarterdeck.

The captain had been standing by watching this orderly
progress of the ship's routine. Now he raised his voice.

"Mr. Buckland!"

"Sir!"

The captain mounted a couple of steps of the quarterdeck ladder so that he might be clearly seen, and raised his
voice so that as many as possible could hear his words.

"Rope-yarn Sunday today."

"Aye aye, sir."

"And double rum for these good men."

"Aye aye, sir."

Buckland did his best to keep the discontent out of his
voice. Coming on top of the captain's previous speech this
was almost too much. A rope-yarn Sunday meant that the

men would spend the rest of the day in idleness. Double
rum in that case most certainly meant fights and quarrels
among the men. Bush, coming aft along the maindeck, was
well aware of the disorder that was spreading among the
crew, pampered by their captain. It was impossible to
maintain discipline when every adverse report made by the
officers was ignored by the captain. Bad characters and
idlers were going unpunished; the willing hands were
beginning to sulk, while the unruly ones were growing
openly restless. "These good men," the captain had said.
The men knew well enough how bad their record had been
during the last week. If the captain called them "good
men" after that, worse still could be expected next week.
And besides all this the men most certainly knew about the
captain's treatment of his lieutenants, of the brutal repri-
mands dealt out to them, the savage punishments. "Today's
wardroom joint is tomorrow's lower-deck stew" said the
proverb, meaning that whatever went on aft was soon
being discussed in a garbled form forward; the men could
not be expected to be obedient to officers whom they knew
to be treated with contempt by the captain. Bush was
worried as he mounted the quarterdeck.

The captain had gone in under the half-deck to his
cabin; Buckland and Roberts were standing by the ham-
mock nettings deep in conversation, and Bush joined them.

"These articles apply to my officers" said Buckland as
he approached.

"Rope-yarn Sunday and double rum" added Roberts.
"All for these good men."

Buckland shot a furtive glance round the deck before
he spoke next. It was pitiful to see the first lieutenant of
a ship of the line taking precautions lest what he should
say should be overheard. But Hornblower and Wellard
were on the other side of the wheel. On the poop the

master was assembling the midshipmen's navigation class
with their sextants to take their noon sights.

"He's mad" said Buckland in as low a voice as the
northeast trade wind would allow.

"We all know that" said Roberts.

Bush said nothing. He was too cautious to commit himself at present.

"Clive won't lift a finger" said Buckland. "He's a ninny
if there ever was one."

Clive was the surgeon.

"Have you asked him?" asked Roberts.

"I tried to. But he wouldn't say a word. He's afraid."

"Don't move from where you are standing, gentlemen"
broke in a loud harsh voice; the well-remembered voice of
the captain, speaking apparently from the level of the deck
on which they stood. All three officers started in surprise.

"Every sign of guilt" blared the voice. "Bear witness to
it, Mr. Hobbs."

They looked round them. The skylight of the captain's
fore cabin was open a couple of inches, and through the
gap the captain was looking at them; they could see his
eyes and his nose. He was a tall man and by standing on
anything low, a book or a footstool, he could look from
under the skylight over the coaming. Rigid, the officers
waited while another pair of eyes appeared under the skylight beside the captain's. They belonged to Hobbs, the
acting-gunner.

"Wait there until I come to you, gentlemen" said the
captain, with a sneer as he said the word "gentlemen".
"Very good, Mr. Hobbs."

The two faces vanished from under the skylight, and
the officers had hardly time to exchange despairing glances
before the captain came striding up the ladder to them.

"A mutinous assembly, I believe" he said.

"No, sir" replied Buckland. Any word that was not a denial would be an admission of guilt, on a charge that could put a rope round his neck.

"Do you give me the lie on my own quarterdeck?" roared the captain. "I was right in suspecting my officers. Plotting. Whispering. Scheming. Planning. And now treating me with gross disrespect. I'll see that you regret this from this minute, Mr. Buckland."

"I intended no disrespect, sir" protested Buckland.

"You give me the lie again to my face! And you others stand by and abet him! You keep him in countenance! I thought better of you, Mr. Bush, until now."

Bush thought it wise to say nothing.

"Dumb insolence, eh?" said the captain. "Eager enough to talk when you think my eye isn't on you, all the same."

The captain glowered round the quarterdeck.

"And you, Mr. Hornblower" he said. "You did not see fit to report this assembly to me. Officer of the watch, indeed! And of course Wellard is in it too. That is only to be expected. But I fancy you will be in trouble with these gentlemen now, Mr. Wellard. You did not keep a sharp enough lookout for them. In fact you are in serious trouble now, Mr. Wellard, without a friend in the ship except for the gunner's daughter, whom you will be kissing again soon."

The captain stood towering on the quarterdeck with his gaze fixed on the unfortunate Wellard, who shrank visibly away from him. To kiss the gunner's daughter was to be bent over a gun and beaten.

"But later will still be sufficient time to deal with you, Mr. Wellard. The lieutenants first, as their lofty rank dictates."

The captain looked round at the lieutenants, fear and triumph strangely alternating in his expression.

"Mr. Hornblower is already on watch and watch" he said. "You others have enjoyed idleness in consequence, and Satan found mischief for your idle hands. Mr. Buckland does not keep a watch. The high and mighty and aspiring first lieutenant."

"Sir——" began Buckland, and then bit off the words which were about to follow. That word "aspiring" undoubtedly implied that he was scheming to gain command of the ship, but a court-martial would not read that meaning into it. Every officer was expected to be an aspiring officer and it would be no insult to say so.

"Sir!" jeered the captain. "Sir! So you have grace enough still to guard your tongue. Cunning, maybe. But you will not evade the consequences of your actions. Mr. Hornblower can stay on watch and watch. But these two gentlemen can report to you when every watch is called, and at two bells, at four bells, and at six bells in every watch. They are to be properly dressed when they report to you, and you are to be properly awake. Is that understood?"

Not one of the dumbfounded trio could speak for a moment.

"Answer me!"

"Aye aye, sir" said Buckland.

"Aye aye, sir" said Bush and Roberts as the captain turned his eyes on them.

"Let there be no slackness in the execution of my orders" said the captain. "I shall have means of knowing if I am obeyed or not."

"Aye aye, sir" said Buckland.

The captain's sentence had condemned him, Bush, and Roberts to be roused and awakened every hour, day and night.

IV

IT was pitch dark down here, absolutely dark, not the tiniest glimmer of light at all. Out over the sea was the moonless night, and here it was three decks down, below the level of the sea's surface—through the oaken skin of the ship could be heard the rush of the water alongside, and the impact of the waves over which the ship rode; the fabric of the ship grumbled to itself with the alternating stresses of the pitch and the roll. Bush hung on to the steep ladder in the darkness and felt for foothold; finding it, he stepped off among the water barrels, and, crouching low, he began to make his way aft through the solid blackness. A rat squeaked and scurried past him, but rats were only to be expected down here in the hold, and Bush went on feeling his way aft unshaken. Out of the blackness before him, through the multitudinous murmurings of the ship, came a slight hiss, and Bush halted and hissed in reply. He was not self-conscious about these conspiratorial goings on. All precautions were necessary, for this was something very dangerous that he was doing.

"Bush!" whispered Buckland's voice.

"Yes."

"The others are here."

Ten minutes before, at two bells in the middle watch, Bush and Roberts had reported to Buckland in his cabin in obedience to the captain's order. A wink, a gesture, a whisper, and the appointment to meet here was made; it was an utterly fantastic state of affairs that the lieutenants of a King's ship should have to act in such a fashion for fear of spies and eavesdroppers, but it had been necessary. Then they had dispersed and by devious routes and different hatchways had made their way here. Hornblower, relieved by Smith on watch, had preceded them.

"We mustn't be here long" whispered Roberts.

Even by his whisper, even in the dark, one could guess at his nervousness. There could be no doubt about this being a mutinous assembly. They could all hang for what they were doing.

"Suppose we declare him unfit for command?" whispered Buckland. "Suppose we put him in irons?"

"We'd have to do it quick and sharp if we do it at all" whispered Hornblower. "He'll call on the hands and they might follow him. And then——"

There was no need for Hornblower to go on with that speech. Everyone who heard it formed a mental picture of corpses swaying at the yard-arms.

"Supposing we do it quick and sharp?" agreed Buckland. "Supposing we get him into irons?"

"Then we go on to Antigua" said Roberts.

"And a court-martial" said Bush, thinking as far ahead as that for the first time in this present crisis.

"Yes" whispered Buckland.

Into that flat monosyllable were packed various moods —inquiry and despair, desperation and doubt.

"That's the point" whispered Hornblower. "He'll give evidence. It'll sound different in court. We've been punished—watch and watch, no liquor. That could happen to anybody. It's no grounds for mutiny."

"But he's spoiling the hands."

"Double rum. Make and mend. It'll sound quite natural in court. It's not for us to criticise the captain's methods— so the court will think."

"But they'll see him."

"He's cunning. And he's no raving lunatic. He can talk —he can find reasons for everything. You've heard him. He'll be plausible."

"But he's held us up to contempt before the hands. He's set Hobbs to spy on us."

"That'll be a proof of how desperate his situation was, surrounded by us criminals. If we arrest him we're guilty until we've proved ourselves innocent. Any court's bound to be on the captain's side. Mutiny means hanging."

Hornblower was putting into words all the doubts that Bush felt in his bones and yet had been unable to express.

"That's right" whispered Bush.

"What about Wellard?" whispered Roberts. "Did you hear him scream the last time?"

"He's only a volunteer. Not even a midshipman. No friends. No family. What's the court going to say when they hear the captain had a boy beaten half a dozen times? They'll laugh. So would we if we didn't know. Do him good, we'd say, the same as it did the rest of us good."

A silence followed this statement of the obvious, broken in the end by Buckland whispering a succession of filthy oaths that could give small vent to his despair.

"He'll bring charges against us" whispered Roberts. "The minute we're in company with other ships. I know he will."

"Twenty-two years I've held my commission" said Buckland. "Now he'll break me. He'll break you as well."

There would be no chance at all for officers charged before a court-martial by their captain with behaving with contempt towards him in a manner subversive of discipline. Every single one of them knew that. It gave an edge to their despair. Charges pressed by the captain with the insane venom and cunning he had displayed up to now might not even end in dismissal from the service—they might lead to the prison and the rope.

"Ten more days before we make Antigua" said Roberts. "If this wind holds fair—and it will."

"But we don't know we're destined for Antigua" said Hornblower. "That's only our guess. It might be weeks—it might be months."

"God help us!" said Buckland.

A slight clatter farther aft along the hold—a noise different from the noises of the working of the ship—made them all start. Bush clenched his hairy fists. But they were reassured by a voice calling softly to them.

"Mr. Buckland—Mr. Hornblower—sir!"

"Wellard, by God!" said Roberts.

They could hear Wellard scrambling towards them.

"The captain, sir!" said Wellard. "He's coming!"

"Holy God!"

"Which way?" snapped Hornblower.

"By the steerage hatchway. I got to the cockpit and came down from there. He was sending Hobbs——"

"Get for'ard, you three" said Hornblower, cutting into the explanation. "Get for'ard and scatter when you're on deck. Quick!"

Nobody stopped to think that Hornblower was giving orders to officers immensely his senior. Every instant of time was of vital importance, and not to be wasted in indecision, or in silly blasphemy. That was apparent as soon as he spoke. Bush turned with the others and plunged forward in the darkness, barking his shins painfully as he fell over unseen obstructions. Bush heard Hornblower say "Come along, Wellard" as he parted from them in his mad flight with the others beside him.

The cable tier—the ladder—and then the extraordinary safety of the lower gundeck. After the utter blackness of

the hold there was enough light here for him to see fairly
distinctly. Buckland and Roberts continued to ascend to
the maindeck; Bush turned to make his way aft. The watch
below had been in their hammocks long enough to be
sound asleep; here to the noises of the ship was added
the blended snoring of the sleepers as the close-hung rows
of hammocks swayed with the motion of the ship in such a
coincidence of timing as to appear like solid masses. Far
down between the rows a light was approaching. It was
a horn lantern with a lighted purser's dip inside it, and
Hobbs, the acting-gunner, was carrying it, and two seamen
were following him as he hurried along. There was an
exchange of glances as Bush met the party. A momentary
hesitation on Hobbs' part betrayed the fact that he would
have greatly liked to ask Bush what he was doing on
the lower gundeck, but that was something no acting-
warrant officer, even with the captain's favour behind him,
could ask of a lieutenant. And there was annoyance in
Hobbs' expression, too; obviously he was hurrying to
secure all the exits from the hold, and was exasperated that
Bush had escaped him. The seamen wore expressions of
simple bewilderment at these goings on in the middle
watch. Hobbs stood aside to let his superior pass, and
Bush strode past him with no more than that one glance.
It was extraordinary how much more confident he felt now
that he was safely out of the hold and disassociated from
any mutinous assembly. He decided to head for his cabin;
it would not be long before four bells when by the captain's
orders he had to report again to Buckland. The messenger
sent by the officer of the watch to rouse him would find
him lying on his cot. But as Bush went on and had progressed as far as the mainmast he arrived in the midst of a
scene of bustle which he would most certainly have taken
notice of if he had been innocent and which consequently

he must (so he told himself) ask about now that he had seen it—he could not possibly walk by without a question or two. This was where the marines were berthed, and they were all of them out of their hammocks hastily equipping themselves—those who had their shirts and trousers on were putting on their crossbelts ready for action.

"What's all this?" demanded Bush, trying to make his voice sound as it would have sounded if he had no knowledge of anything irregular happening in the ship except this.

"Dunno, sir" said the private he addressed. "We was just told to turn out—muskets an' side arms and ball cartridge, sir."

A sergeant of marines looked out through the screen which divided the non-commissioned officers' bay from the rest of the deck.

"Captain's orders, sir" he said; and then with a roar at the men, "Come on! Slap it about, there!"

"Where's the captain, then?" asked Bush with all the innocence he could muster.

"Aft some'eres, sir. 'E sent for the corpril's guard same time as we was told to turn out."

Four marine privates and a corporal supplied the sentry who stood day and night outside the captain's cabin. A single order was all that was needed to turn out the guard and provide the captain with at least a nucleus of armed and disciplined men ready for action.

"Very well, sergeant" said Bush, and he tried to look puzzled and to hurry naturally aft to find out what was going on. But he knew what fear was. He felt he would do anything rather than continue this walk to encounter whatever was awaiting him at the end of it. Whiting, the captain of marines, made his appearance, sleepy and unshaven, belting on his sword over his shirt.

"What in hell——?" he began, as he saw Bush.

"Don't ask *me*!" said Bush, striving after that natural appearance. So tense and desperate was he at that moment that his normally quiescent imagination was hard at work. He could imagine the prosecutor in the deceptive calm of a court-martial saying to Whiting, "Did Mr. Bush appear to be his usual self?" and it was frightfully necessary that Whiting should be able to answer, "Yes." Bush could even imagine the hairy touch of a rope round his neck. But next moment there was no more need for him to simulate surprise or ignorance. His reactions were genuine.

"Pass the word for the doctor" came the cry. "Pass the word, there."

And here came Wellard, white-faced, hurrying.

"Pass the word for the doctor. Call Dr. Clive."

"Who's hurt, Wellard?" asked Bush.

"The c-captain, sir."

Wellard looked distraught and shaken, but now Hornblower made his appearance behind him. Hornblower was pale, too, and breathing hard, but he seemed to have command of himself. The glance which he threw round him in the dim light of the lanterns passed over Bush without apparent recognition.

"Get Dr. Clive!" he snapped at one midshipman peering out from the midshipmen's berth; and then to another, "You, there. Run for the first lieutenant. Ask him to come below here. Run!"

Hornblower's glance took in Whiting and travelled forward to where the marines were snatching their muskets from the racks.

"Why are your men turning out, Captain Whiting?"

"Captain's orders."

"Then you can form them up. But I do not believe there is any emergency."

Only then did Hornblower's glance comprehend Bush.

"Oh, Mr. Bush. Will you take charge, sir, now that you're here? I've sent for the first lieutenant. The captain's hurt —badly hurt, I'm afraid, sir."

"But what's happened?" asked Bush.

"The captain's fallen down the hatchway, sir" said Hornblower.

In the dim light Hornblower's eyes stared straight into Bush's, but Bush could read no message in them. This after part of the lower gundeck was crowded now, and Hornblower's definite statement, the first that had been made, raised a buzz of excitement. It was the sort of undisciplined noise that most easily roused Bush's wrath, and, perhaps fortunately, it brought a natural reaction from him.

"Silence, there!" he roared. "Get about your business."

When Bush glowered round at the excited crowd it fell silent.

"With your permission I'll go below again, sir" said Hornblower. "I must see after the captain."

"Very well, Mr. Hornblower" said Bush; the stereo-typed phrase had been uttered so often before that it escaped sounding stilted.

"Come with me, Mr. Wellard" said Hornblower, and turned away.

Several new arrivals made their appearance as he did so —Buckland, his face white and strained, Roberts at his shoulder, Clive in his shirt and trousers walking sleepily from his cabin. All of them started a little at the sight of the marines forming line on the cumbered deck, their musket barrels glinting in the feeble light of the lanterns.

"Would you come at once, sir?" asked Hornblower, turning back at sight of Buckland.

"I'll come" said Buckland.

"What in the name of God is going on?" asked Clive.

"The captain's hurt" said Hornblower curtly. "Come at once. You'll need a light."

"The captain?" Clive blinked himself wider awake. "Where is he? Give me that lantern, you. Where are my mates? You, there, run and rouse my mates. They sling their hammocks in the sick bay."

So it was a procession of half a dozen that carried their lanterns down the ladder—the four lieutenants, Clive, and Wellard. While waiting at the head of the ladder Bush stole a side glance at Buckland; his face was working with anxiety. He would infinitely rather have been walking a shot-torn deck with grape flying round him. He rolled an inquiring eye at Bush, but with Clive within earshot Bush dared say no word—he knew no more than Buckland did, for that matter. There was no knowing what was awaiting them at the foot of the ladder—arrest, ruin, disgrace, perhaps death.

The faint light of a lantern revealed the scarlet tunic and white crossbelts of a marine, standing by the hatchway. He wore the chevrons of a corporal.

"Anything to report?" demanded Hornblower.

"No, sir. Nothink, sir."

"Captain's down there unconscious. There are two marines guarding him," said Hornblower to Clive, pointing down the hatchway, and Clive swung his bulk painfully onto the ladder and descended.

"Now, corporal" said Hornblower, "tell the first lieutenant all you know about this."

The corporal stood stiffly at attention. With no fewer than four lieutenants eyeing him he was nervous, and he probably had a gloomy feeling based on his experience of the service that when there was trouble among the higher ranks it was likely to go ill with a mere corporal who was unfortunate enough to be involved, however innocently. He stood rigid, trying not to meet anybody's eye.

"Speak up, man" said Buckland, testily. He was nervous as well, but that was understandable in a first lieutenant whose captain had just met with a serious accident.

"I was corporal of the guard, sir. At two bells I relieved the sentry at the captain's door."

"Yes?"

"An'—an'—then I went to sleep again."

"Damn it" said Roberts. "Make your report."

"I was woke up, sir" went on the corporal, "by one of the gennelmen. Gunner, I think 'e is."

"Mr. Hobbs?"

"That may be 'is name, sir. 'E said, 'Cap'n's orders, and guard turn out.' So I turns out the guard, sir, an' there's the cap'n with Wade, the sentry I'd posted. 'E 'ad pistols in 'is 'ands, sir."

"Who—Wade?"

"No, sir, the cap'n, sir."

"What was his manner like?" demanded Hornblower.

"Well, sir——" the corporal did not want to offer any criticism of a captain, not even to a lieutenant.

"Belay that, then. Carry on."

"Cap'n says, sir, 'e says 'e says, sir, 'Follow me'; an' then 'e says to the gennelman 'e says, 'Do your duty, Mr. Hobbs.' So Mr. Hobbs, 'e goes one way, sir, and we comes with the captain down 'ere, sir. 'There's mutiny brewing' says the cap'n, 'black bloody mutiny. We've got to catch the mutineers. Catch 'em red 'anded' says the cap'n."

The surgeon's head appeared in the hatchway.

"Give me another of those lanterns" he said.

"How's the captain?" demanded Buckland.

"Concussion and some fractures, I would say."

"Badly hurt?"

"No knowing yet. Where are my mates? Ah, there you are, Coleman. Splints and bandages, man, as quick as you can get 'em. And a carrying-plank and a canvas and lines. Run, man! You, Pierce, come on down and help me."

So the two surgeon's mates had hardly made their appearance than they were hurried away.

"Carry on, corporal" said Buckland.

"I dunno what I said, sir."

"The captain brought you down here."

"Yessir. 'E 'ad 'is pistols in 'is 'ands, sir, like I said, sir. 'E sent one file for'ard 'Stop every bolt'ole' 'e says; an' 'e says, 'You, corporal, take these two men down an' search.' 'E—'e was yellin', like. 'E 'ad 'is pistols in 'is 'ands."

The corporal looked anxiously at Buckland as he spoke.

"That's all right, corporal" said Buckland. "Just tell the truth."

The knowledge that the captain was unconscious and perhaps badly hurt had reassured him, just as it had reassured Bush.

"So I took the other file down the ladder, sir" said the corporal. "I went first with the lantern, seein' as 'ow I didn't 'ave no musket with me. We got down to the foot of the ladder in among those cases down there, sir. The cap'n, 'e was yellin' down the hatchway. ''Urry' he says. ''Urry. Don't let 'em escape. 'Urry.' So we started climbin' for'ard over the stores, sir."

The corporal hesitated as he approached the climax of his story. He might possibly have been seeking a crude dramatic effect, but more likely he was still afraid of being entangled in circumstances that might damage him despite his innocence.

"What happened then?" demanded Buckland.

"Well, sir——"

Coleman reappeared at this moment, encumbered with various gear including a light six-foot plank he had been carrying on his shoulder. He looked to Buckland for permission to carry on, received a nod, laid the plank on the deck along with the canvas and lines, and disappeared with the rest down the ladder.

"Well?" said Buckland to the corporal.

"I dunno what 'appened, sir."

"Tell us what you know."

"I 'eard a yell, sir. An' a crash. I 'adn't 'ardly gone ten yards, sir. So I came back with the lantern."

"What did you find?"

"It was the cap'n, sir. Layin' there at the foot of the ladder. Like 'e was dead, sir. 'E'd fallen down the 'atchway, sir."

"What did you do?"

"I tried to turn 'im over, sir. 'Is face was all bloody-like. 'E was stunned, sir. I thought 'e might be dead but I could feel 'is 'eart."

"Yes?"

"I didn't know what I ought to do, sir. I didn't know nothink about this 'ere meeting, sir."

"But what *did* you do, in the end?"

"I left my two men with the cap'n, sir, an' I come up to give the alarm. I didn't know who to trust, sir."

There was irony in this situation—the corporal frightened lest he should be taken to task about a petty question as to whether he should have sent a messenger or come himself, while the four lieutenants eyeing him were in danger of hanging.

"Well?"

"I saw Mr. Hornblower, sir." The relief in the corporal's voice echoed the relief he must have felt at finding someone to take over his enormous responsibility. "'E was with young Mr. Wellard, I think 'is name is. Mr. Hornblower, 'e told me to stand guard 'ere, sir, after I told 'im about the cap'n."

"It sounds as if you did right, corporal" said Buckland, judicially.

"Thank 'ee, sir. Thank 'ee, sir."

Coleman came climbing up the ladder, and with another glance at Buckland for permission passed the gear he had left down to someone else under the hatchway. Then he descended again. Bush was looking at the corporal who, now his tale was told, was self-consciously awkward again under the concentrated gaze of four lieutenants.

"Now, corporal" said Hornblower, speaking unexpectedly and with deliberation. "You have no idea how the captain came to fall down the hatchway?"

"No, sir. Indeed I haven't, sir."

Hornblower shot one single glance at his colleagues, one and no more. The corporal's words and Hornblower's glance were vastly reassuring.

"He was excited, you say? Come on, man, speak up."

"Well, yessir." The corporal remembered his earlier unguarded statement, and then in a sudden flood of loquacity he went on. "'E was yellin' after us down the hatchway, sir. I expect 'e was leanin' over. 'E must 'ave been leanin' when the ship pitched, sir. 'E could catch 'is foot on the coamin' and fall 'ead first, sir."

"That's what must have happened" said Hornblower.

Clive came climbing up the ladder and stepped stiffly over the coaming.

"I'm going to sway him up now." he said. He looked at the four lieutenants and then put his hand in the bosom of his shirt and took out a pistol. "This was lying at the captain's side."

"I'll take charge of that" said Buckland.

"There ought to be another one down there, judging by what we've just heard," said Roberts, speaking for the first time. He spoke overloudly, too; excitement had worked on him, and his manner might appear suspicious to any-one with anything to suspect. Bush felt a twinge of annoyance and fear.

"I'll have 'em look for it after we've got the captain up" said Clive. He leaned over the hatchway and called down, "Come on up."

Coleman appeared first, climbing the ladder with a pair of lines in his hand, and after him a marine, clinging awkwardly to the ladder with one arm while the other sup-ported a burden below him.

"Handsomely, handsomely, now" said Clive.

Coleman and the marine, emerging, drew the end of the plank up after them; swathed mummy-like in the canvas and bound to the plank was the body of the captain. That was the best way in which to mount ladders carrying a man with broken bones. Pierce, the other surgeon's mate, came climbing up next, holding the foot of the plank steady. The lieutenants clustered round to give a hand as the plank was hoisted over the coaming. In the light of the lanterns Bush could see the captain's face above the canvas. It was still and expressionless, what there was to be seen of it, for a white bandage concealed one eye and the nose. One temple was still stained with the traces of blood which the doctor had not entirely wiped away.

"Take him to his cabin" said Buckland.

That was the definitive order. This was an important moment. The captain being incapacitated, it was the first lieutenant's duty to take command, and those five words indicated that he had done so. In command, he could even give orders for dealing with the captain. But although this was a momentous step, it was one of routine; Buckland had assumed temporary command of the ship, during the captain's absences, a score of times before. Routine had carried him through this present crisis; the habits of thirty years of service in the navy, as midshipman and lieutenant, had enabled him to carry himself with his usual bearing towards his juniors, to act normally even though he did not know what dreadful fate awaited him at any moment in the immediate future.

And yet Bush, turning his eyes on him now that he had assumed command, was not too sure about the permanence of the effect of habit. Buckland was clearly a little shaken. That might be attributed to the natural reaction of an officer with responsibility thrust upon him in such startling circumstances. So an unsuspicious person—someone without knowledge of the hidden facts—might conclude. But Bush, with fear in his heart, wondering and despairing about what the captain would do when he recovered consciousness, could see that Buckland shared his fear. Chains —a court-martial—the hangman's rope; thoughts of these were unmanning Buckland. And the lives, certainly the whole futures, of the officers in the ship might depend on Buckland's actions.

"Pardon, sir" said Hornblower.

"Yes?" said Buckland; and then with an effort, "Yes, Mr. Hornblower?"

"Might I take the corporal's statement in writing now, while the facts are clear in his memory?"

"Very good, Mr. Hornblower."

"Thank you, sir" said Hornblower. There was nothing to be read in his expression at all, nothing except a respectful attention to duty. He turned to the corporal. "Report to me in my berth after you have reposted the sentry."

"Yessir."

The doctor and his party had already carried the captain away. Buckland was making no effort to move from the spot. It was as if he was paralysed.

"There's the matter of the captain's other pistol, sir" said Hornblower, respectfully as ever.

"Oh yes." Buckland looked round him.

"Here's Wellard, sir."

"Oh yes. He'll do."

"Mr. Wellard" said Hornblower, "go down with a lantern and see if you can find the other pistol. Bring it to the first lieutenant on the quarterdeck."

"Aye aye, sir."

Wellard had recovered from most of his agitation; he had not taken his eyes from Hornblower for some time. Now he picked up the lantern and went down the ladder with it. What Hornblower had said about the quarterdeck penetrated into Buckland's mind, and he began to move off with the others following him. On the lower gundeck Captain Whiting saluted him.

"Any orders, sir?"

No doubt the word that the captain was incapacitated and that Buckland was in command had sped through the ship like wildfire. It took Buckland's numbed brain a second or two to function.

"No, captain" he said at length; and then, "Dismiss your men."

When they reached the quarterdeck the trade wind was still blowing briskly from over the starboard quarter, and the *Renown* was soaring along over the magic sea. Over their heads the great pyramids of sails were reaching up —up—up towards the uncounted stars; with the easy motion of the ship the mastheads were sweeping out great circles against the sky. On the port quarter a half-moon had just lifted itself out of the sea and hung, miraculously, above the horizon, sending a long glittering trail of silver towards the ship. The dark figures of the men on deck stood out plainly against the whitened planks.

Smith was officer of the watch. He came eagerly up to them as they came up the companionway. For the last hour and more he had been pacing about in a fever, hearing the noise and bustle down below, hearing the rumours which had coursed through the ship, and yet unable to leave his post to find out what was really going on.

"What's happened, sir?" he asked.

Smith had not been in the secret of the meeting of the other lieutenants. He had been less victimised by the captain, too. But he could not help being aware of the prevailing discontent; he must know that the captain was insane. Yet Buckland was not prepared for this question. He had not thought about it and had no particular reply. In the end it was Hornblower who answered.

"The captain fell down the hold" he said; his tone was even and with no particular stress. "They've just carried him to his cabin unconscious."

"But how in God's name did he come to fall down the hold?" asked the bewildered Smith.

"He was looking for mutineers" said Hornblower, in that same even tone.

"I see" said Smith. "But——"

There he checked himself. That even tone of Hornblower's had warned him that this was a delicate subject; if he pursued it the question of the captain's sanity would arise, and he would be committed to an opinion on it. He did not want to ask any more questions in that case.

"Six bells, sir" reported the quartermaster to him.

"Very good" said Smith, automatically.

"I must take the marine corporal's deposition, sir" said Hornblower. "I come on watch at eight bells."

If Buckland were in command he could put an end to the ridiculous order that Hornblower should stand watch and watch, and that Bush and Roberts should report to him hourly. There was a moment's awkward pause. No one knew how long the captain would remain unconscious, nor in what condition he would regain consciousness. Wellard came running up to the quarterdeck.

"Here's the other pistol, sir" he said, handing it to Buckland, who took it, at the same time drawing its fellow from his pocket; he stood rather helplessly with them in his hands.

"Shall I relieve you of those, sir?" asked Hornblower, taking them. "And Wellard might be of help to me with the marine's deposition. Can I take him with me, sir?"

"Yes" said Buckland.

Hornblower turned to go below, followed by Wellard.

"Oh, Mr. Hornblower——" said Buckland.

"Sir?"

"Nothing" said Buckland, the inflection in his voice revealing the indecision under which he laboured.

"Pardon, sir, but I should take some rest if I were you" said Hornblower, standing at the head of the companionway. "You've had a tiring night."

Bush was in agreement with Hornblower; not that he cared at all whether Buckland had had a tiring night or not, but because if Buckland were to retire to his cabin there would be no chance of his betraying himself—and his associates—by an unguarded speech. Then it dawned upon Bush that this was just what Hornblower had in mind. And at the same time he was aware of regret at Hornblower's leaving them, and knew that Buckland felt the same regret. Hornblower was level-headed, thinking fast whatever danger menaced him. It was his example which had given a natural appearance to the behaviour of all of them since the alarm down below. Perhaps Horn-blower had a secret unshared with them; perhaps he knew more than they did about how the captain came to fall down the hold—Bush was puzzled and anxious about that —but if such was the case Hornblower had given no sign of it.

'When in God's name is that damned doctor going to report?" said Buckland, to no one in particular.

"Why don't you turn in, sir, until he does?" said Bush.

"I will." Buckland hesitated before he went on speaking. "You gentlemen had best continue to report to me every hour as the captain ordered."

"Aye aye, sir" said Bush and Roberts.

That meant, as Bush realised, that Buckland would take no chances; the captain must hear, when he should recover consciousness, that his orders had been carried out. Bush was anxious—desperate—as he went below to try to snatch half an hour's rest before he would next have to report. He could not hope to sleep. Through the slight partition that divided his cabin from the next he could hear a drone of voices as Hornblower took down the marine corporal's statement in writing.

V

B REAKFAST was being served in the wardroom. It was
a more silent and less cheerful meal even than
breakfast there usually was. The master, the purser,
the captain of marines, had said their conventional "good
mornings" and had sat down to eat without further conversation. They had heard—as had everyone in the ship
—that the captain was recovering consciousness.

Through the scuttles in the side of the ship came two
long ,hafts of sunlight, illuminating the crowded little
place and swinging back and forward across the wardroom
with the easy motion of the ship; the fresh, delightful air
of the northeast trades came in through the hooked-open
door. The coffee was hot; the biscuit, only three weeks on
board, could not have been more than a month or two in
store before that, because it had hardly any weevils in it.
The wardroom cook had intelligently taken advantage of
the good weather to fry the remains of last night's salt pork
with some of the ship's dwindling store of onions. A
breakfast of fried slivers of salt pork with onions, hot
coffee and good biscuit, fresh air and sunshine and fair
weather; the wardroom should have been a cheerful place.
Instead there was brooding anxiety, apprehension, tense
uneasiness. Bush looked across the table at Hornblower,
drawn and pale and weary; there were many things Bush
wanted to say to him but they had to remain unsaid, at
least at present, while the shadow of the captain's madness
darkened the sunlit ship.

Buckland came walking into the wardroom with the

surgeon following him, and everyone looked up question-
ingly—practically everyone stood up to hear the news.

"He's conscious" said Buckland, and looked round at
Clive for him to elaborate on that statement.

"Weak" said Clive.

Bush looked round at Hornblower hoping that he would
ask the questions that Bush wanted asked. Hornblower's
face was set in a mask without expression. His glance
was fixed penetratingly on Clive, but he did not open his
mouth. It was Lomax, the purser, who asked the question
in the end.

"Is he sensible?"

"Well——" said Clive, glancing sidelong at Buckland.
Clearly the last thing Clive wanted to do was to commit
himself definitely regarding the captain's sanity. "He's too
weak at present to be sensible."

Lomax fortunately was inquisitive enough and bull-
headed enough not to be deterred by Clive's reluctance.

"What about this concussion?" he asked. "What's it
done to him?"

"The skull is intact" said Clive. "There are extensive
scalp lacerations. The nose is broken. The clavicle—that's
the collar-bone—and a couple of ribs. He must have fallen
headfirst down the hatchway, as might be expected if he
tripped over the coaming."

"But how on earth did he come to do that?" asked
Lomax.

"He has not said" answered Clive. "I think he does not
remember."

"What?"

"That is a usual state of affairs" said Clive. "One might
almost call it symptomatic. After a severe concussion the
patient usually displays a lapse of memory, extending back
to many hours before the injury."

Bush stole a glance at Hornblower again. His face was still expressionless, and Bush tried to follow his example, both in betraying no emotion and in leaving the questioning to others. And yet this was great, glorious, magnificent news which could not be too much elaborated on for Bush's taste.

"Where does he think he is?" went on Lomax.

"Oh, he knows he's in this ship" said Clive, cautiously.

Now Buckland turned upon Clive; Buckland was hollow-cheeked, unshaven, weary, but he had seen the captain in his berth, and he was in consequence a little more ready to force the issue.

"In your opinion is the captain fit for duty?" he demanded.

"Well——" said Clive again.

"Well?"

"Temporarily, perhaps not."

That was an unsatisfactory answer, but Buckland seemed to have exhausted all his resolution in extracting it. Hornblower raised a mask-like face and stared straight at Clive.

"You mean he is incapable at present of commanding this ship?"

The other officers murmured their concurrence in this demand for a quite definite statement, and Clive, looking round at the determined faces, had to yield.

"At present, yes."

"Then we all know where we stand" said Lomax, and there was satisfaction in his voice which was echoed by everyone in the wardroom except Clive and Buckland.

To deprive a captain of his command was a business of terrible, desperate importance. King and Parliament had combined to give Captain Sawyer command of the *Renown*, and to reverse their appointment savoured of treason, and anyone even remotely connected with the transaction might be tainted for the rest of his life with the unsavoury odour of insubordination and rebellion. Even the most junior master's mate in later years applying for some new appointment might be remembered as having been in the *Renown* when Sawyer was removed from his command and might have his application refused in consequence. It was necessary that there should be the appearance of the utmost legality in an affair which, under the strictest interpretation, could never be entirely legal.

"I have here Corporal Greenwood's statement, sir" said Hornblower, "signed with his mark and attested by Mr. Wellard and myself."

"Thank you" said Buckland, taking the paper; there was some slight hesitation in Buckland's gesture as though the document were a firecracker likely to go off unexpectedly. But only Bush, who was looking for it, could have noticed the hesitation. It was only a few hours since Buckland had been a fugitive in peril of his life, creeping through the bowels of the ship trying to avoid detection, and the names of Wellard and Greenwood, reminding him of this, were a shock to his ears. And like a demon conjured up by the saying of his name, Wellard appeared at that moment at the wardroom door.

"Mr. Roberts sent me down to ask for orders, sir" he said.

Roberts had the watch, and must be fretting with worry about what was going on below decks. Buckland stood in indecision.

"Both watches are on deck, sir" said Hornblower, deferentially.

Buckland looked an inquiry at him.

"You could tell this news to the hands, sir" went on Hornblower.

He was making a suggestion, unasked, to his superior officer, and so courting a snub. But his manner indicated the deepest respect, and nothing besides but eagerness to save his superior all possible trouble.

"Thank you" said Buckland.

Anyone could read in his face the struggle that was going on within him; he was still shrinking from committing himself too deeply—as if he was not already committed! —and he was shrinking from the prospect of making a speech to the assembled hands, even while he realised the necessity of doing so. And the necessity grew greater the more he thought about it—rumours must be flying about the lower deck, where the crew, already unsettled by the captain's behaviour, must be growing more restive still in the prevailing uncertainty. A hard, definite statement must be made to them; it was vitally necessary. Yet the greater the necessity the greater the responsibility that Buckland bore, and he wavered obviously between these two frightening forces.

"All hands, sir?" prompted Hornblower, very softly.

"Yes" said Buckland, desperately taking the plunge.

"Very well, Mr. Wellard" said Hornblower.

Bush caught the look that Hornblower threw to Wellard with the words. There was a significance in it which might be interpreted as of a nature only to be expected when one junior officer was telling another to do something quickly before a senior could change his mind—that was how an uninitiated person would naturally interpret it— but to Bush, clairvoyant with fatigue and worry, there was some other significance in that glance. Wellard was pale and weak with fatigue and worry too; he was being reassured. Possibly he was being told that a secret was still safe.

"Aye aye, sir" said Wellard, and departed.

The pipes twittered through the ship.

"All hands! All hands!" roared the bosun's mates. "All hands fall in abaft the mainmast! All hands!"

Buckland went nervously up on deck, but he acquitted himself well enough at the moment of trial. In a harsh expressionless voice he told the assembled hands that the accident to the captain, which they all must have heard about, had rendered him incapable at present of continuing in command.

"But we'll all go on doing our duty" said Buckland, staring down at the level plain of upturned faces.

Bush, looking with him, picked out the grey head and paunchy figure of Hobbs, the acting-gunner, the captain's toady and informer. Things would be different for Mr. Hobbs in future—at least as long as the captain's disability endured. That was the point; as long as the captain's disability endured. Bush looked down at Hobbs and wondered how much he knew, how much he guessed—how much he would swear to at a court-martial. He tried to read the future in the fat old man's face, but his clairvoyance failed him. He could guess nothing.

When the hands were dismissed there was a moment of bustle and confusion, as the watches resumed their duties and the idlers streamed off below. It was there, in the noise and confusion of a crowd, that momentary privacy and freedom from observation could best be found. Bush intercepted Hornblower by the mizzenmast bitts and could ask the question that he had been wanting to ask for hours; the question on which so much depended.

"How did it happen?" asked Bush.

The bosun's mates were bellowing orders; the hands were scurrying hither and thither; all round the two of them was orderly confusion, a mass of people intent on their own business, while they stood face to face, isolated, with the beneficent sunshine streaming down on them, lighting up the set face which Hornblower turned towards his questioner.

"How did *what* happen, Mr. Bush?" said Hornblower.

"How did the captain fall down the hatchway?"

As soon as he had said the words Bush glanced back over his shoulder in sudden fright lest he should have been overheard. These might be hanging words. When he looked back Hornblower's face was quite expressionless.

"I think he must have overbalanced" he said, evenly, looking straight into Bush's eyes; and then he went on, "If you will excuse me, sir, I have some duties to attend to."

Later in the day every wardroom officer was introduced in turn to the captain's cabin to see with his own eyes what sort of wreck lay there. Bush saw only a feeble invalid, lying in the half-light of the cabin, the face almost covered with bandages, the fingers of one hand moving minutely, the other hand concealed in a sling.

"He's under an opiate" explained Clive in the wardroom. "I had to administer a heavy dose to enable me to try and set the fractured nose."

"I expect it was spread all over his face" said Lomax brutally. "It was big enough."

"The fracture was very extensive and comminuted" agreed Clive.

There were screams the next morning from the captain's cabin, screams of terror as well as of pain, and Clive and his mates emerged eventually sweating and worried. Clive went instantly to report confidentially to Buckland, but everyone in the ship had heard those screams or had been told about them by men who had; the surgeon's mates, questioned eagerly in the gunroom by the other warrant officers, could not maintain the monumental discretion that Clive aimed at in the wardroom. The wretched invalid was undoubtedly insane; he had fallen into a paroxysm of terror when they had attempted to examine the fractured nose, flinging himself about with a madman's strength so that, fearing damage to the other broken bones, they had had to swathe him in canvas as in a strait-jacket, leaving only his left arm out. Laudanum and an extensive bleeding had reduced him to insensibility in the end, but later in the day when Bush saw him he was conscious again, a weeping, pitiful object, shrinking in fear from every face that he saw, persecuted by shadows, sobbing—it was a dreadful thing to see that burly man sobbing like a child— over his troubles, and trying to hide his face from a world which to his tortured mind held no friendship at all and only grim enmity.

"It frequently happens" said Clive pontifically—the longer the captain's illness lasted the more freely he would discuss it—"that an injury, a fall, or a burn, or a fracture, will completely unbalance a mind that previously was a little unstable."

"A little unstable!" said Lomax. "Did he turn out the marines in the middle watch to hunt for mutineers in the hold? Ask Mr. Hornblower here, ask Mr. Bush, if they thought he was a little unstable. He had Hornblower doing watch and watch, and Bush and Roberts and Buckland himself out of bed every hour day and night. He was as mad as a hatter even then."

It was extraordinary how freely tongues wagged now in the ship, now that there was no fear of reports being made to the captain.

"At least we can make seamen out of the crew now" said Carberry, the master, with a satisfaction in his voice that was echoed round the wardroom. Sail drill and gun drill, tautened discipline and hard work, were pulling together a crew that had fast been disintegrating. It was what Buckland obviously delighted in, what he had been itching to do from the moment they had left the Eddystone behind, and exercising the crew helped to lift his mind out of the other troubles that beset it.

For now there was a new responsibility, that all the wardroom discussed freely in Buckland's absence—Buckland was already fenced in by the solitude that surrounds the captain of a ship of war. This was Buckland's sole responsibility, and the wardroom could watch Buckland wrestling with it, as they would watch a prizefighter in the ring; there even were bets laid on the result, as to whether or not Buckland would take the final plunge, whether or not he would take the ultimate step that would proclaim himself as in command of the *Renown* and the captain as incurable.

Locked in the captain's desk were the captain's papers, and among those papers were the secret orders addressed to him by the Lords of the Admiralty. No other eyes than the captain's had seen those orders as yet; not a soul in the ship could make any guess at their contents. They might be merely routine orders, directing the *Renown* perhaps to join Admiral Bickerton's squadron; but also they might reveal some vital diplomatic secret of the kind that no mere lieutenant could be entrusted with. On the one hand Buckland could continue to head for Antigua, and there he could turn over his responsibilities to whoever was the senior officer. There might be some junior captain who could be transferred to the *Renown*; to read the orders and carry off the ship on whatever mission was allotted her. On the other hand Buckland could read the orders now; they might deal with some matter of the greatest urgency. Antigua was a convenient landfall for ships to make from England, but from a military point of view it was not so desirable, being considerably to leeward of most of the points of strategic importance.

If Buckland took the ship down to Antigua and then she had to beat back to windward he might be sharply rapped on the knuckles by My Lords of the Admiralty; yet if he read the secret orders on that account he might be reprimanded for his presumption. The wardroom could guess at his predicament and each individual officer could congratulate himself upon not being personally involved while wondering what Buckland would do about it.

Bush and Hornblower stood side by side on the poop, feet wide apart on the heaving deck, as they steadied themselves and looked through their sextants at the horizon. Through the darkened glass Bush could see the image of the sun reflected from the mirror. With infinite pains he moved the arm round, bringing the image down closer and closer to the horizon. The pitch of the ship over the long blue rollers troubled him, but he persevered, decided in the end that the image of the sun was just sitting on the horizon, and clamped the sextant. Then he could read and record the measurement. As a concession to newfangled prejudices, he decided to follow Hornblower's example and observe the altitude also from the opposite point of the horizon. He swung round and did so, and as he recorded his reading he tried to remember what he had to do about half the difference between the two readings. And the index error, and the "dip". He looked round to find that Hornblower had already finished his observation and was standing waiting for him.

"That's the greatest altitude I've ever measured" remarked Hornblower. "I've never been as far south as this before. What's your result?"

They compared readings.

"That's accurate enough" said Hornblower. "What's the difficulty?"

"Oh, I can shoot the sun" said Bush. "No trouble about

that. It's the calculations that bother me—those damned corrections."

Hornblower raised an eyebrow for a moment. He was accustomed to taking his own observations each noon and making his own calculations of the ship's position, in order to keep himself in practice. He was aware of the mechanical difficulty of taking an accurate observation in a moving ship, but—although he knew of plenty of other instances—he still could not believe that any man could really find the subsequent mathematics difficult. They were so simple to him that when Bush had asked him if he could join him in their noontime exercise for the sake of improving himself he had taken it for granted that it was only the mechanics of using a sextant that troubled Bush. But he politely concealed his surprise.

"They're easy enough" he said, and then he added "sir." A wise officer, too, did not make too much display of his superior ability when speaking to his senior. He phrased his next speech carefully.

"If you were to come below with me, sir, you could check through my calculations."

Bush listened in patience to Hornblower's explanations. They made the problem perfectly clear for the moment— it was by a hurried last-minute reading up that Bush had been able to pass his examination for lieutenant, although it was seamanship and not navigation that got him through —but Bush knew by bitter experience that tomorrow it would be hazy again.

"Now we can plot the position" said Hornblower, bending over the chart.

Bush watched as Hornblower's capable fingers worked the parallel rulers across the chart; Hornblower had long bony hands with something of beauty about them, and it was actually fascinating to watch them doing work at which they were so supremely competent. The powerful fingers picked up the pencil and ruled a line.

"There's the point of interception" said Hornblower. "Now we can check against the dead reckoning."

Even Bush could follow the simple steps necessary to plot the ship's course by dead reckoning since noon yesterday. The pencil in the steady fingers made a tiny *x* on the chart.

"We're still being set to the s'uth'ard, you see" said Hornblower. "We're not far enough east yet for the Gulf Stream to set us to the nor'ard."

"Didn't you say you'd never navigated these waters before?" asked Bush.

"Yes."

"Then how——? Oh, I suppose you've been studying."

To Bush it was as strange that a man should read up beforehand and be prepared for conditions hitherto unknown as it was strange to Hornblower that a man should find trouble in mathematics.

"At any rate, there we are" said Hornblower, tapping the chart with the pencil.

"Yes" said Bush.

They both looked at the chart with the same thought in mind.

"What d'ye think Number One'll do?" asked Bush.

Buckland might be legally in command of the ship, but it was too early yet to speak of him as the captain—"the captain" was still that weeping figure swathed in canvas on the cot in the cabin.

"Can't tell" answered Hornblower, "but he makes up his mind now or never. We lose ground to loo'ard every day from now, you see."

"What'd *you* do?" Bush was curious about this junior lieutenant who had shown himself ready of resources and so guarded in speech.

"I'd read those orders" said Hornblower instantly. "I'd rather be in trouble for having done something than for not having done anything."

"I wonder" said Bush. On the other hand a definite action could be made the subject of a court-martial charge far more easily than the omission to do something; Bush felt this, but he had not the facility with words to express it easily.

"Those orders may detach us on independent service" went on Hornblower. "God, what a chance for Buckland!"

"Yes" said Bush.

The eagerness in Hornblower's expression was obvious. If ever a man yearned for an independent command and the consequent opportunity to distinguish himself it was Hornblower. Bush wondered faintly if he himself was as anxious to have the responsibility of the command of a ship of the line in troubled waters. He looked at Hornblower with an interest which he knew to be constantly increasing. Hornblower was a man always ready to adopt the bold course, a man who infinitely preferred action to inaction; widely read in his profession and yet a practical seaman, as Bush had already had plenty of opportunity to observe. A student yet a man of action; a fiery spirit and yet discreet—Bush remembered how tactfully he had acted during the crisis following the captain's injury and how dexterously he had handled Buckland.

And—and—what was the truth about that injury to the captain? Bush darted a more searching glance than ever at Hornblower as he followed up that train of thought. Bush's mind did not consciously frame the words "motive" and "opportunity" to itself—it was not that type of mind—but it felt its way along an obscure path of reasoning which might well have been signposted with those words. He wanted to ask again the question he had asked once before, but to do so would not merely invite but would merit a rebuff. Hornblower was established in a strong position and Bush could be sure that he would never abandon it through indiscretion or impatience. Bush looked at the lean eager face, at the long fingers drumming on the chart. It was not right or fit or proper that he should feel any admiration or even respect for Hornblower, who was not merely his junior in age by a couple of years—that did not matter—but was his junior as a lieutenant. The dates on their respective commissions really did matter; a junior was someone for whom it should be impossible to feel respect by the traditions of the service. Anything else would be unnatural, might even savour of the equalitarian French ideas which they were engaged in fighting. The thought of himself as infected with Red Revolutionary notions made Bush actually uneasy, and yet as he stirred uncomfortably in his chair he could not wholly discard those notions.

"I'll put these things away" said Hornblower, rising from his chair. "I'm exercising my lower-deck guns' crews after the hands have had their dinner. And I have the first dogwatch after that."

VI

THE lower-deck guns had been secured, and the sweating crews came pouring up on deck. Now that the *Renown* was as far south as 30° north latitude the lower gundeck, even with the ports open for artillery exercise, was a warm place, and hauling those guns in and running them out was warm work. Hornblower had kept the crews hard at it, one hundred and eighty men, who afterwards came pouring up into the sunshine and the fresh air of the trade wind to receive the good-humoured chaff of the rest of the crew who had not been working so hard but who knew perfectly well that their turn would come soon.

The guns' crews wiped their steaming foreheads and flung jests—jagged and unpolished like the flints in the soil from which they had sprung—back at their tormentors. It was exhilarating to an officer to see the high spirits of the men and to be aware of the good temper that prevailed; in the three days that had elapsed since the change in command the whole atmosphere of the ship had improved. Suspicion and fear had vanished; after a brief sulkiness the hands had found that exercise and regular work were stimulating and satisfactory.

Hornblower came aft, the sweat running down him, and touched his hat to Roberts, who was officer of the watch, where he stood chatting with Bush at the break of the poop. It was an unusual request that Hornblower made, and Roberts and Bush stared at him with surprise.

"But what about the deck, Mr. Hornblower?" asked Roberts.

"A hand can swab it off in two minutes, sir" replied Hornblower, wiping his face and looking at the blue sea overside with a longing that was obvious to the most casual glance. "I have fifteen minutes before I relieve you, sir—plenty of time."

"Oh, very well, Mr. Hornblower."

"Thank you, sir" said Hornblower, and he turned eagerly away with another touch of his hat, while Roberts and Bush exchanged glances which were as much amused as puzzled. They watched Hornblower give his orders.

"Captain of the waist! Captain of the waist, there!"

"Sir?"

"Get the wash-deck pump rigged at once."

"Rig the wash-deck pump, sir?"

"Yes. Four men for the handles. One for the hose. Jump to it, now. I'll be with you in two minutes."

"Aye aye, sir."

The captain of the waist set about obeying the strange order after a glance at the receding figure. Hornblower was as good as his word; it was only two minutes before he returned, but now he was naked except for a towel draped sketchily round him. This was all very strange.

"Give away" he said to the men at the pump handles.

They were dubious about all this, but they obeyed the order, and in alternate pairs they threw their weight upon the handles. Up—down, up—down; clank—clank. The seaman holding the hose felt it stir in his hands as the water from far overside came surging up along it; and next moment a clear stream of water came gushing out of it.

"Turn it on me" said Hornblower, casting his towel aside and standing naked in the sunshine. The hoseman hesitated.

"Hurry up, now!"

As dubiously as ever the hoseman obeyed orders, turning

the jet upon his officer, who rotated first this way and then that as it splashed upon him; an amused crowd was gathering to watch.

"Pump, you sons of seacooks!" said Hornblower; and obediently the men at the pump handles, now grinning broadly, threw all their weight on the handles, with such enthusiasm that their feet left the deck as they hauled down upon them and the clear water came hurtling out through the hose with considerable force. Hornblower twirled round and round under the stinging impact, his face screwed up in painful ecstasy.

Buckland had been standing aft at the taffrail, lost in thought and gazing down at the ship's wake, but the clanking of the pump attracted his attention and he strolled forward to join Roberts and Bush and to look at the strange spectacle.

"Hornblower has some odd fancies" he remarked, but he smiled as he said it—a rather pathetic smile, for his face bore the marks of the anxieties he was going through.

"He seems to be enjoying himself, sir" said Bush.

Bush, looking at Hornblower revolving under the sparkling stream, was conscious of a prickling under his shirt in his heavy uniform coat, and actually had the feeling that it might be pleasurable to indulge in that sort of shower bath, however injurious it might be to the health.

"'Vast pumping!" yelled Hornblower. "Avast, there!"

The hands at the pumps ceased their labours, and the jet from the hose died away to a trickle, to nothing.

"Captain of the waist! Secure the pump. Get the deck swabbed."

"Aye aye, sir."

Hornblower grabbed his towel and came trotting back along the maindeck. He looked up at the group of officers with a grin which revealed his exhilaration and high spirits.

"Dunno if it's good for discipline" commented Roberts, as Hornblower disappeared; and then, with a tardy flash of insight, "I suppose it's all right."

"I suppose so" said Buckland. "Let's hope he doesn't get himself a fever, checking the perspiration like that."

"He showed no sign of one, sir" said Bush; lingering in Bush's mind's eye was the picture of Hornblower's grin. It blended with his memory of Hornblower's eager expression when they were discussing what Buckland had best do in the dilemma in which he found himself.

"Ten minutes to eight bells, sir" reported the quarter-master.

"Very well" said Roberts.

The wet patch on the deck was now almost dry; a faint steam rose from it as the sun, still fierce at four o'clock in the afternoon, beat on it.

"Call the watch" said Roberts.

Hornblower came running up to the quarterdeck with his telescope; he must have pulled on his clothes with the orderly rapidity that marked all his actions. He touched his hat to the quarterdeck and stood by to relieve Roberts.

"You feel refreshed after your bath?" asked Buckland.

"Yes, sir, thank you."

Bush looked at the pair of them, the elderly, worried first lieutenant and the young fifth lieutenant, the older man pathetically envying the youngster's youth. Bush was learning something about personalities. He would never be able to reduce the results of his observations to a tabular system, and it would never occur to him to do so, but he could learn without doing so; his experience and observations would blend with his native wit to govern his judgments, even if he were too self-conscious to philosophise over them. He was aware that naval officers (he knew almost nothing of mankind on land) could be divided into

active individuals and passive individuals, into those eager
for responsibility and action and into those content to
wait until action was forced on them. Before that he had
learned the simpler lesson that officers could be divided
into the efficient and the blunderers, and also into the
intelligent and the stupid—this last division was nearly the
same as the one immediately preceding, but not quite.
There were the officers who could be counted on to act
quickly and correctly in an emergency, and those who
could not—again the dividing line did not quite coincide
with the preceding. And there were officers with discretion
and officers with none, patient officers and impatient ones,
officers with strong nerves and officers with weak nerves.
In certain cases Bush's estimates had to contend with his
prejudices—he was liable to be suspicious of brains and of
originality of thought and of eagerness for activity, especially because in the absence of some of the other desirable
qualities these things might be actual nuisances. The final
and most striking difference Bush had observed during ten
years of continuous warfare was that between the leaders
and the led, but that again was a difference of which Bush
was conscious without being able to express it in words,
and especially not in words as succinct or as definite as
these; but he was actually aware of the difference even
though he was not able to bring himself to define it.

But he had that difference at the back of his mind,
all the same, as he looked at Buckland and Hornblower
chatting together on the quarterdeck. The afternoon watch
had ended, and the first dogwatch had begun, with Hornblower as officer of the watch. It was the traditional
moment for relaxation; the heat of the day had passed,
and the hands collected forward, some of them to gaze
down at the dolphins leaping round the bows, while the
officers who had been dozing during the afternoon in their

cabins came up to the quarterdeck for air and paced up and down in little groups deep in conversation.

A ship of war manned for active service was the most crowded place in the world—more crowded than the most rundown tenement in Seven Dials—but long and hard experience had taught the inhabitants how to live even in those difficult conditions. Forward there were groups of men yarning, men skylarking; there were solitary men who had each preempted a square yard of deck for himself and sat, cross-legged, with tools and materials about them, doing scrimshaw work—delicate carvings on bone—or embroidery or whittling at models oblivious to the tumult about them. Similarly aft on the crowded quarterdeck the groups of officers strolled and chatted, avoiding the other groups without conscious effort.

It was in accordance with the traditions of the service that these groups left the windward side of the quarterdeck to Buckland as long as he was on deck; and Buckland seemed to be making a long stay this afternoon. He was deep in conversation with Hornblower, the two of them pacing up and down beside the quarterdeck carronades, eight yards forward, eight yards back again; long ago the navy had discovered that when the walking distance was so limited conversation must not be interrupted by the necessarily frequent turns. Every pair of officers turned inwards as they reached the limits of their walk, facing each other momentarily and continuing the conversation without a break, and walking with their hands clasped behind them as a result of the training they had all received as midshipmen not to put their hands in their pockets.

So walked Buckland and Hornblower, and curious glances were cast at them by the others, for even on this golden evening, with the blue-enamel sea overside and the sun sinking to starboard with the promise of a magnificent sunset, everyone was conscious that in the cabin just below their feet lay a wretched insane man, half-swathed in a strait-jacket; and Buckland had to make up his mind how to deal with him. Up and down, up and down walked Buckland and Hornblower. Hornblower seemed to be as deferential as ever, and Buckland seemed to be asking questions; but some of the replies he received must have been unexpected, for more than once Buckland stopped in the middle of a turn and stood facing Hornblower, apparently repeating his question, while Hornblower seemed to be standing his ground both literally and figuratively, sturdy and yet respectful, as Buckland stood with the sun illuminating his haggard features.

Perhaps it had been a fortunate chance that had made Hornblower decide to take a bath under the wash-deck pump—this conversation had its beginnings in that incident.

"Is that a council of war?" said Smith to Bush, looking across at the pair.

"Not likely" said Bush.

A first lieutenant would not deliberately ask the advice or even the opinion of one so junior. Yet—yet—it might be possible, starting with idle conversation about different matters.

"Don't tell me they're discussing Catholic Emancipation" said Lomax.

It was just possible, Bush realised guiltily, that they were discussing something else—that question as to how the captain had come to fall down the hatchway. Bush found himself automatically looking round the deck for Wellard when that thought occurred to him. Wellard was skylarking in the main rigging with the midshipmen and master's mates as if he had not a care in the world. But it could not be that question which Buckland and

Hornblower were discussing. Their attitudes seemed to indicate that theories and not facts were the subject of the debate.

"Anyway, they've settled it" said Smith.

Hornblower was touching his hat to Buckland, and Buckland was turning to go below again. Several curious pairs of eyes looked across at Hornblower now that he was left solitary, and as he became conscious of their regard he strolled over to them.

"Affairs of state?" asked Lomax, asking the question which everyone wanted asked.

Hornblower met his gaze with a level glance.

"No" he said, and smiled.

"It certainly looked like matters of importance" said Smith.

"That depends on the definition" answered Hornblower.

He was still smiling, and his smile gave no clue at all regarding his thoughts. It would be rude to press him further; it was possible that he and Buckland had been discussing some private business. Nobody looking at him could guess.

"Come off those hammocks, there!" bellowed Hornblower; the skylarking midshipmen were not breaking one of the rules of the ship, but it was a convenient moment to divert the conversation.

Three bells rang out; the first dogwatch was three-quarters completed.

"Mr. Roberts, sir!" suddenly called the sentry at the smokers' slow match by the hatchway. "Passing the word for Mr. Roberts!"

Roberts turned from the group.

"Who's passing the word for me?" he asked, although with the captain ill there could only be one man in the ship who could pass the word for the second lieutenant.

"Mr. Buckland, sir. Mr. Buckland passing the word for Mr. Roberts."

"Very well," said Roberts, hurrying down the companion.

The others exchanged glances. This might be the moment of decision. Yet on the other hand it might be only a routine matter. Hornblower took advantage of the distraction to turn away from the group and continue his walk on the weather side of the ship; he walked with his chin nearly down on his breast, his drooping head balanced by the hands behind his back. Bush thought he looked weary.

Now there came a fresh cry from below, repeated by the sentry at the hatchway.

"Mr. Clive! Passing the word for Mr. Clive. Mr. Buckland passing the word for Mr. Clive!"

"Oh-ho!" said Lomax in significant tones, as the surgeon hurried down.

"Something happens" said Carberry, the master.

Time went on without either the second lieutenant or the surgeon reappearing. Smith, under his arm the telescope that was the badge of his temporary office, touched his hat to Hornblower and prepared to relieve him as officer of the watch as the second dogwatch was called. In the east the sky was turning dark, and the sun was setting over the starboard quarter in a magnificent display of red and gold; from the ship towards the sun the surface of the sea was gilded and glittering, but close overside it was the richest purple. A flying fish broke the surface and went skimming along, leaving a transient, momentary furrow behind it like a groove in enamel.

"Look at that!" exclaimed Hornblower to Bush.

"A flying fish" said Bush, indifferently.

"Yes! There's another!"

Hornblower leaned over to get a better view.

"You'll see plenty of them before this voyage is over" said Bush.

"But I've never seen one before."

The play of expression on Hornblower's face was curious. One moment he was full of eager interest; the next he assumed an appearance of stolid indifference as a man might pull on a glove. His service at sea so far, varied though it might be, had been confined to European waters; years of dangerous activity on the French and Spanish coasts in a frigate, two years in the *Renown* in the Channel fleet, and he had been eagerly looking forward to the novelties he would encounter in tropical waters. But he was talking to a man to whom these things were no novelty, and who evinced no excitement at the sight of the first flying fish of the voyage. Hornblower was not going to be outdone in stolidity and self-control; if the wonders of the deep failed to move Bush they were not going to evoke any childish excitement in Hornblower, at least any apparent excitement if Hornblower could suppress it. He was a veteran, and he was not going to appear like a raw hand.

Bush looked up to see Roberts and Clive ascending the companionway in the gathering night, and turned eagerly towards them. Officers came from every part of the quarterdeck to hear what they had to say.

"Well, sir?" asked Lomax.

"He's done it" said Roberts.

"He's read the secret orders, sir?" asked Smith.

"As far as I know, yes."

"Oh!"

There was a pause before someone asked the inevitable silly question.

"What did they say?"

"They are secret orders" said Roberts, and now there

was a touch of pomposity in his voice—it might be to compensate for his lack of knowledge, or it might be because Roberts was now growing more aware of the dignity of his position as second in command. "If Mr. Buckland had taken me into his confidence I still could not tell you."

"True enough" said Carberry.

"What did the captain do?" asked Lomax.

"Poor devil" said Clive. With all attention turned to him Clive grew expansive. "We might be fiends from the pit! You should have seen him cower away when we came in. Those morbid terrors grow more acute."

Clive awaited a request for further information, and even though none was forthcoming he went on with his story.

"We had to find the key to his desk. You would have thought we were going to cut his throat, judging by the way he wept and tried to hide. All the sorrows of the world—all the terrors of hell torment that wretched man."

"But you found the key?" persisted Lomax.

"We found it. And we opened his desk."

"And then?"

"Mr. Buckland found the orders. The usual linen envelope with the Admiralty seal. The envelope had been already opened."

"Naturally" said Lomax. "Well?"

"And now, I suppose" said Clive, conscious of the anti-climax, "I suppose he's reading them."

"And we are none the wiser."

There was a disappointed pause.

"Bless my soul!" said Carberry. "We've been at war since '93. Nearly ten years of it. D'ye still expect to know what lies in store for you? The West Indies today—Halifax tomorrow. We obey orders. Helm-a-lee—let go and haul. A bellyful of grape or champagne in a captured flagship.

Who cares? We draw our four shillings a day, rain or shine."

"Mr. Carberry!" came the word from below. "Mr. Buckland passing the word for Mr. Carberry."

"Bless my soul!" said Carberry again.

"Now you can earn your four shillings a day" said Lomax.

The remark was addressed to his disappearing back, for Carberry was already hastening below.

"A change of course" said Smith. "I'll wager a week's pay on it."

"No takers" said Roberts.

It was the most likely new development of all, for Carberry, the master, was the officer charged with the navigation of the ship.

Already it was almost full night, dark enough to make the features of the speakers indistinct, although over to the westward there was still a red patch on the horizon, and a faint red trail over the black water towards the ship. The binnacle lights had been lit and the brighter stars were already visible in the dark sky, with the mastheads seeming to brush past them, with the motion of the ship, infinitely far over their heads. The ship's bell rang out, but the group showed no tendency to disperse. And then interest quickened. Here were Buckland and Carberry returning, ascending the companionway; the group drew on one side to clear them a passage.

"Officer of the watch!" said Buckland.

"Sir!" said Smith, coming forward in the darkness.

"We're altering course two points. Steer southwest."

"Aye aye, sir. Course southwest. Mr. Abbott, pipe the hands to the braces."

The *Renown* came round on her new course, with her sails trimmed to the wind which was now no more than a point on her port quarter. Carberry walked over to the binnacle and looked into it to make sure the helmsman was exactly obeying his orders.

"Another pull on the weather forebrace, there!" yelled Smith. "Belay!"

The bustle of the change of course died away.

"Course sou'west, sir" reported Smith.

"Very good, Mr. Smith" said Buckland, by the rail.

"Pardon, sir" said Roberts, greatly daring, addressing him as he loomed in the darkness. "Can you tell us our mission, sir?"

"Not our mission. That is still secret, Mr. Roberts."

"Very good, sir."

"But I'll tell you where we're bound. Mr. Carberry knows already."

"Where, sir?"

"Santo Domingo. Scotchman's Bay."

There was a pause while this information was being digested.

"Santo Domingo," said someone, meditatively.

"Hispaniola" said Carberry, explanatorily.

"Hayti" said Hornblower.

"Santo Domingo—Hayti—Hispaniola" said Carberry. "Three names for the same island."

"Hayti!" exclaimed Roberts, some chord in his memory suddenly touched. "That's where the blacks are in rebellion."

"Yes" agreed Buckland.

Anyone could guess that Buckland was trying to say that word in as noncommittal a tone as possible; it might be because there was a difficult diplomatic situation with regard to the blacks, and it might be because fear of the captain was still a living force in the ship.

LIEUTENANT HORNBLOWER

VII

LIEUTENANT Buckland, in acting command of H.M.S.
Renown, of seventy-four guns, was on the quarterdeck of his ship peering through his telescope at the
low mountains of Santo Domingo. The ship was rolling
in a fashion unnatural and disturbing, for the long Atlantic
swell, driven by the northeast trades, was passing under her
keel while she lay hove-to to the final puffs of the land
breeze which had blown since midnight and was now
dying away as the fierce sun heated the island again. The
Renown was actually wallowing, rolling her lower deck
gunports under, first on one side and then on the other,
for what little breeze there was was along the swell and
did nothing to stiffen her as she lay with her mizzen topsail backed. She would lie right over on one side, until
the gun tackles creaked with the strain of holding the guns
in position, until it was hard to keep a foothold on the
steep-sloping deck; she would lie there for a few harrowing
seconds, and then slowly right herself, making no pause at
all at the moment when she was upright and her deck
horizontal, and continue, with a clattering of blocks and a
rattle of gear in a sickening swoop until she was as far over
in the opposite direction, gun tackles creaking and unwary
men slipping and sliding, and lie there unresponsive until the
swell had rolled under her and she repeated her behaviour.

"For God's sake" said Hornblower, hanging on to a
belaying pin in the mizzen fife rail to save himself from
sliding down the deck into the scuppers, "can't he make up
his mind?"

There was something in Hornblower's stare that made Bush look at him more closely.

"Seasick?" he asked, with curiosity.

"Who wouldn't be?" replied Hornblower. "How she rolls!"

Bush's cast-iron stomach had never given him the least qualm, but he was aware that less fortunate men suffered from seasickness even after weeks at sea, especially when subjected to a different kind of motion. This funereal rolling was nothing like the free action of the *Renown* under sail.

"Buckland has to see how the land lies," he said in an effort to cheer Hornblower up.

"How much more does he want to see?" grumbled Hornblower. "There's the Spanish colours flying on the fort up there. Everyone on shore knows now that a ship of the line is prowling about, and the Dons won't have to be very clever to guess that we're not here on a yachting trip. Now they've all the time they need to be ready to receive us."

"But what else could he do?"

"He could have come in in the dark with the sea breeze. Landing parties ready. Put them ashore at dawn. Storm the place before they knew there was any danger. Oh, God!"

The final exclamation had nothing to do with what went before. It was wrenched out of Hornblower by the commotion of his stomach. Despite his deep tan there was a sickly green colour in his cheeks.

"Hard luck" said Bush.

Buckland still stood trying to keep his telescope trained on the coast despite the rolling of the ship. This was Scotchman's Bay—the Bahia de Escocesa, as the Spanish charts had it. To the westward lay a shelving beach; the big rollers here broke far out and ran in creamy white up to the water's edge with diminishing force, but to the eastward the shore line rose in a line of tree-covered hills standing bluffly with their feet in blue water; the rollers burst against them in sheets of spray that climbed far up the cliffs before falling back in a smother of white. For thirty miles those hills ran beside the sea, almost due east and west; they constituted the Samaná peninsula, terminating in Samaná Point. According to the charts the peninsula was no more than ten miles wide; behind them, round Samaná Point, lay Samaná Bay, opening into the Mona Passage and a most convenient anchorage for privateers and small ships of war which could lie there, under the protection of the fort on the Samaná peninsula, ready to slip out and harass the West Indian convoys making use of the Mona Passage. The *Renown* had been given orders to clear out this raiders' lair before going down to leeward to Jamaica—everyone in the ship could guess that—but now that Buckland confronted the problem he was not at all sure how to solve it. His indecision was apparent to all the curious lookers-on who clustered on the *Renown's* deck.

The main topsail suddenly flapped like thunder, and the ship began to turn slowly head to sea; the land breeze was expiring, and the trade winds, blowing eternally across the Atlantic, were resuming their dominion. Buckland shut his telescope with relief. At least that was an excuse for postponing action.

"Mr. Roberts!"

"Sir!"

"Lay her on the port tack. Full and by!"

"Aye aye, sir."

The after guard came running to the mizzen braces, and the ship slowly paid off. Gradually the topsails caught the wind, and she began to lie over, gathering way as she did so. She met the next roller with her port bow, thrusting boldly into it in a burst of spray. The tautened weather-rigging began to sing a more cheerful note, blending with the music of her passage through the water. She was a live thing again, instead of rolling like a corpse in the trough. The roaring trade wind pressed her over, and she went surging along, rising and swooping as if with pleasure, leaving a creamy wake behind her on the blue water while the sea roared under the bows.

"Better?" asked Bush of Hornblower.

"Better in one way" was the reply. Hornblower looked over at the distant hills of Santo Domingo. "I could wish we were going into action and not running away to think about it."

"What a fire-eater!" said Bush.

"A fire-eater? Me? Nothing like that—quite the opposite. I wish—oh, I wish for too much, I suppose."

There was no explaining some people, thought Bush, philosophically. He was content to bask in the sunshine now that its heat was tempered by the ship's passage through the wind. If action and danger lay in the future he could await it in stolid tranquillity; and he certainly could congratulate himself that he did not have to carry Buckland's responsibility of carrying a ship of the line and seven hundred and twenty men into action. The prospect of action at least took one's mind off the horrid fact that confined below lay an insane captain.

At dinner in the wardroom he looked over at Hornblower, fidgety and nervous. Buckland had announced his intention of taking the bull by the horns the next morning, of rounding Samaná Point and forcing his way straight up the bay. It would not take many broadsides from the *Renown* to destroy any shipping that lay there at anchor. Bush thoroughly approved of the scheme. Wipe out the privateers, burn them, sink them, and then it would be time to decide what, if anything, should be done next. At the meeting in the wardroom, when Buckland asked if any officer had any questions, Smith had asked sensibly about the tides, and Carberry had given him the information; Roberts had asked a question or two about the situation on the south shore of the bay; but Hornblower at the foot of the table had kept his mouth shut, although looking with eager attention at each speaker in turn.

During the dogwatches Hornblower had paced the deck by himself, head bent in meditation; Bush noticed the fingers of the hands behind his back twisting and twining nervously, and he experienced a momentary doubt. Was it possible that this energetic young officer was lacking in physical courage? That phrase was not Bush's own—he had heard it used maliciously somewhere or other years ago. It was better to use it now than to tell himself outright that he suspected Hornblower might be a coward. Bush was not a man of large tolerance; if a man were a coward he wanted no more to do with him.

Half-way through next morning the pipes shrilled along the decks; the drums of the marines beat a rousing roll.

"Clear the decks for action! Hands to quarters! Clear for action!"

Bush came down to the lower gundeck, which was his station for action; under his command was the whole deck and the seventeen twenty-four-pounders of the starboard battery, while Hornblower commanded under him those of the port side. The hands were already knocking down the screens and removing obstructions. A little group of the surgeon's crew came along the deck; they were carrying a strait-jacketed figure bound to a plank. Despite the jacket and the lashings it writhed feebly and wept pitifully—the captain being carried down to the safety of the cable tier while his cabin was cleared for action. A hand or two in the bustle found time to shake their heads over the unhappy figure, but Bush checked them soon enough. He wanted to be able to report the lower gundeck cleared for action with creditable speed.

Hornblower made his appearance, touched his hat to Bush, and stood by to supervise his guns. Most of this lower deck was in twilight, for the stout shafts of sunlight that came down the hatchways did little to illuminate the farther parts of the deck with its sombre red paint. Half a dozen ship's boys came along, each one carrying a bucket of sand, which they scattered in handfuls over the deck. Bush kept a sharp eye on them, because the guns' crews depended on that sand for firm foothold. The water buckets beside each gun were filled; they served a dual purpose, to dampen the swabs that cleaned out the guns and for immediate use against fire. Round the mainmast stood a ring of extra fire buckets; in tubs at either side of the ship smouldered the slow matches from which the gun captains could rekindle their linstocks when necessary. Fire and water. The marine sentries came clumping along the deck in their scarlet coats and white crossbelts, the tops of their shakos brushing the deck beams over their heads. Corporal Greenwood posted one at each hatchway, bayonet fixed and musket loaded. Their duty was to see that no unauthorised person ran down to take shelter in the safety of that part of the ship comfortably below waterline. Mr. Hobbs, the acting-gunner, with his mates and helpers made a momentary appearance on their way down to the magazine. They were all wearing list slippers to obviate any chance of setting off loose powder which would be bound to be strewn about down there in the heat of action.

Soon the powder boys came running up, each with a charge for the guns. The breechings of the guns were cast off and the crews stood by the tackles, waiting for the word to open the ports and run out the guns. Bush darted his glance along both sides. The gun captains were all at their posts. Ten men stood by every gun on the starboard side, five by every gun on the port side—maximum and minimum crews for twenty-four-pounders. It was Bush's responsibility to see to it that whichever battery came into action the guns were properly manned. If both sides had to be worked at once he had to make a fair division, and when the casualties began and guns were put out of service he had to redistribute the crews. The petty officers and warrant officers were reporting their subdivisions ready for action, and Bush turned to the midshipman beside him whose duty was to carry messages.

"Mr. Abbott, report the lower deck cleared for action. Ask if the guns should be run out."

"Aye aye, sir."

A moment before the ship had been full of noise and bustle, and now everything down here was still and quiet save for the creaking of the timbers; the ship was rising and swooping rhythmically over the sea—Bush as he stood by the mainmast was automatically swaying with the ship's motion. Young Abbott came running down the ladder again.

"Mr. Buckland's compliments, sir, and don't run the guns out yet."

"Very good."

Hornblower was standing farther aft, in line with the ringbolts of the train tackles; he had looked round to hear what message Abbott bore, and now he turned back again. He stood with his feet apart, and Bush saw him put one hand into the other, behind his back, and clasp it firmly. There was a rigidity about the set of his shoulders and in the way he held his head that might be significant of anything, eagerness for action or the reverse. A gun captain addressed a remark to Hornblower, and Bush watched him turn to answer it. Even in the half-light of the lower deck Bush could see there were signs of strain in his expression, and that smile might be forced. Oh well, decided Bush, as charitably as he could, men often looked like that before going into action.

Silently the ship sailed on; even Bush had his ears cocked, trying to hear what was going on above him so as to draw deductions about the situation. Faintly down the hatchway came the call of a seaman.

"No bottom, sir. No bottom with this line."

So there was a man in the chains taking casts with the lead, and they must be drawing near the land; everyone down on the lower deck drew the same conclusion and started to remark about it to his neighbour.

"Silence, there!" snapped Bush.

Another cry from the leadsman, and then a bellowed order. Instantly the lower deck seemed to be filled solid with noise. The maindeck guns were being run out; in the confined space below every sound was multiplied and reverberated by the ship's timbers so that the gun-trucks rolling across the planking made a noise like thunder. Everyone looked to Bush for orders, but he stood steady; he had received none. Now a midshipman appeared descending the ladder.

"Mr. Buckland's compliments, sir, and please to run your guns out."

He had squealed his message without ever setting foot on deck, and everyone had heard it. There was an instant buzz round the deck, and excitable people began to reach for the gunports to open them.

"Still!" bellowed Bush. Guiltily all movement ceased.

"Up ports!"

The twilight of the lower deck changed to daylight as the ports opened; little rectangles of sunshine swayed about on the deck on the port side, broadening and narrowing with the motion of the ship.

"Run out!"

With the ports open the noise was not so great; the crews flung their weight on the tackles and the trucks

roared as the guns thrust their muzzles out. Bush stepped
to the nearest gun and stooped to peer out through the
open port. There were the green hills of the island at
extreme gunshot distance; here the cliffs were not nearly so
abrupt, and there was a jungle-covered shelf at their feet.

"Hands wear ship!"

Bush could recognise Roberts' voice hailing from the
quarterdeck. The deck under his feet steadied to the
horizontal, and the distant hills seemed to swing with
the vessel. The masts creaked as the yards came round.
That must be Samaná Point which they were rounding.
The motion of the ship had changed far more than would
be the result of mere alteration of course. She was not
only on an even keel but she was in quiet water, gliding
along into the bay. Bush squatted down on his heels by the
muzzle of a gun and peered at the shore. This was the
south side of the peninsula at which he was looking,
presenting a coastline toward the bay nearly as steep as the
one on the seaward side. There was the fort on the crest
and the Spanish flag waving over it. The excited midshipman came scuttling down the ladder like a squirrel.

"Sir! Sir! Will you try a ranging shot at the batteries
when your guns bear?"

Bush ran a cold eye over him.

"Whose orders?" he asked.

"M—Mr. Buckland's, sir."

"Then say so. Very well. My respects to Mr. Buckland,
and it will be a long time before my guns are within range."

"Aye aye, sir."

There was smoke rising from the fort, and not powder
smoke either. Bush realised with something like a quiver of
apprehension that probably it was smoke from a furnace for
heating shot; soon the fort would be hurling red-hot shot at
them, and Bush could see no chance of retaliation; he would

never be able to elevate his guns sufficiently to reach the fort, while the fort, from its commanding position on the crest, could reach the ship easily enough. He straightened himself up and walked over to the port side to where Hornblower, in a similar attitude, was peering out beside a gun.

"There's a point running out here" said Hornblower. "See the shallows there? The channel must bend round them. And there's a battery on the point—look at the smoke. They're heating shot."

"I daresay" said Bush.

Soon they would be under a sharp crossfire. He hoped they would not be subjected to it for too long. He could hear orders being shouted on deck, and the masts creaked as the yards came round; they were working the *Renown* round the bend.

"The fort's opened fire, sir" reported the master's mate in charge of the forward guns on the starboard side.

"Very well, Mr. Purvis." He crossed over and looked out. "Did you see where the shot fell?"

"No, sir."

"They're firing on this side, too, sir" reported Hornblower.

"Very well."

Bush saw the fort spurting white cannon smoke. Then straight in the line between his eye and the fort, fifty yards from the side of the ship, a pillar of water rose up from the golden surface, and within the same instant of time something crashed into the side of the ship just above Bush's head. A ricochet had bounded from the surface and had lodged somewhere in the eighteen inches of oak that constituted the ship's side. Then followed a devil's tattoo of crashes; a well-aimed salvo was striking home.

"I might just reach the battery on this side now, sir" said Hornblower.

"Then try what you can do."

Now here was Buckland himself, hailing fretfully down the hatchway.

"Can't you open fire yet, Mr. Bush?"

"This minute, sir."

Hornblower was standing by the centre twenty-four-pounder. The gun captain slid the rolling handspike under the gun carriage, and heaved with all his weight. Two men at each side tackle tugged under his direction to point the gun true. With the elevating coign quite free from the breech the gun was at its highest angle of elevation. The gun captain flipped up the iron apron over the touchhole, saw that the hole was filled with powder, and with a shout of "Stand clear" he thrust his smouldering linstock into it. The gun bellowed loud in the confined space; some of the smoke came drifting back through the port.

"Just below, sir" reported Hornblower, standing at the next port. "When the guns are hot they'll reach it."

"Carry on, then."

"Open fire, first division!" yelled Hornblower.

The four foremost guns crashed out almost together.

"Second division!"

Bush could feel the deck heaving under him with the shock of the discharge and the recoil. Smoke came billowing back into the confined space, acrid, bitter; and the din was paralysing.

"Try again, men!" yelled Hornblower. "Division captains, see that you point true!"

There was a frightful crash close beside Bush and something screamed past him to crash into the deck beam near his head. Something flying through an open gunport had struck a gun on its reinforced breech. Two men had fallen close beside it, one lying still and the other twisting and turning in agony. Bush was about to give an order regarding them when his attention was drawn to something more important. There was a deep gash in the deck beam by his head and from the depths of the gash smoke was curling. It was a red-hot shot that had struck the breech of the gun and had apparently flown into fragments. A large part—the largest part—had sunk deep into the beam and already the wood was smouldering.

"Fire buckets here!" roared Bush.

Ten pounds of red-hot glowing metal lodged in the dry timbers of the ship could start a blaze in a few seconds. At the same time there was a rush of feet overhead, the sound of gear being moved about, and then the clank-clank of pumps. So on the maindeck they were fighting fires too. Hornblower's guns were thundering on the port side, the gun-trucks roaring over the planking. Hell was unchained, and the smoke of hell was eddying about him.

The masts creaked again with the swing of the yards; despite everything the ship had to be sailed up the tortuous channel. He peered out through a port, but his eye told him, as he forced himself to gauge the distance calmly, that the fort on the crest was still beyond range. No sense in wasting ammunition. He straightened himself and looked round the murky deck. There was something strange in the feel of the ship under his feet. He teetered on his toes to put his wild suspicions to the test. There was the slightest perceptible slope to the deck—a strange rigidity and permanence about it. Oh my God! Hornblower was looking round at him and making an urgent gesture downwards to confirm the awful thought. The *Renown* was aground. She must have run so smoothly and slowly up a mudbank as to lose her speed without any jerk perceptible. But she must have put her bows far up on the bank for the slope of the deck to be noticeable. There were more rending crashes as other shots from the shore struck home, a fresh hurrying and bustle as the fire parties ran to deal with the danger. Hard aground, and doomed to be slowly shot to pieces by those cursed forts, if the shots did not set them on fire to roast alive on the mudbank. Hornblower was beside him, his watch in his hand.

"Tide's still rising" he said. "It's an hour before high water. But I'm afraid we're pretty hard aground."

Bush could only look at him and swear, pouring out filth from his mouth as the only means of relieving his overwrought feelings.

"Steady there, Duff!" yelled Hornblower, looking away from him at a gun's crew gathered round their gun. "Swab that out properly! D'ye want your hands blown off when you load?"

By the time Hornblower looked round at Bush again the latter had regained his self-control.

"An hour to high water, you say?" he asked.

"Yes, sir. According to Carberry's calculations."

"God help us!"

"My shot's just reaching the battery on that point, sir. If I can keep the embrasures swept I'll slow their rate of fire even if I don't silence them."

Another crash as a shot struck home, and another.

"But the one across the channel's out of range."

"Yes" said Hornblower.

The powder boys were running through all the bustle with fresh charges for the guns. And here was the messenger-midshipman threading his way through them.

"Mr. Bush, sir! Will you please report to Mr. Buckland, sir? And we're aground, under fire, sir."

"Shut your mouth. I leave you in charge here, Mr. Hornblower."

"Aye aye, sir."

The sunlight on the quarterdeck was blinding. Buckland

was standing hatless at the rail, trying to control the
working of his features. There was a roar and a spluttering
of steam as someone turned the jet of a hose on a fiery
fragment lodged in the bulkhead. Dead men in the scuppers; wounded being carried off. A shot, or the splinters it
had sent flying, must have killed the man at the wheel so
that the ship, temporarily out of control, had run aground.

"We have to kedge off," said Buckland.

"Aye aye, sir."

That meant putting out an anchor and heaving in on the
cable with the capstan to haul the ship off the mud by main
force. Bush looked round him to confirm what he had
gathered regarding the ship's position from his restricted
view below. Her bows were on the mud; she would have to
be hauled off stern first. A shot howled close overhead,
and Bush had to exert his self-control not to jump.

"You'll have to get a cable out aft through a stern port."

"Aye aye, sir."

"Roberts'll take the stream anchor off in the launch."

"Aye aye, sir."

The fact that Buckland omitted the formal "Mister" was
significant of the strain he was undergoing and of the
emergency of the occasion.

"I'll take the men from my guns, sir" said Bush.

"Very good."

Now was the time for discipline and training to assert
themselves; the *Renown* was fortunate in having a crew
more than half composed of seasoned men drilled in the
blockade of Brest. At Plymouth she had only been filled
up with pressed men. What had merely been a drill, an
evolution, when the *Renown* was one of the Channel Fleet,
was now an operation on which the life of the ship
depended, not something to be done perfunctorily in competition with the rest of the squadron. Bush gathered his

guns' crews around him and set about the task of rousing
out a cable and getting it aft to a port, while overhead
Roberts' men were manning stay tackles and yard tackles
to sway out the launch.

Down below the heat between the decks was greater even
than above with the sun glaring down. The smoke from
Hornblower's guns was eddying thick under the beams;
Hornblower was holding his hat in his hand and wiping
his streaming face with his handkerchief. He nodded as
Bush appeared; there was no need for Bush to explain the
duty on which he was engaged. With the guns still thundering and the smoke still eddying, powder boys still running
with fresh charges and fire parties bustling with their
buckets, Bush's men roused out the cable. The hundred
fathoms of it weighed a trifle over a couple of tons; clear
heads and skilled supervision were necessary to get the unwieldy cable laid out aft, but Bush was at his best doing
work which called for single-minded attention to a single
duty. He had it clear and faked down along the deck by the
time the cutter was under the stern to receive the end, and
then he watched the vast thing gradually snake out through
the after port without a hitch. The launch came into his line
of vision as he stood looking out, with the vast weight of the
stream anchor dangling astern; it was a relief to know that
the tricky business of getting the anchor into her had been
successfully carried out. The second cutter carried the
spring cable from the hawse-hole. Roberts was in command; Bush heard him hail the cutter as the three boats
drew off astern. There was a sudden jet of water among
the boats; one or other, if not both, of the batteries ashore
had shifted targets; a shot now into the launch would be a
disaster, and one into a cutter would be a serious setback.

"Pardon, sir" said Hornblower's voice beside him, and
Bush turned back from looking out over the glittering water.

D

"Well?"

"I could take some of the foremost guns and run 'em aft" said Hornblower. "Shifting the weight would help."

"So it would" agreed Bush; Hornblower's face was streaked and grimy with his exertions, as Bush noted while he considered if he had sufficient authority to give the order on his own responsibility. "Better get Buckland's permission. Ask him in my name if you like."

"Aye aye, sir."

These lower-deck twenty-four-pounders weighed more than two tons each; the transfer of some from forward aft would be an important factor in getting the bows off the mudbank. Bush took another glance through the port. James, the midshipman in the first cutter, was turning to look back to check that the cable was out in exact line with the length of the ship. There would be a serious loss of tractive effort if there was an angle in the cable from anchor to capstan. Launch and cutter were coming together in preparation for dropping the anchor. All round them the water suddenly boiled to a salvo from the shore; the skipping jets of the ricochets showed that it was the fort on the hill that was firing at them—and making good practice for that extreme range. The sun caught an axe blade as it turned in the air in the sternsheets of the launch; Bush saw the momentary flash. They were letting the anchor drop from where it hung from the gallows in the stern. Thank God.

Hornblower's guns were still bellowing out, making the ship tremble with their recoil, and at the same time a splintering crash over his head told him that the other battery was still firing on the ship and still scoring hits. Everything was still going on at once; Hornblower had a gang of men at work dragging aft the foremost twenty-four-pounder on the starboard side—a ticklish job with the rolling handspike under the transom of the carriage. The trucks squealed horribly as the men struggled to turn the cumbersome thing and thread their way along the crowded deck. But Bush could spare Hornblower no more than a glance as he hurried up to the maindeck to see for himself what was happening at the capstan.

The men were already taking their places at the capstan bars under the supervision of Smith and Booth; the maindeck guns were being stripped of the last of their crews to supply enough hands. Naked to the waist, the men were spitting on their hands and testing their foothold—there was no need to tell them how serious the situation was; no need for Booth's knotted rattan.

"Heave away!" hailed Buckland from the quarterdeck.

"Heave away!" yelled Booth. "Heave, and wake the dead!"

The men flung their weight on the bars and the capstan came round, the pawls clanking rapidly as the capstan took up the slack. The boys with the nippers at the messenger had to hurry to keep pace. Then the intervals between the clanking of the pawls became longer as the capstan turned more slowly. More slowly; clank—clank —clank. Now the strain was coming; the bitts creaked as the cable tightened. Clank—clank. That was a new cable, and it could be expected to stretch a trifle.

The sudden howl of a shot—what wanton fate had directed it here of all places in the ship? Flying splinters and prostrate men; the shot had ploughed through the whole crowded mass. Red blood was pouring out, vivid in the sunshine; in understandable confusion the men drew away from the bloody wrecks.

"Stand to your posts!" yelled Smith. "You, boys! Get those men out of the way. Another capstan bar here! Smartly now!"

The ball which had wrought such fearful havoc had not

spent all its force on human flesh; it had gone on to shatter the cheekpiece of a gun carriage and then to lodge in the ship's side. Nor had human blood quenched it; smoke was rising on the instant from where it rested. Bush himself seized a fire bucket and dashed its contents on the glowing ball; steam blended with the smoke and the water spat and sputtered. No single fire bucket could quench twenty-four pounds of red-hot iron, but a fire party came running up to flood the smouldering menace.

The dead and the wounded had been dragged away and the men were at the capstan bars again.

"Heave!" shouted Booth. Clank—clank—clank. Slowly and more slowly still turned the capstan. Then it came to a dead stop while the bitts groaned under the strain.

"Heave! Heave!"

Clank! Then reluctantly, and after a long interval, clank! Then no more. The merciless sun beat down upon the men's straining backs; their horny feet sought for a grip against the cleats on the deck as they shoved and thrust against the bars. Bush went below again, leaving them straining away; he could, and did, send plenty of men up from the lower gundeck to treble-bank the capstan bars. There were men still hard at work in the smoky twilight hauling the last possible gun aft, but Hornblower was back among his guns supervising the pointing. Bush set his foot on the cable. It was not like a rope, but like a wooden spar, as rigid and unyielding. Then through the sole of his shoe Bush felt the slightest tremor, the very slightest; the men at the capstan were putting their reinforced strength against the bars. The clank of one more pawl gained rever-berated along the ship's timbers; the cable shuddered a trifle more violently and then stiffened into total rigidity again. It did not creep over an eighth of an inch under Bush's foot, although he knew that at the capstan a hundred and fifty men were straining their hearts out at the bars. One of Hornblower's guns went off; Bush felt the jar of the recoil through the cable. Faintly down the hatchways came the shouts of encouragement from Smith and Booth at the capstan, but not an inch of gain could be noted at the cable. Hornblower came and touched his hat to Bush.

"D'you notice any movement when I fire a gun, sir?" As he asked the question he turned and waved to the captain of a midship gun which was loaded and run out. The gun captain brought the linstock down on the touchhole, and the gun roared out and came recoiling back through the smoke. Bush's foot on the cable recorded the effect.

"Only the jar—no—yes." Inspiration came to Bush. To the question he asked Bush already knew the answer Hornblower would give. "What are you thinking of?"

"I could fire all my guns at once. That might break the suction, sir."

So it might, indeed. The *Renown* was lying on mud, which was clutching her in a firm grip. If she could be severely shaken while the hawser was maintained at full tension the grip might be broken.

"I think it's worth trying, by God" said Bush.

"Very good, sir. I'll have my guns loaded and ready in three minutes, sir." Hornblower turned to his battery and funnelled his hands round his mouth. "Cease fire! Cease fire, all!"

"I'll tell 'em at the capstan" said Bush.

"Very good, sir." Hornblower went on giving his orders. "Load and double-shot your guns. Prime and run out."

That was the last that Bush heard for the moment as he went up on the maindeck and made his suggestion to Smith, who nodded in instant agreement.

"'Vast heaving!" shouted Smith, and the sweating men at the bars eased their weary backs.

An explanation was necessary to Buckland on the quarterdeck; he saw the force of the argument. The unfortunate man, who was watching the failure of his first venture in independent command, and whose ship was in such deadly peril, was gripping at the rail and wringing it with his two hands as if he would twist it like a corkscrew. In the midst of all this there was a piece of desperately important news that Smith had to give.

"Roberts is dead" he said, out of the side of his mouth.

"No!"

"He's dead. A shot cut him in two in the launch."

"Good God!"

It was to Bush's credit that he felt sorrow at the death of Roberts before his mind recorded the fact that he was now first lieutenant of a ship of the line. But there was no time now to think of either sorrow or rejoicing, not with the *Renown* aground and under fire. Bush hailed down the hatchway.

"Below, there! Mr. Hornblower!"

"Sir!"

"Are your guns ready?"

"Another minute, sir."

"Better take the strain" said Bush to Smith; and then, louder, down the hatchway, "Await my order, Mr. Hornblower."

"Aye aye, sir."

The men settled themselves at the capstan bars again, braced their feet, and heaved.

"Heave!" shouted Booth. "Heave!"

The men might be pushing at the side of a church, so little movement did they get from the bars after the first inch.

"Heave!"

Bush left them and ran below. He set his foot on the rigid cable and nodded to Hornblower. The fifteen guns—

two had been dragged aft from the port side—were run out and ready, the crews awaiting orders.

"Captains, take your linstocks!" shouted Hornblower. "All you· others, stand clear! Now, I shall give you the words 'one, two, three'. At 'three' you touch your linstocks down. Understand?"

There was a buzz of agreement.

"All ready? All linstocks glowing?" The gun captains swung them about to get them as bright as possible. "Then one—two—three!"

Down came the linstocks on the touchholes, and almost simultaneously the guns roared out; even with the inevitable variation in the amounts of powder in the touchholes there was not a second between the first and the last of the fifteen explosions. Bush, his foot on the cable, felt the ship heave with the recoil—double-shotting the guns had increased the effect. The smoke came eddying into the sweltering heat, but Bush had no attention to give to it The cable moved under his foot with the heave of the ship. Surely it was moving along. It was! He had to shift the position of his foot. The clank of a newly gained pawl on the windlass could be heard by everyone. Clank— clank. Someone in the smoke started to cheer and others took it up.

"Silence!" bellowed Hornblower.

Clank—clank—clank. Reluctant sounds; but the ship was moving. The cable was coming in slowly, like a mortally wounded monster. If only they could keep her on the move! Clank—clank—clank. The interval between the sounds was growing shorter—even Bush had to admit that to himself. The cable was coming in faster—faster.

"Take charge here, Mr. Hornblower" said Bush, and sprang for the maindeck. If the ship were free there would be urgent matters for the first lieutenant to attend to. The capstan pawls seemed almost to be playing a merry tune, so rapidly did they sound as the capstan turned.

Undoubtedly there was much to be attended to on deck. There were decisions which must be made at once. Bush touched his hat to Buckland.

"Any orders, sir?"

Buckland turned unhappy eyes on him.

"We've lost the flood" he said.

This must be the highest moment of the tide; if they were to touch ground again, kedging off would not be so simple an operation.

"Yes, sir" said Bush.

The decision could only lie with Buckland; no one else could share the responsibility. But it was terribly hard for a man to have to admit defeat in his very first command. Buckland looked as if for inspiration round the bay, where the red-and-gold flags of Spain flew above the banked-up powder smoke of the batteries—no inspiration could be found there.

"We can only get out with the land breeze" said Buckland.

"Yes, sir."

There was almost no longer for the land breeze to blow, either, thought Bush; Buckland knew it as well as he did. A shot from the fort on the hill struck into the main chains at that moment, with a jarring crash and a shower of splinters. They heard the call for the fire party, and with that Buckland reached the bitter decision.

"Heave in on the spring cable" he ordered. "Get her round head to sea."

"Aye aye, sir."

Retreat—defeat; that was what that order meant. But defeat had to be faced; even with that order given there was much that had to be done to work the ship out of the imminent danger in which she lay. Bush turned to give the orders.

" 'Vast heaving at the capstan, there!"

The clanking ceased and the *Renown* rode free in the muddy, churned-up waters of the bay. To retreat she would have to turn tail, reverse herself in that confined space, and work her way out to sea. Fortunately the means were immediately available: by heaving in on the bow cable which had so far lain idle between hawsehole and anchor the ship could be brought short round.

"Cast off the stern cable messenger!"

The orders came quickly and easily; it was a routine piece of seamanship, even though it had to be carried out under the fire of red-hot shot. There were the boats still manned and afloat to drag the battered vessel out of harm's way if the precarious breeze should die away. Round came the *Renown's* bows under the pull of the bow cable as the capstan set to work upon it. Even though the wind was dying away to a sweltering calm movement was obvious— but the shock of defeat and the contemplation of that accursed artillery! While the capstan was dragging the ship up to her anchor the necessity for keeping the ship on the move occurred to Bush. He touched his hat to Buckland again.

"Shall I warp her down the bay, sir?"

Buckland had been standing by the binnacle staring vacantly at the fort. It was not a question of physical cowardice—that was obvious—but the shock of defeat and the contemplation of the future had made the man temporarily incapable of logical thought. But Bush's question prodded him back into dealing with the current situation.

"Yes" said Buckland, and Bush turned away, happy to have something useful to do which he well knew how to do.

Another anchor had to be cockbilled at the port bow, another cable roused out. A hail to James, in command of the boats since Roberts' death, told him of the new evolution and called him under the bows for the anchor to be lowered down to the launch—the trickiest part of the whole business. Then the launch's crew bent to their oars and towed ahead, their boat crank with the ponderous weight that it bore dangling aft and with the cable paying out astern of it. Yard by yard, to the monotonous turning of the capstan, the *Renown* crept up to her first anchor, and when that cable was straight up and down the flutter of a signal warned James, now far ahead in the launch, to drop the anchor his boat carried and return for the stream anchor which was about to be hauled up. The stern cable, now of no more use, had to be unhitched and got in, the effort of the capstan transferred from one cable to the other, while the two cutters were given lines by which they could contribute their tiny effort to the general result, towing the ponderous ship and giving her the smallest conceivable amount of motion which yet was valuable when it was a matter of such urgency to withdraw the ship out of range.

Down below Hornblower was at work dragging forward the guns he had previously dragged aft; the rumble and squeal of the trucks over the planking was audible through the ship over the monotonous clanking of the capstan. Overhead blazed the pitiless sun, softening the pitch in the seams, while yard after painful yard, cable's length after cable's length, the ship crept on down the bay out of range of the red-hot shot, over the glittering still water; down the bay of Samaná until at last they were out of range, and could pause while the men drank a niggardly half-pint of warm odorous water before turning back to their labours. To bury the dead, to repair the damages, and to digest the realisation of defeat. Maybe to wonder if the captain's malign influence still persisted, mad and helpless though he was

VIII

WHEN the tropic night closed down upon the battered *Renown*, as she stood off the land under easy sail, just enough to stiffen her to ride easily over the Atlantic rollers that the trade wind, reinforced by the sea breeze, sent hurrying under her bows, Buckland sat anxiously discussing the situation with his new first lieutenant. Despite the breeze, the little cabin was like an oven; the two lanterns which hung from the deck beams to illuminate the chart on the table seemed to heat the room unbearably. Bush felt the perspiration prickling under his uniform, and his stock constricted his thick neck so that every now and again he put two fingers into it and tugged, without relief. It would have been the simplest matter in the world to take off his heavy uniform coat and unhook his stock, but it never crossed his mind that he should do so. Bodily discomfort was something that one bore without complaint in a hard world; habit and pride both helped.

"Then you think we should bear up for Jamaica?" asked Buckland.

"I wouldn't go as far as to advise it, sir" replied Bush, cautiously.

The responsibility was Buckland's, entirely Buckland's, by the law of the navy, and Bush was a little irked at Buckland's trying to share it.

"But what else can we do?" asked Buckland. "What do you suggest?"

Bush remembered the plan of campaign Hornblower had sketched out to him, but he did not put it instantly

forward; he had not weighed it sufficiently in his mind—
he did not even know if he thought it practicable. Instead
he temporised.

"If we head for Jamaica it'll be with our tail between
our legs, sir" he said.

"That's perfectly true" agreed Buckland, with a helpless
gesture. "There's the captain——"

"Yes" said Bush. "There's the captain."

If the *Renown* were to report to the admiral at Kingston
with a resounding success to her record there might not
be too diligent an inquiry into past events; but if she came
limping in, defeated, battered, it would be far more likely
that inquiry might be made into the reasons why her
captain had been put under restraint, why Buckland had
read the secret orders, why he had taken upon himself the
responsibility of making the attack upon Samaná.

"It was young Hornblower who said the same thing to
me" complained Buckland pettishly. "I wish I'd never
listened to him."

"What did you ask him, sir?" asked Bush.

"Oh, I can't say that I asked him anything" replied
Buckland, pettishly again. "We were yarning together on
the quarterdeck one evening. It was his watch."

"I remember, sir" prompted Bush.

"We talked. The infernal little whippersnapper said just
what you were saying—I don't remember how it started. But
then it was a question of going to Antigua. Hornblower
said that it would be better if we had the chance to achieve
something before we faced an inquiry about the captain.
He said it was my opportunity. So it was, I suppose. My
great chance. But with Hornblower talking you'd think I
was going to be posted captain tomorrow. And now——"

Buckland's gesture indicated how much chance he
thought he had of ever being posted captain now.

Bush thought about the report Buckland would have to make: nine killed and twenty wounded; the *Renown's* attack ignominiously beaten off; Samaná Bay as safe a refuge for privateers as ever. He was glad he was not Buckland, but at the same time he realised that there was grave danger of his being tarred with the same brush. He was first lieutenant now, he was one of the officers who had acquiesced, if nothing more, in the displacement of Sawyer from command, and it would take a victory to invest him with any virtue at all in the eyes of his superiors.

"Damn it" said Buckland in pathetic self-defence, "we did our best. Anyone could run aground in that channel. It wasn't our fault that the helmsman was killed. Nothing could get up the bay under that crossfire."

"Hornblower was suggesting a landing on the seaward side. In Scotchman's Bay, sir." Bush was speaking as cautiously as he could.

"Another of Hornblower's suggestions?" said Buckland.

"I think that's what he had in mind from the start, sir. A landing and a surprise attack."

Probably it was because the attempt had failed, but Bush now could see the unreason of taking a wooden ship into a situation where red-hot cannon balls could be fired into her.

"What do *you* think?"

"Well, sir——"

Bush was not sure enough about what he thought to be able to express himself with any clarity. But if they had failed once they might as well fail twice; as well be hanged for a sheep as for a lamb. Bush was a sturdy soul; it went against his grain to yield in face of difficulties, and he was irritated at the thought of a tame retreat after a single repulse. The difficulty was to devise an alternative plan of campaign. He tried to say all these things to Buckland, and was sufficiently carried away to be incautious.

"I see" said Buckland. In the light of the swaying lamps the play of the shadows on his face accentuated the struggle in his expression. He came to a sudden decision. "Let's hear what he has to say."

"Aye aye, sir. Smith has the watch. Hornblower has the middle—I expect he has turned in until he's called."

Buckland was as weary as anyone in the ship—wearier than most, it seemed likely. The thought of Hornblower stretched at ease in his cot while his superiors sat up fretting wrought Buckland up to a pitch of decision that he might not otherwise have reached, determining him to act at once instead of waiting till the morrow.

"Pass the word for him" he ordered.

Hornblower came into the cabin with commendable promptitude, his hair tousled and his clothes obviously hastily thrown on. He threw a nervous glance round the cabin as he entered; obviously he suffered from not unreasonable doubts as to why he had been summoned thus into the presence of his superiors.

"What plan is this I've been hearing about?" asked Buckland. "You had some suggestion for storming the fort, I understand, Mr. Hornblower."

Hornblower did not answer immediately; he was marshalling his arguments and reconsidering his first plan in the light of the new situation—Bush could see that it was hardly fair that Hornblower should be called upon to state his plan now that the *Renown* had made one attempt and had failed after sacrificing the initial advantage of surprise. But Bush could see that he was reordering his ideas.

"I thought a landing might have more chance, sir" he said. "But that was before the Dons knew there was a ship of the line in the neighbourhood."

"And now you don't think so?"

Buckland's tone was a mixture of relief and disappointment—relief that he might not have to reach any further decisions, and disappointment that some easy way of gaining success was not being put forward. But Hornblower had had time now to sort out his ideas, and to think about times and distances. That showed in his face.

"I think something might well be tried, sir, as long as it was tried at once."

"At once?" This was night, the crew were weary, and Buckland's tone showed surprise at the suggestion of immediate activity. "You don't mean tonight?"

"Tonight might be the best time, sir. The Dons have seen us driven off with our tail between our legs—excuse me, sir, but that's how it'll look to them, at least. The last they saw of us was beating out of Samaná Bay at sunset. They'll be pleased with themselves. You know how they are, sir. An attack at dawn from another quarter, overland, would be the last thing they'd expect."

That sounded like sense to Bush, and he made a small approving noise, the most he would venture towards making a contribution to the debate.

"How would you make this attack, Mr. Hornblower?" asked Buckland.

Hornblower had his ideas in order now; the weariness disappeared and there was a glow of enthusiasm in his face.

"The wind's fair for Scotchman's Bay, sir. We could be back there in less than two hours—before midnight. By the time we arrive we can have the landing party told off and prepared. A hundred seamen and the marines. There's a good landing beach there—we saw it yesterday. The country inland must be marshy, before the hills of the peninsula start again, but we can land on the peninsula side of the marsh. I marked the place yesterday, sir."

"Well?"

Hornblower swallowed the realisation that it was possible for a man not to be able to continue from that point with a single leap of his imagination.

"The landing party can make their way up to the crest without difficulty, sir. There's no question of losing their way—the sea one side and Samaná Bay on the other. They can move forward along the crest. At dawn they can rush the fort. What with the marsh and the cliffs the Dons'll keep a poor lookout on that side, I fancy, sir."

"You make it sound very easy, Mr. Hornblower. But— a hundred and eighty men?"

"Enough, I think, sir."

"What makes you think so?"

"There were six guns firing at us from the fort, sir. Ninety men at most—sixty more likely. Ammunition party; men to heat the furnaces. A hundred and fifty men altogether; perhaps as few as a hundred."

"But why should that be all they had?"

"The Dons have nothing to fear on that side of the island. They're holding out against the blacks, and the French, maybe, and the English in Jamaica. There's nothing to tempt the blacks to attack 'em across the marshes. It's south of Samaná Bay that the danger lies. The Don'll have every man that can carry a musket on that side. That's where the cities are. That's where this fellow Toussaint, or whatever his name is, will be threatening 'em, sir."

The last word of this long speech came as a fortunate afterthought; Hornblower clearly was restraining himself from pointing out the obvious too didactically to his superior officer. And Bush could see Buckland squirm in discomfort at this casual mention of blacks and French. Those secret orders—which Bush had not been allowed to read—must lay down some drastic instructions regarding the complicated political situation in Santo Domingo, where the revolted slaves, the French, and the Spaniards (nominal allies though these last might be, elsewhere in the world) all contended for the mastery.

"We'll leave the blacks and the French out of this" said Buckland, confirming Bush's suspicions.

"Yes, sir. But the Dons won't" said Hornblower, not very abashed. "They're more afraid of the blacks than of us at present."

"So you think this attack might succeed?" asked Buckland, desperately changing the subject.

"I think it might, sir. But time's getting on."

Buckland sat looking at his two juniors in painful indecision, and Bush felt full sympathy for him. A second bloody repulse—possibly something even worse, the cutting off and capitulation of the entire landing party—would be Buckland's certain ruin.

"With the fort in our hands, sir" said Hornblower, "we can deal with the privateers up the bay. They could never use it as an anchorage again."

"That's true" agreed Buckland. It would be a neat and economical fulfilment of his orders; it would restore his credit.

The timbers of the ship creaked rhythmically as the *Renown* rode over the waves. The trade wind came blowing into the cabin, relieving it of some of its stuffiness, breathing cooler air on Bush's sweaty face.

"Damn it" said Buckland with sudden reckless decision, "let's do it."

"Very good, sir" said Hornblower.

Bush had to restrain himself from saying something that would express his pleasure; Hornblower had used a neutral tone—too obvious pushing of Buckland along the path of action might have a reverse effect and goad him into reversing his decision even now.

And although this decision had been reached there was another one, almost equally important, which had to be reached at once.

"Who will be in command?" asked Buckland. It could only be a rhetorical question; nobody except Buckland could possibly supply the answer, and to Bush and Hornblower this was obvious. They could only wait.

"It'd be poor Roberts' duty if he had lived" said Buckland, and then he turned to look at Bush.

"Mr. Bush, you will take command."

"Aye aye, sir."

Bush got up from his chair and stood with his head bowed uneasily under the deck timbers above.

"Who do you want to take with you?"

Hornblower had been on his feet during the whole interview; now he shifted his weight self-consciously from one foot to the other.

"Do you require me any more, sir?" he said to Buckland.

Bush could not tell by looking at him what emotions were at work in him; he had the pose merely of a respectful, attentive officer. Bush thought about Smith, the remaining lieutenant in the ship. He thought about Whiting, the captain of marines, who would certainly have to take part in the landing. There were midshipmen and master's mates to be used as subordinate officers. He was going to be responsible for a risky and desperate operation of war—now it was his own credit, as well as Buckland's, that was at stake. Whom did he want at his side at this, one of the most important moments in his career? Another lieutenant, if he asked for one, would be second in command, might expect to have a voice in the decisions to be made.

"Do we need Mr. Hornblower any more, Mr. Bush?" asked Buckland.

Hornblower would be an active subordinate in command. A restless one, would be another way of expressing it. He would be apt to criticise, in thought at least. Bush did not think he cared to exercise command with Hornblower listening to his every order. This whole internal debate of Bush's did not take definite shape, with formal arguments pro and con; it was rather a conflict of prejudices and instincts, the result of years of experience, which Bush could never have expressed in words. He decided he needed neither Hornblower nor Smith at the moment before he looked again at Hornblower's face. Hornblower was trying to remain impassive; but Bush could see, with sympathetic insight, how desperately anxious he was to be invited to join in the expedition. Any officer would want to go, of course, would yearn to be given an opportunity to distinguish himself, but actuating Hornblower was some motive more urgent than this. Hornblower's hands were at his sides, in the "attention" position, but Bush noticed how the long fingers tapped against his thighs, restrained themselves, and then tapped again uncontrollably. It was not cool judgment that finally brought Bush to his decision, but something quite otherwise. It might be called kindliness; it might be called affection. He had grown fond of this volatile, versatile young man, and he had no doubts now as to his physical courage.

"I'd like Mr. Hornblower to come with me, sir" he said; it seemed almost without his volition that the words came from his mouth; a softhearted elder brother might have said much the same thing, burdening himself with the presence of a much younger brother out of kindness of heart when contemplating some pleasant day's activities.

And as he spoke he received a glance in return from Hornblower that stifled at birth any regrets he may have felt at allowing his sentiments to influence his judgment.

There was so much of relief, so much of gratitude, in the way Hornblower looked at him that Bush experienced a kindly glow of magnanimity; he felt a bigger and better man for what he had done. Naturally he did not for a moment see anything incongruous about Hornblower's being grateful for a decision that would put him in peril of his life.

"Very well, Mr. Bush" said Buckland; typically, he wavered for a space after agreeing. "That will leave me with only one lieutenant."

"Carberry could take watch, sir" replied Bush. "And there are several among the master's mates who are good watch-keeping officers."

It was as natural for Bush to argue down opposition once he had committed himself as it might be for a fish to snap at a lure.

"Very well" said Buckland again, almost with a sigh. "And what is it that's troubling you, Mr. Hornblower?"

"Nothing, sir."

"There was something you wanted to say. Out with it."

"Nothing important, sir. It can wait. But I was wondering about altering course, sir. We can head for Scotchman's Bay now and waste no time."

"I suppose we can." Buckland knew as well as any officer in the navy that the whims of wind and weather were unpredictable, and that action upon any decision at sea should in consequence never be delayed, but he was likely to forget it unless he were prodded. "Oh, very well. We'd better get her before the wind, then. What's the course?"

After the bustle of wearing the ship round had died away Buckland led the way back to his cabin and threw himself wearily into his chair again. He put on a whimsical air to conceal the anxiety which was now consuming him afresh.

"We've satisfied Mr. Hornblower for a moment" he said. "Now let's hear what you need, Mr. Bush."

The discussion regarding the proposed expedition proceeded along normal lines; the men to be employed, the equipment that was to be issued to them, the rendezvous that had to be arranged for next morning. Hornblower kept himself studiously in the background as these points were settled.

"Any suggestions, Mr. Hornblower?" asked Bush at length. Politeness, if not policy as well, dictated the question.

"Only one, sir. We might have with us some boat grapnels with lines attached. If we have to scale the walls they might be useful."

"That's so" agreed Bush. "Remember to see that they're issued."

"Aye aye, sir."

"Do you need a messenger, Mr. Hornblower?" asked Buckland.

"It might be better if I had one, sir."

"Anyone in particular?"

"I'd prefer to have Wellard, sir, if you've no objection He's cool-headed and thinks quickly."

"Very well." Buckland looked hard at Hornblower at the mention of Wellard's name, but said nothing more on the subject for the moment.

"Anything else? No? Mr. Bush? All settled?"

"Yes, sir" said Bush.

Buckland drummed with his fingers on the table. The recent alteration of course had not been the decisive move; it did not commit him to anything. But the next order would. If the hands were roused out, arms issued to them, instructions given for a landing, he could hardly draw back. Another attempt; maybe another failure; maybe a disaster. It was not in his power to command success, while it was certainly in his power to obviate failure by simply not risking it. He looked up and met the gaze of his two subordinates turned on him remorselessly. No, it was too late now—he had been mistaken when he thought he could draw back. He could not.

"Then it only remains to issue the orders" he said. "Will you see to it, if you please?"

"Aye aye, sir" said Bush.

He and Hornblower were about to leave the cabin when Buckland asked the question he had wanted to ask for so long. It necessitated an abrupt change of subject, even though the curiosity that inspired the question had been reawakened by Hornblower's mention of Wellard. But Buckland, full of the virtuous glow of having reached a decision, felt emboldened to ask the question; it was a moment of exaltation in any case, and confidences were possible.

"By the way, Mr. Hornblower" he said, and Hornblower halted beside the door, "how did the captain come to fall down the hatchway?"

Bush saw the expressionless mask take the place of the eager look on Hornblower's face. The answer took a moment or two to come.

"I think he must have overbalanced, sir" said Hornblower, with the utmost respect and a complete absence of feeling in his voice. "The ship was lively that night, you remember, sir."

"I suppose she was" said Buckland; disappointment and perplexity were audible in his tone. He stared at Hornblower, but there was nothing to be gleaned from that face. "Oh, very well then. Carry on."

"Aye aye, sir."

IX

THE sea breeze had died away with the cooling of the land, and it was that breathless time of night when air pressures over island and ocean were evenly balanced. Not many miles out at sea the trade winds could blow, as they blew eternally, but here on the beach a humid calm prevailed. The long swell of the Atlantic broke momentarily at the first hint of shallows far out, but lived on, like some once vigorous man now feeble after an illness, to burst rhythmically in foam on the beach to the westward; here, where the limestone cliffs of the Samaná peninsula began, there was a sheltered corner where a small watercourse had worn a wide gully in the cliff, at the most easterly end of the wide beach. And sea and surf and beach seemed to be afire; in the dark night the phosphorescence of the water was vividly bright, heaving up with the surf, running up the beach with the breakers, and lighting up the oar blades as the launches pulled to shore. The boats seemed to be floating on fire which derived new life from their passage; each launch left a wake of fire behind it, with a vivid streak on either side where the oar blades had bitten into the water.

Both landing and ascent were easy at the foot of the gully; the launches nuzzled their bows into the sand and the landing party had only to climb out, thigh-deep in the water—thigh-deep in liquid fire—holding their weapons and cartridge boxes high to make sure they were not wetted. Even the experienced seamen in the party were impressed by the brightness of the phosphorescence; the raw hands were excited by it enough to raise a bubbling chatter which called for a sharp order to repress it. Bush was one of the earliest to climb out of his launch; he splashed ashore and stood on the unaccustomed solidity of the beach while the others followed him; the water streamed down out of his soggy trouser legs.

A dark figure appeared before him, coming from the direction of the other launch.

"My party is all ashore, sir" it reported.

"Very good, Mr. Hornblower."

"I'll start up the gully with the advanced guard then, sir?"

"Yes, Mr. Hornblower. Carry out your orders."

Bush was tense and excited, as far as his stoical training and phlegmatic temperament would allow him to be; he would have liked to plunge into action at once, but the careful scheme worked out in consultation with Hornblower did not allow it. He stood aside while his own party was being formed up and Hornblower called the other division to order.

"Starbowlines! Follow me closely. Every man is to keep in touch with the man ahead of him. Remember your muskets aren't loaded—it's no use snapping them if we meet an enemy. Cold steel for that. If any one of you is fool enough to load and fire he'll get four dozen at the gangway tomorrow. That I promise you. Woolton!"

"Sir!"

"Bring up the rear. Now follow me, you men, starting from the right of the line."

Hornblower's party filed off into the darkness. Already the marines were coming ashore, their scarlet tunics black against the phosphorescence. The white crossbelts were faintly visible side by side in a rigid two-deep line as they formed up, the non-commissioned officers snapping low-voiced orders at them. With his left hand still resting on his sword hilt Bush checked once more with his right hand that his pistols were in his belt and his cartridges in his pocket. A shadowy figure halted before him with a military click of the heels.

"All present and correct, sir. Ready to march off" said Whiting's voice.

"Thank you. We may as well start. Mr. Abbott!"

"Sir!"

"You have your orders. I'm leaving with the marine detachment now. Follow us."

"Aye aye, sir."

It was a long hard climb up the gully; the sand soon was replaced by rock, flat ledges of limestone, but even among the limestone there was a sturdy vegetation, fostered by the tropical rains which fell profusely on this northern face. Only in the bed of the watercourse itself, dry now with all the water having seeped into the limestone, was there a clear passage, if clear it could be called, for it was jagged and irregular, with steep ledges up which Bush had to heave himself. In a few minutes he was streaming with sweat, but he climbed on stubbornly. Behind him the marines followed clumsily, boots clashing, weapons and equipment clinking, so that anyone might think the noise would be heard a mile away. Someone slipped and swore.

"Keep a still tongue in yer 'ead!" snapped a corporal.

"Silence!" snarled Whiting over his shoulder.

Onward and upward; here and there the vegetation was lofty enough to cut off the faint light from the stars, and Bush had to grope his way along over the rock, his breath coming with difficulty, powerfully built man though he was. Fireflies showed here and there as he climbed; it was years since he had seen fireflies last, but he paid no attention to them now. They excited irrepressible comment among the marines following him, though; Bush felt a bitter rage against the uncontrolled louts who were imperilling everything—their own lives as well as the success of the expedition—by their silly comments.

"I'll deal with 'em, sir" said Whiting, and dropped back to let the column overtake him.

Higher up a squeaky voice, moderated as best its owner knew how, greeted him from the darkness ahead.

"Mr. Bush, sir?"

"Yes."

"This is Wellard, sir. Mr. Hornblower sent me back here to act as guide. There's grassland beginning just above here."

"Very well" said Bush.

He halted for a space, wiping his streaming face with his coat sleeve, while the column closed up behind him. It was not much farther to climb when he moved on again; Wellard led him past a clump of shadowy trees, and, sure enough, Bush felt grass under his feet, and he could walk more freely, uphill still, but only a gentle slope compared with the gully. There was a low challenge ahead of them.

"Friend" said Wellard. "This is Mr. Bush here."

"Glad to see you, sir" said another voice—Hornblower's.

Hornblower detached himself from the darkness and came forward to make his report.

"My party is formed up just ahead, sir. I've sent Saddler and two reliable men on as scouts."

"Very good" said Bush, and meant it.

The marine sergeant was reporting to Whiting.

"All present, sir, 'cept for Chapman, sir. 'E's sprained 'is ankle, or 'e says 'e 'as, sir. Left 'im be'ind back there, sir."

"Let your men rest, Captain Whiting" said Bush.

Life in the confines of a ship of the line was no sort of training for climbing cliffs in the tropics, especially as the day before had been exhausting. The marines lay down, some of them with groans of relief which drew the unmistakable reproof of savage kicks from the sergeant's toe.

"We're on the crest here, sir" said Hornblower. "You can see over into the bay from that side there."

"Three miles from the fort, d'ye think?"

Bush did not mean to ask a question, for he was in command, but Hornblower was so ready with his report that Bush could not help doing so.

"Perhaps. Less than four, anyway, sir. Dawn in four hours from now, and the moon rises in half an hour."

"Yes."

"There's some sort of track or path along the crest, sir, as you'd expect. It should lead to the fort."

"Yes."

Hornblower was a good subordinate, clearly. Bush realised now that there would naturally be a track along the crest of the peninsula—that would be the obvious thing—but the probability had not occurred to him until that moment.

"If you will permit me, sir" went on Hornblower, "I'll leave James in command of my party and push on ahead with Saddler and Wellard and see how the land lies."

"Very good, Mr. Hornblower."

Yet no sooner had Hornblower left than Bush felt a vague irritation. It seemed that Hornblower was taking too much on himself. Bush was not a man who would tolerate any infringement upon his authority. However, Bush was distracted from this train of thought by the arrival of the second division of seamen, who came sweating and gasping up to join the main body. With the memory of his own weariness when he arrived still fresh in his mind Bush allowed them a rest period before he should push on with his united force. Even in the darkness a cloud of insects had discovered the sweating force, and a host of them sang round Bush's ears and bit him viciously at every opportunity. The crew of the *Renown* had been long at sea and were tender and desirable in consequence. Bush slapped at himself and swore, and every man in his command did the same.

"Mr. Bush, sir?"

It was Hornblower back again.

"Yes?"

"It's a definite trail, sir. It crosses a gully just ahead, but it's not a serious obstacle."

"Thank you, Mr. Hornblower. We'll move forward. Start with your division, if you please."

"Aye aye, sir."

The advance began. The domed limestone top of the peninsula was covered with long grass, interspersed with occasional trees. Off the track walking was a little difficult on account of the toughness and irregularity of the bunches of high grass, but on the track it was comparatively easy. The men could move along it in something like a solid body, well closed up. Their eyes, thoroughly accustomed to the darkness, could see in the starlight enough to enable them to pick their way. The gully that Hornblower had reported was only a shallow depression with easily sloping sides and presented no difficulty.

Bush plodded on at the head of the marines with Whiting at his side, the darkness all about him like a warm blanket. There was a kind of dreamlike quality about the march, induced perhaps by the fact that Bush had not slept for twenty-four hours and was stupid with the fatigues he had undergone during that period. The path was ascending gently—naturally, of course, since it was rising to the highest part of the peninsula where the fort was sited.

"Ah!" said Whiting suddenly.

The path had wandered to the right, away from the sea and towards the bay, and now they had crossed the backbone of the peninsula and opened up the view over the bay. On their right they could see clear down the bay to the sea, and there it was not quite dark, for above the horizon a little moonlight was struggling through the clouds that lay at the lower edge of the sky.

"Mr. Bush, sir?"

This was Wellard, his voice more under command this time.

"Here I am."

"Mr. Hornblower sent me back again, sir. There's another gully ahead, crossing the path. An' we've come across some cattle, sir. Asleep on the hill. We disturbed 'em, and they're wandering about."

"Thank you, I understand" said Bush.

Bush had the lowest opinion of the ordinary man and the subordinary man who constituted the great bulk of his command. He knew perfectly well that if they were to blunder into cattle along this path they would think they were meeting the enemy. There would be excitement and noise, even if there was no shooting.

"Tell Mr. Hornblower I am going to halt for fifteen minutes."

"Aye aye, sir."

A rest and opportunity to close up the column were desirable for the weary men in any case, as long as there was time to spare. And during the rest the men could be personally and individually warned about the possibility of encountering cattle. Bush knew that merely to pass the word back down the column would be unsatisfactory, actually unsafe, with these tired and slow-witted men. He gave the order and the column came to a halt, of course with sleepy men bumping into the men in front of them with a clatter and a murmur that the whispered curses of the petty officers with difficulty suppressed. While the warning was being circulated among the men lying in the grass another trouble was reported to Bush by a petty officer.

"Seaman Black, sir. 'E's drunk."

"Drunk?"

" 'E must 'ave 'ad sperrits in 'is canteen, sir. You can smell it on 'is breff. Dunno 'ow 'e got it, sir."

With a hundred and eighty seamen and marines under his command one man at least was likely to be drunk. The ability of the British sailor to get hold of liquor and his readiness to over-indulge in it were part of his physical make-up, like his ears or his eyes.

"Where is he now?"

" 'E made a noise, sir, so I clipped 'im on the ear'ole an' 'e's quiet now, sir."

There was much left untold in that brief sentence, as Bush could guess, but he had no reason to make further inquiry while he thought of what to do.

"Choose a steady seaman and leave him with Black when we go on."

"Aye aye, sir."

So the landing party was the weaker now by the loss of the services not only of the drunken Black but of the man who must be left behind to keep him out of mischief. But it was lucky that there were not more stragglers than there had been up to now.

As the column moved forward again Hornblower's unmistakable gangling figure showed up ahead, silhouetted against the faint moonlight. He fell into step beside Bush and made his report.

"I've sighted the fort, sir."

"You have?"

"Yes, sir. A mile ahead from here, or thereabouts, there's another gully. The fort's beyond that. You can see it against the moon. Maybe half a mile beyond, maybe less. I've left Wellard and Saddler at the gully with orders to halt the advance there."

"Thank you."

Bush plodded on over the uneven surface. Now despite his fatigue he was growing tense again, as the tiger having scented his prey braces his muscles for the spring. Bush was a fighting man, and the thought of action close ahead acted as a stimulant to him. Two hours to sunrise; time and to spare.

"Half a mile from the gully to the fort?" he asked.

"Less than that, I should say, sir."

"Very well. I'll halt there and wait for daylight."

"Yes, sir. May I go on to join my division?"

"You may, Mr. Hornblower."

Bush and Whiting were holding down the pace of the march to a slow methodical step, adapted to the capacity of the slowest and clumsiest man in the column; Bush at this moment was checking himself from lengthening his stride under the spur of the prospect of action. Hornblower went plunging ahead; Bush could see his awkward gait but found himself approving of his subordinate's overflowing energy. He began to discuss with Whiting plans for the final assault.

There was a petty officer waiting for them at the approach to the gully. Bush passed the word back for the column to be ready to halt, and then halted it. He went forward to reconnoitre; with Whiting and Hornblower beside him he stared forward at the square silhouette of the fort against the sky. It even seemed possible to see the dark line of the flagpole. Now his tenseness was eased; the scowl that had been on his face in the last stages of the advance had softened into an expression of good humour, which was wasted in the circumstances.

The arrangements were quickly made, the orders whispered back and forth, the final warnings given. It was the most dangerous moment so far, as the men had to be moved up into the gully and deployed ready for a rush. One whisper from Whiting called for more than a moment's cogitation from Bush.

"Shall I give permission for the men to load, sir?"

"No" answered Bush at length. "Cold steel."

It would be too much of a risk to allow all those muskets to be loaded in the dark. There would not only be the noise of the ramrods, but there was also the danger of some fool pulling a trigger. Hornblower went off to the left, Whiting with his marines to the right, and Bush lay down in the midst of his division in the centre. His legs ached with their unaccustomed exercise, and as he lay his head was inclined to swim with fatigue and lack of sleep. He roused himself and sat up so as to bring himself under control again. Except for his weariness he did not find the waiting period troublesome to him; years of life at sea with its uncounted eventless watches, and years of war with its endless periods of boredom, had inured him to waiting. Some of the seamen actually slept as they lay in the rocky gully; more than once Bush heard snores begin, abruptly cut off by the nudges of the snorers' neighbours.

Now there, at last, right ahead, beyond the fort—was the sky a little paler? Or was it merely that the moon had climbed above the cloud? All round about save there the sky was like purple velvet, still spangled with stars. But there—there—undoubtedly there was a pallor in the sky which had not been there before. Bush stirred and felt again at the uncomfortable pistols in his belt. They were at half-cock; he must remember to pull the hammers back. On the horizon there was a suspicion, the merest suggestion, of a redness mingled with the purple of the sky.

"Pass the word down the line" said Bush. "Prepare to attack."

He waited for the word to pass, but in less time than was possible for it to have reached the ends of the line there were sounds and disturbances in the gully. The damned fools who were always to be found in any body of men had started to rise as soon as the word had reached them, probably without even bothering to pass the word on themselves. But the example would be infectious, at least; beginning at the wings, and coming back to the centre where Bush was, a double ripple of men rising to their feet went along the line. Bush rose too. He drew his sword, balanced it in his hand, and when he was satisfied with his grip he drew a pistol with his left hand and pulled back the hammer. Over on the right there was a sudden clatter of metal; the marines were fixing their bayonets. Bush could see the faces now of the men to right and to left of him.

"Forward!" he said, and the line came surging up out of the gully. "Steady, there!"

He said the last words almost loudly; sooner or later the hotheads in the line would start to run, and later would be better than sooner. He wanted his men to reach the fort in a single wave, not in a succession of breathless individuals. Out on the left he heard Hornblower's voice saying "Steady" as well. The noise of the advance must reach the fort now, must attract the attention even of sleepy, careless Spanish sentries. Soon a sentry would call for his sergeant, the sergeant would come to see, would hesitate a moment, and then give the alarm. The fort bulked square in front of Bush, still shadowy black against the newly red sky; he simply could not restrain himself

E

from quickening his step, and the line came hurrying forward along with him. Then someone raised a shout, and then the other hotheads shouted, and the whole line started to run, Bush running with them.

Like magic, they were at the edge of the ditch, a six-foot scarp, almost vertical, cut in the limestone.

"Come on!" shouted Bush.

Even with his sword and his pistol in his hands he was able to precipitate himself down the scarp, turning his back to the fort and clinging to the edge with his elbows before allowing himself to drop. The bottom of the dry ditch was slippery and irregular, but he plunged across it to the opposite scarp. Yelling men clustered along it, hauling themselves up.

"Give me a hoist!" shouted Bush to the men on either side of him, and they put their shoulders to his thighs and almost threw him up bodily. He found himself on his face, lying on the narrow shelf above the ditch at the foot of the ramparts. A few yards along a seaman was already trying to fling his grapnel up to the top. It came thundering down, missing Bush by no more than a yard, but the seaman without a glance at him snatched it back, poised himself again, and flung the grapnel up the ramparts. It caught, and the seaman, setting his feet against the ramparts and grasping the line with his hands, began to climb like a madman. Before he was half-way up another seaman had grabbed the line and started to scale the ramparts after him, and a yelling crowd of excited men gathered round contending for the next place. Farther along the foot of the ramparts another grapnel had caught and another crowd of yelling men were gathered about the line. Now there was musketry fire; a good many loud reports, and a whiff of powder smoke came to Bush's nostrils in sharp contrast with the pure night air that he had been breathing.

Round on the other face of the fort on his right the marines would be trying to burst in through the embrasures of the guns; Bush turned to his left to see what could be done there. Almost instantly he found his reward; here was the sally port into the fort—a wide wooden door bound with iron, sheltered in the angle of the small projecting bastion at the corner of the fort. Two idiots of seamen were firing their muskets up at the heads that were beginning to show above—not a thought for the door. The average seaman was not fit to be trusted with a musket. Bush raised his voice so that it pealed like a trumpet above the din.

"Axemen here! Axemen! Axemen!"

There were still plenty of men down in the ditch who had not yet had time to scale the scarp; one of them, waving an axe, plunged through the crowd and began to climb up. But Silk, the immensely powerful bosun's mate who commanded a section of seamen in Bush's division, came running along the shelf and grabbed the axe. He began to hew at the door, with tremendous methodical blows, gathering his body together and then flinging the axehead into the wood with all the strength in his body. Another axeman arrived, elbowed Bush aside, and started to hack at the door as well, but he was neither as accomplished nor as powerful. The thunder of their blows resounded in the angle. The iron-barred wicket in the door opened, with a gleam of steel beyond the bars. Bush pointed his pistol and fired. Silk's axe drove clean through the door, and he wrenched the blade free; then, changing his aim, he began to swing the axe in a horizontal arc at the middle part of the door. Three mighty blows and he paused to direct the other axeman where to strike. Silk struck again and again; then he put down the axe, set his fingers in the jagged hole that had opened, his foot against the door, and with one frightful muscle-tearing effort he rent away a whole section of the door. There was a beam across the gap he had opened; Silk's axe crashed onto it and through it, and again. With a hoarse shout Silk plunged, axe in hand, through the jagged hole.

"Come along, men!" yelled Bush, at the top of his lungs, and plunged through after him.

This was the open courtyard of the fort. Bush stumbled over a dead man and looked up to see a group of men before him, in their shirts, or naked; coffee-coloured faces with long disordered moustaches; men with cutlasses and pistols. Silk flung himself upon them like a maniac, the axe swinging. A Spaniard fell under the axe; Bush saw a severed finger fall to the ground as the axe crashed through the Spaniard's ineffectual guard. Pistols banged and smoke eddied about as Bush rushed forward too. There were other men swarming after him. Bush's sword clashed against a cutlass and then the group turned and fled. Bush swung with his sword at a naked shoulder fleeing before him, and saw a red wound open in the flesh and heard the man scream. The man he was pursuing vanished somewhere, like a wraith, and Bush, hurrying on to find other enemies, met a red-coated marine, hatless, his hair wild and his eyes blazing, yelling like a fiend. Bush actually had to parry the bayonet-thrust the marine made at him.

"Steady, you fool!" shouted Bush, only conscious after the words had passed his lips that they were spoken at the top of his voice.

There was a hint of recognition in the marine's mad eyes, and he turned aside, his bayonet at the charge, and rushed on. There were other marines in the background; they must have made their way in through the embrasures. They were all yelling, all drunk with fighting. And here was another rush of seamen, swarming down from the ramparts

they had scaled. On the far side there were wooden buildings; his men were swarming round them and shots and
screams were echoing from them. Those must be the
barracks and storehouses, and the garrison must have fled
there for shelter from the fury of the stormers.

Whiting appeared, his scarlet tunic filthy, his sword
dangling from his wrist. His eyes were bleary and cloudy.

"Call 'em off," said Bush, grasping at his own sanity
with a desperate effort.

It took Whiting a moment to recognise him and to
understand the order.

"Yes, sir" he said.

A fresh flood of seamen came pouring into view beyond
the buildings; Hornblower's division had found its way
into the fort on the far side, evidently. Bush looked round
him and called to a group of his own men who appeared
at that moment.

"Follow me" he said, and pushed on.

A ramp with an easy slope led up the side of the ramparts. A dead man lay there, half-way up, but Bush gave
the corpse no more attention than it deserved. At the top
was the main battery, six huge guns pointing through the
embrasures. And beyond was the sky, all bloody-red with
the dawn. A third of the way up to the zenith reached the
significant colour, but even while Bush halted to look at it
a golden gleam of sun showed through the clouds on the
horizon, and the red began to fade perceptibly; blue sky
and white clouds and blazing golden sun took its place.
That was the measure of the time the assault had taken;
only the few minutes from earliest dawn to tropical sunrise. Bush stood and grasped this astonishing fact—it could
have been late afternoon as far as his own sensations went.

Here from the gun platform the whole view of the bay
opened up. There was the opposite shore; the shallows

where the *Renown* had grounded (was it only yesterday?),
the rolling country lifting immediately into the hills of that
side, with the sharply defined shape of the other battery
at the foot of the point. To the left the peninsula dropped
sharply in a series of jagged headlands, stretching like
fingers out into the blue, blue ocean; farther round still
was the sapphire surface of Scotchman's Bay, and there,
with her backed mizzen topsail catching brilliantly the
rising sun, lay the *Renown*. At that distance she looked like
a lovely toy; Bush caught his breath at the sight of her, not
because of the beauty of the scene but with relief. The sight
of the ship, and the associated memories which the sight
called up in his mind, brought his sanity flooding back;
there were a thousand things to be done now.

Hornblower appeared up the other ramp; he looked like
a scarecrow with his disordered clothes. He held sword in
one hand and pistol in the other, just as did Bush. Beside
him Wellard swung a cutlass singularly large for him, and
at his heels were a score or more of seamen still under
discipline, their muskets, with bayonets fixed, held before
them ready for action.

"Morning, sir" said Hornblower. His battered cocked
hat was still on his head for him to touch it, and he made
a move to do so, checking himself at the realisation that
his sword was in his hand.

"Good morning" said Bush, automatically.

"Congratulations, sir" said Hornblower. His face was
white, and the smile on his lips was like the grin of a
corpse. His beard sprouted over his lips and chin.

"Thank you" said Bush.

Hornblower pushed his pistol into his belt and then
sheathed his sword.

"I've taken possession of all that side, sir" he went on,
with a gesture behind him. "Shall I carry on?"

"Yes, carry on, Mr. Hornblower."

"Aye aye, sir."

This time Hornblower could touch his hat. He gave a rapid order posting a petty officer and men over the guns.

"You see, sir" said Hornblower, pointing "a few got away."

Bush looked down the precipitous hillside that fell to the bay and could see a few figures down there.

"Not enough to trouble us" he said; his mind was just beginning to work smoothly now.

"No, sir. I've forty prisoners under guard at the main gate. I can see Whiting's collecting the rest. I'll go on now, sir, if I may."

"Very well, Mr. Hornblower."

Somebody at least had kept a clear head during the fury of the assault. Bush went on down the farther ramp. A petty officer and a couple of seamen stood there on guard; they came to attention as Bush appeared.

"What are you doing?" he asked.

"This yere's the magazine, zur" said the petty officer— Ambrose, captain of the foretop, who had never lost the broad Devon acquired in his childhood, despite his years in the navy. "We'm guarding of it."

"Mr. Hornblower's orders?"

"Iss, zur."

A forlorn party of prisoners were squatting by the main gate. Hornblower had reported the presence of them. But there were guards he had said nothing about: a sentry at the well; guards at the gate; Woolton, the steadiest petty officer of them all, at a long wooden building beside the gate, and six men with him.

"What's your duty?" demanded Bush.

"Guarding the provision store, sir. There's liquor here."

"Very well."

If the madmen who had made the assault—that marine, for instance, whose bayonet-thrust Bush had parried—had got at the liquor there would be no controlling them at all.

Abbott, the midshipman in subordinate command of Bush's own division, came hurrying up.

"What the hell d'ye think you've been doing?" demanded Bush, testily. "I've been without you since the attack began."

"Sorry, sir" apologised Abbott. Of course he had been carried away by the fury of the attack, but that was no excuse; certainly no excuse when one remembered young Wellard still at Hornblower's side and attending to his duties.

"Get ready to make the signal to the ship" ordered Bush. "You ought to have been ready to do that five minutes ago. Clear three guns. Who was it who was carrying the flag? Find him and bend it on over the Spanish colours. Jump to it, damn you."

Victory might be sweet, but it had no effect on Bush's temper, now that the reaction had set in. Bush had had no sleep and no breakfast, and even though perhaps only ten minutes had elapsed since the fort had been captured, his conscience nagged at him regarding those ten minutes; there were many things he ought to have done in that time.

It was a relief to turn away from the contemplation of his own shortcomings and to settle with Whiting regarding the safeguarding of the prisoners. They had all been fetched out of the barrack buildings by now; a hundred half-naked men, and at least a score of women, their hair streaming down their backs and their scanty clothing clutched about them. At a more peaceful moment Bush would have had an eye for those women, but as it was he merely felt irritated at the thought of an additional complication to deal with, and his eyes only took note of them as such.

Among the men there was a small sprinkling of Negroes and mulattoes, but most of them were Spaniards. Nearly all the dead men who lay here and there were fully clothed, in white uniforms with blue facings—they were the sentinels and the main guard who had paid the penalty for their lack of watchfulness.

"Who was in command?" asked Bush of Whiting.

"Can't tell, sir."

"Well, ask them, then."

Bush had command of no language at all save his own, and apparently neither had Whiting, judging by his unhappy glance.

"Please, sir——" This was Pierce, surgeon's mate, trying to attract his attention. "Can I have a party to help carry the wounded into the shade?"

Before Bush could answer him Abbott was hailing from the gun platform.

"Guns clear, sir. May I draw powder charges from the magazines?"

And then before Bush could give permission here was young Wellard, trying to elbow Pierce on one side so as to command Bush's attention.

"Please, sir. Please, sir. Mr. Hornblower's respects, sir, an' could you please come up to the tower there, sir. Mr. Hornblower says it's urgent, sir."

Bush felt at that moment as if one more distraction would break his heart.

X

A<small>T</small> each corner of the fort there was a small bastion built out, to give flanking fire along the walls, and on top of the southwest bastion stood a little watch-tower which carried the flagstaff. Bush and Hornblower stood on the tower, the broad Atlantic behind them and before them the long gulf of the bay of Samaná. Over their heads waved two flags: the White Ensign above, the red and gold of Spain below. Out in the *Renown* they might not be able to make out the colours, but they would certainly see the two flags. And when having heard the three signal guns boom out they trained their telescopes on the fort they must have seen the flags slowly flutter down and rise again, dip and rise again. Three guns; two flags twice dipped. That was the signal that the fort was in English hands, and the *Renown* had seen it, for she had braced up her mizzen topsail and begun the long beat back along the coast of the peninsula.

Bush and Hornblower had with them the one telescope which a hasty search through the fort had brought to light; when one of them had it to his eye the other could hardly restrain his twitching fingers from snatching at it. At the moment Bush was looking through it, training it on the farther shore of the bay, and Hornblower was stabbing with an index finger at what he had been looking at a moment before.

"You see, sir?" he asked. "Farther up the bay than the battery. There's the town—Savana, it's called. And beyond that there's the shipping. They'll up anchor any minute now."

"I see 'em" said Bush, the glass still at his eye. "Four small craft. No sail hoisted—hard to tell what they are."

"Easy enough to guess, though, sir."

"Yes, I suppose so" said Bush.

There would be no need for big men of war here, immediately adjacent to the Mona Passage. Half the Caribbean trade came up through here, passing within thirty miles of the bay of Samaná. Fast, handy craft, with a couple of long guns each and a large crew, could dash out and snap up prizes and retire to the protection of the bay, where the crossed fire of the batteries could be relied on to keep out enemies, as the events of yesterday had proved. The raiders would hardly have to spend a night at sea.

"They'll know by now we've got this fort" said Hornblower. "They'll guess that *Renown* will be coming round after 'em. They can sweep, and tow, and kedge. They'll be out of the bay before you can say Jack Robinson. And from Engano Point it's a fair wind for Martinique."

"Very likely" agreed Bush.

With a simultaneous thought they turned to look at the *Renown*. With her stern to them, her sails braced sharp on the starboard tack, she was making her way out to sea; it would be a long beat before she could go about in the certainty of being able to weather Cape Samaná. She looked lovely enough out there, with her white sails against the rich blue, but it would be hours before she could work round to stop the bolt hole. Bush turned back and considered the sheltered waters of the bay.

"Better man the guns and make ready for 'em" he said.

"Yes, sir" said Hornblower. He hesitated. "We won't have 'em under fire for long. They'll be shallow draught. They can hug the point over there closer than *Renown* could."

"But it won't take much to sink 'em, either" said Bush. "Oh, I see what you're after."

"Red-hot shot might make all the difference, sir" said Hornblower.

"Repay 'em in their own coin" said Bush, with a grin of satisfaction. Yesterday the *Renown* had endured the hellish fire of red-hot shot. To Bush the thought of roasting a few Dagoes was quite charming.

"That's right, sir" said Hornblower.

He was not grinning like Bush. There was a frown on his face; he was oppressed with the thought that the privateers might escape to continue their depredations elsewhere, and any means to reduce their chances should be used.

"But can you do it?" asked Bush suddenly. "D'ye know how to heat shot?"

"I'll find out, sir."

"I'll wager no man of ours knows how."

Shot could only be heated in a battery on land; a seagoing ship, constructed of inflammable material, could not run the risk of going into action with a flaming furnace inside her. The French, in the early days of the Revolutionary War, had made some disastrous experiments in the hope of finding a means of countering England's naval superiority, but after a few ships had set themselves on fire they had given up the attempt. Seagoing men now left the use of the heated weapon to shore-based garrison artillery.

"I'll try and find out for myself, sir" said Hornblower. "There's the furnace down there and all the gear."

Hornblower stood in the sunshine, already far too hot to be comfortable. His face was pale, dirty, and bearded, and in his expression eagerness and weariness were oddly at war.

"Have you had any breakfast yet?" asked Bush.

"No, sir." Hornblower looked straight at him. "Neither have you, sir."

"No" grinned Bush.

He had not been able to spare a moment for anything like that, with the whole defence of the fort to be organised. But he could bear fatigue and hunger and thirst, and he doubted if Hornblower could.

"I'll get a drink of water at the well, sir" said Hornblower.

As he said the words, and the full import came to him, a change in his expression was quite obvious. He ran the tip of his tongue over his lips; Bush could see that the lips were cracked and parched and that the tongue could do nothing to relieve them. The man had drunk nothing since he had landed twelve hours ago—twelve hours of desperate exertion in a tropical climate.

"See that you do, Mr. Hornblower" said Bush. "That's an order."

"Aye aye, sir."

Bush found the telescope leaving his hand and passing into Hornblower's.

"May I have another look, sir, before I go down? By George, I thought as much. That two-master's warping out, sir. Less than an hour before she's within range. I'll get the guns manned, sir. Take a look for yourself, sir."

He went darting down the stone stairs of the tower, having given back the telescope, but half-way down he paused.

"Don't forget your breakfast, sir" he said, his face upturned to Bush. "You've plenty of time for that."

Bush's glance through the telescope confirmed what Hornblower had said. At least one of the vessels up the bay was beginning to move. He turned and swept the rest of the land and water with a precautionary glance before handing the telescope to Abbott, who during all this conversation had been standing by, silent in the presence of his betters.

"Keep a sharp lookout" said Bush.

Down in the body of the fort Hornblower was already issuing rapid orders, and the men, roused to activity, were on the move. On the gun platform they were casting loose the remaining guns, and as Bush descended from the platform he saw Hornblower organising other working parties, snapping out orders with quick gestures. At the sight of Bush he turned guiltily and walked over to the well. A marine was winding up the bucket, and Hornblower seized it. He raised the bucket to his lips, leaning back to balance the weight; and he drank and drank, water slopping in quantities over his chest as he drank, water pouring over his face, until the bucket was empty, and then he put it down with a grin at Bush, his face still dripping water. The very sight of him was enough to make Bush, who had already had one drink from the well, feel consumed with thirst all over again.

By the time Bush had drunk there was the usual group of people clamouring for his attention, for orders and information, and by the time he had dealt with them there was smoke rising from the furnace in the corner of the courtyard, and a loud crackling from inside it. Bush walked over. A seaman, kneeling, was plying a pair of bellows; two other men were bringing wood from the pile against the ramparts. When the furnace door was opened the blast of heat that rose into Bush's face was enough to make him step back. Hornblower turned up with his hurried pace.

"How's the shot, Saddler?" he asked.

The petty officer picked up some rags, and, with them to shield his hands, laid hold of two long handles that projected from the far side of the furnace, balancing two projecting from the near side. When he drew them out it became apparent that all four handles were part of a large iron grating, the centre of which rested inside the furnace above the blazing fuel. Lying on the grating were rows of shot, still black in the sunshine. Saddler shifted his quid, gathered his saliva, and spat expertly on the nearest one. The spittle boiled off, but not with violence.

"Not very hot yet, sir" said Saddler.

"Us'll fry they devils" said the man with the bellows, unexpectedly; he looked up, as he crouched on his knees, with ecstasy in his face at the thought of burning his enemies alive.

Hornblower paid him no attention.

"Here, you bearer men" he said, "let's see what you can do."

Hornblower had been followed by a file of men, every pair carrying a piece of apparatus formed of two iron bars joined with iron crosspieces. The first pair approached. Saddler took a pair of tongs and gingerly worked a hot shot onto the bearer.

"Move on, you two" ordered Hornblower. "Next!"

When a shot lay on every bearer Hornblower led his men away.

"Now let's see you roll those into the guns" he said.

Bush followed, consumed with curiosity. The procession moved up the ramp to the gun platform, where now crews had been told off to every gun; the guns were run back with the muzzles well clear of the embrasures. Tubs of water stood by each pair of guns.

"Now, you rammers" said Hornblower, "are your dry wads in? Then in with your wet wads."

From the tubs the seamen brought out round flat discs of fibre, dripping with water.

"Two to a gun" said Hornblower.

The wet wads were thrust into the muzzles of the guns and then were forced down the bores with the club-ended ramrods.

"Ram 'em home" said Hornblower. "Now, bearers."

It was not such an easy thing to do, to put the ends of the bearing-stretchers at the muzzles of the guns and then to tilt so as to induce the hot shot to roll down into the bore.

"The Don must've exercised with these guns better than we'd give 'em credit for" said Hornblower to Bush, "judging by the practice they made yesterday. Rammers!"

The ramrods thrust the shot home against the charges; there was a sharp sizzling noise as each hot shot rested against the wet wads.

"Run up!"

The guns' crews seized the tackles and heaved, and the ponderous guns rolled slowly forward to point their muzzles out through the embrasures.

"Aim for the point over there and fire!"

With handspikes under the rear axles the guns were traversed at the orders of the captains; the priming tubes were already in the touchholes and each gun was fired as it bore. The sound of the explosions was very different here on the stone platform from when guns were fired in the confined spaces of a wooden ship. The slight wind blew the smoke sideways.

"Pretty fair!" said Hornblower, shading his eyes to watch the fall of the shot; and, turning to Bush, "That'll puzzle those gentlemen over there. They'll wonder what in the world we're firing at."

"How long" asked Bush, who had watched the whole process with a fascinated yet horrified interest, "before a hot shot burns through those wads and sets off the gun itself?"

"That is one of the things I do not know, sir" answered Hornblower with a grin. "It would not surprise me if we found out during the course of today."

"I dare say" said Bush; but Hornblower had swung round and was confronting a seaman who had come running up to the platform.

"What d'ye think you're doing?"

"Bringing a fresh charge, sir" said the man, surprised, indicating with a gesture the cartridge-container he carried.

"Then get back and wait for the order. Get back, all of you."

The ammunition carriers shrank back before his evident anger.

"Swab out!" ordered Hornblower to the guns' crews, and as the wetted sponges were thrust into the muzzles he turned to Bush again. "We can't be too careful, sir. We don't want any chance of live charges and red-hot shot coming together on this platform."

"Certainly not" agreed Bush.

He was both pleased and irritated that Hornblower should have dealt so efficiently with the organisation of the battery.

"Fresh charges!" yelled Hornblower, and the ammunition carriers he had previously sent back came trotting up the ramp again. "These are English cartridges, sir, I'll wager."

"Why do you say that?"

"West-Country serge, stitched and choked exactly like ours, sir. Out of English prizes, I fancy."

It was most probable; the Spanish forces which held this end of the island against the insurgents most likely depended on renewing their stores from English ships captured in the Mona Passage. Well, with good fortune they would take no more prizes—the implication, forcing itself on Bush's mind despite his many preoccupations, made him stir uneasily as he stood by the guns with his hands clasped behind him and the sun beating down on his face. The Dons would be in a bad way with their source of supplies cut off. They would not be able to hold out long against the rebellious blacks that hemmed them in here in the eastern end of Santo Domingo.

"Ram those wads handsomely, there, Cray" said Hornblower. "No powder in that bore, or we'll have 'Cray D.D.' in the ship's books."

There was a laugh at that—"D.D." in the ship's books meant "discharged, dead"—but Bush was not paying attention. He had scrambled up the parapet and was staring out at the bay.

"They're standing down the bay" he said. "Stand by, Mr. Hornblower."

"Aye aye, sir."

Bush strained his sight to look at the four vessels creeping down the fairway. As he watched he saw the first one hoisting sail on both masts. Apparently she was taking advantage of a flaw of wind, blowing flukily in the confined and heated waters, to gain some of the desperately necessary distance towards the sea and safety.

"Mr. Abbott, bring down that glass!" shouted Hornblower.

As Abbott descended the steps Hornblower addressed a further comment to Bush.

"If they're making a bolt for it the moment they know we've got the fort it means they're not feeling too secure over there, sir."

"I suppose not."

"You might have expected 'em to try to recapture the fort one way or another. They could land a force up the peninsula and come down to attack us. I wonder why they're not trying that, sir? Why do they just unstick and run?"

"They're only Dagoes" said Bush. He refused to speculate further about the enemy's motives while action was imminent, and he grabbed the glass from Abbott's hands.

Through the telescope details were far plainer. Two large schooners with several guns a-side; a big lugger, and a vessel whose rig they still could not determine, as she was the farthest away and, with no sail set, was towing behind her boats out from the anchorage.

"It'll be long range, Mr. Hornblower" said Bush.

"Yes, sir. But they hit us with these same guns yesterday."

"Make sure of your aim. They won't be long under fire."

"Aye aye, sir."

The vessels were not coming down together. If they had done so they might stand a better chance, as the fort would only be able to fire on one at a time. But the panic feeling of every man for himself must have started them off as soon as each one separately could get under way—and perhaps the deep channel was too narrow for vessels in company. Now the leading schooner had taken in her sail again; the wind here, what there was of it, was foul for her when she turned to port along the channel. She had two boats out quickly enough to tow her; Bush's telescope could reveal every detail.

"Some time yet before she's in range, sir" said Hornblower. "I'll take a look at the furnace, with your permission."

"I'll come too" said Bush.

At the furnace the bellows were still being worked and the heat was tremendous—but it was far hotter when Saddler drew out the grating that carried the heated shot. Even in the sunshine they could see the glow of the spheres; as the heat rose from them the atmosphere above them wavered so that everything below was vague and distorted. It could be a scene in Hell. Saddler spat on the nearest cannon ball and the saliva leaped with an instant hiss from the smooth surface of the sphere, falling from it without contact to dance and leap on the grating under it until with a final hiss it vanished entirely. A second attempt by Saddler brought the same result.

"Hot enough, sir?" asked Saddler.

"Yes" said Hornblower.

Bush had often enough as a midshipman taken a smoothing-iron forward to the galley to heat it when there had been particular need to iron a shirt or a neckcloth; he remembered how he had made the same test of the temperature of the iron. It was a proof that the iron was dangerously hot to use when the spittle refused to make contact with it, but the shot was far hotter than that, infinitely hotter.

Saddler thrust the grating back into the furnace and wiped his streaming face with the rags that had shielded his hands.

"Stand by, you bearer men" said Hornblower. "You'll be busy enough soon."

With a glance at Bush for permission he was off again, back to the battery, hurrying with awkward galvanic strides. Bush followed more slowly; he was weary with all his exertions, and it crossed his mind as he watched Hornblower hurrying up the ramp that Hornblower had probably been more active than he and was not blessed with nearly as powerful a physique. By the time he came up to him Hornblower was watching the leading schooner again.

"Her scantling'll be weak" said Hornblower. "These twenty-four-pounders'll go clean through her most of the time, even at long range."

"Plunging shot" said Bush. "Maybe they'll go out through her bottom."

"Maybe so" said Hornblower, and then added "sir." Even after all his years of service he was liable to forget that important monosyllable when he was thinking deeply.

"She's setting sail again!" said Bush. "They've got her head round."

"And the tows have cast off" added Hornblower. "Not long now."

He looked down the line of guns, all charged and primed, the quoins withdrawn so that they were at their highest elevation, the muzzles pointing upward as though awaiting the shot to be rolled into them. The schooner was moving perceptibly down the channel towards them. Hornblower turned and walked down the row; behind his back one hand was twisting impatiently within the other; he came back and turned again, walking jerkily down the row—he seemed incapable of standing still, but when he caught Bush's eye on him he halted guiltily, forcing himself, with an obvious effort, to stand still like his superior officer. The schooner crept on, a full half-mile ahead of the next vessel.

"You might try a ranging shot" said Bush at length.

"Aye aye, sir" said Hornblower with instant agreement, like a river bursting through a broken dam. It seemed as if he had been compelling himself to wait until Bush should speak.

"Furnace, there!" hailed Hornblower. "Saddler! Send up one shot."

The bearers came plodding up the ramp, carrying carefully between them the glowing cannon ball. The bright redness of it was quite obvious—even the heat that it gave off was distinctly perceptible. The wet wads were rammed down the bore of the nearest gun, the shot bearer was hoisted up level with its muzzle, and, coaxed into motion with wad-hook and rammer, the fiery shot was rolled in. There was an instant hissing and spluttering of steam as the ball came into contact with the wet wads; Bush wondered again how long it would be before the wads were burned through and the charge set off; the recoil would make it decidedly uncomfortable for anyone who happened to be aiming the gun at that moment.

"Run up!" Hornblower was giving the orders. The gun's crew heaved at the tackles and the gun rumbled forward

Hornblower took his place behind the gun and, squatting down, he squinted along it.

"Trail right!" Tackles and handspikes heaved the gun around. "A touch more! Steady! No, a touch left. Steady!"

Somewhat to Bush's relief Hornblower straightened himself and came from behind the gun. He leaped onto the parapet with his usual uncontrollable vigour and shaded his eyes; Bush at one side kept his telescope trained on the schooner.

"Fire!" said Hornblower.

The momentary hiss of the priming was drowned in the instant bellow of the gun. Bush saw the black line of the shot's path across the blue of the sky, reaching upward during the time it might take to draw a breath, sinking downward again; a strange sort of line, an inch long if he had to say its length, constantly renewing itself in front and constantly disappearing at its back end, and pointing straight at the schooner. It was still pointing at her, just above her—to that extent did the speed of the shot outpace the recording of retina and brain—when Bush saw the splash, right in line with the schooner's bows. He took his eye from the telescope as the splash disappeared, to to find Hornblower looking at him.

"A cable's length short" he said, and Hornblower nodded agreement.

"We can open fire then, sir?" asked Hornblower.

"Yes, carry on, Mr. Hornblower."

The words were hardly out of his mouth before Hornblower was hailing again.

"Furnace, there! Five more shot!"

It took Bush a moment or two to see the point of that order. But clearly it was inadvisable to have hot shot and powder charges brought up on the platform at the same time; the gun that had been fired would have to remain unloaded until the other five had fired as well. Hornblower came down and stood at Bush's side again.

"I couldn't understand yesterday why they always fired salvos at us, sir" he said, "that reduced the rate of fire to the speed of the slowest gun. But I see now."

"So do I" said Bush.

"All your wet wads in?" demanded Hornblower of the guns' crews. "Certain? Carry on, then."

The shot were coaxed into the muzzles of the guns; they hissed and spluttered against the wads.

"Run up. Now take your aim. Make sure of it, captains."

The hissing and spluttering continued as the guns were trained.

"Fire when your gun bears!"

Hornblower was up on the parapet again; Bush could see perfectly well through the embrasure of the idle gun. The five guns all fired within a second or two of each other; through Bush's telescope the sky was streaked by the passage of their shot.

"Sponge out!" said Hornblower; and then, louder, "Six charges!"

He came down to Bush.

"One splash pretty close" said Bush.

"Two very short" said Hornblower "and one far out on the right. I know who fired that one and I'll deal with him."

"One splash I didn't see" said Bush.

"Nor did I, sir. Clean over, perhaps. But possibly a hit."

The men with the charges came running up to the platform, and the eager crews seized them and rammed them home and the dry wads on top of the charges.

"Six shot!" shouted Hornblower to Saddler; and then, to the gun captains, "Prime. Put in your wet wads."

"She's altered course" said Bush. "The range can't have changed much."

"No, sir. Load and run up! Excuse me, sir."

He went hurrying off to take his stand by the left-hand gun, which presumably was the one which had been incorrectly laid previously.

"Take your aim carefully" he called from his new position. "Fire when you're sure."

Bush saw him squat behind the left-hand gun, but he himself applied his attention to observing the results of the shooting.

The cycle repeated itself; the guns roared, the men came running with fresh charges, the red-hot shot were brought up. The guns were fired again before Hornblower came back to Bush's side.

"You're hitting, I think" said Bush. He turned back to look again through his glass. "I think—by God, yes! Smoke! Smoke!"

A faint black cloud was just visible between the schooner's masts. It thinned again, and Bush could not be perfectly sure. The nearest gun bellowed out, and a chance flaw of wind blew the powder smoke about them as they stood together, blotting out their view of the schooner.

"Confound it all!" said Bush, moving about restlessly in search of a better viewpoint.

The other guns went off almost simultaneously and added to the smoke.

"Bring up fresh charges!" yelled Hornblower, with the smoke eddying round him. "See that you swab those guns out properly."

The smoke eddied away, revealing the schooner, apparently unharmed, still creeping along the bay, and Bush cursed in his disappointment.

"The range is shortening and the guns are hot now" said Hornblower; and then, louder, "Gun captains! Get your quoins in!"

He hurried off to supervise the adjustment of the guns' elevation, and it was some seconds before he hailed again for hot shot to be brought up. In that time Bush noticed that the schooner's boats, which had been pulling in company with the schooner, were turning to run alongside her. That could mean that the schooner's captain was now sure that the flaws of wind would be sufficient to carry her round the point and safely to the mouth of the bay. The guns went off again in an irregulaɪ salvo, and Bush saw a trio of splashes rise from the water's surface close on the near side of the schooner.

"Fresh charges!" yelled Hornblower.

And then Bush saw the schooner swing round, presenting her stern to the battery and heading straight for the shallows of the further shore.

"What in hell——" said Bush to himself.

Then he saw a sudden fountain of black smoke appear spouting from the schooner's deck, and while this sight was rejoicing him he saw the schooner's booms swing over as she took the ground. She was afire and had been deliberately run ashore. The smoke was dense about her hull, and while he held her in his telescope he saw her big white mainsail above the smoke suddenly disintegrate and disappear—the flames had caught it and whisked it away into nothing. He took the telescope from his eye and looked round for Hornblower, who was standing on the parapet again. Powder and smoke had grimed his face, already dark with the growth of his beard, and his teeth showed strangely white as he grinned. The gunners were cheering, and the cheering was being echoed by the rest of the landing party in the fort.

Hornblower was gesticulating to make the gunners cease their noise so that he could be heard down in the fort as he countermanded his call for more shot.

"Belay that order, Saddler! Take those shot back, bearer men!"

He jumped down and approached Bush.

"That's done it" said the latter.

"The first one, anyway."

A great jet of smoke came from the burning wreck, reaching up and up from between her masts; the mainmast fell as they watched, and as it fell the report of the explosion came to their ears across the water; the fire had reached the schooner's powder store, and when the smoke cleared a little they could see that she now lay on the shore in two halves, blown asunder in the middle. The foremast still stood for a moment on the forward half, but it fell as they watched it; bows and stern were blazing fiercely, while the boats with the crew rowed away across the shallows.

"A nasty sight" said Hornblower.

But Bush could see nothing unpleasant about the sight of an enemy burning. He was exulting. "With half his men in the boats he didn't have enough hands to spare to fight the fires when we hit him" he said.

"Maybe a shot went through her deck and lodged in her hold" said Hornblower.

The tone of his voice made Bush look quickly at him, for he was speaking thickly and harshly like a drunken man; but he could not be drunk, although the dirty hairy face and blood-shot eyes might well have suggested it. The man was fatigued. Then the dull expression on Hornblower's face was replaced once more by a look of animation, and when he spoke his voice was natural again.

"Here comes the next" he said. "She must be nearly in range."

The second schooner, also with her boats in attendance, was coming down the channel, her sails set. Hornblower turned back to the guns.

"D'you see the next ship to aim at?" he called; and received a fierce roar of agreement, before he turned round to hail Saddler. "Bring up those shot, bearer men."

The procession of bearers with the glowing shot came up the ramp again—frightfully hot shot; the heat as each one went by—twenty-four pounds of white-hot iron—was like the passage of a wave. The routine of rolling the fiendish things into the gun muzzles proceeded. There were some loud remarks from the men at the guns, and one of the shot fell with a thump on the stone floor of the battery, and lay there glowing. Two other guns were still not loaded.

"What's wrong there?" demanded Hornblower.

"Please, sir——"

Hornblower was already striding over to see for himself. From the muzzle of one of the three loaded guns there was a curl of steam; in all three there was a wild hissing as the hot shot rested on the wet wads.

"Run up, train, and fire" ordered Hornblower. "Now what's the matter with you others? Roll that thing out of the way."

"Shot won't fit, sir" said more than one voice as someone with a wad-hook awkwardly rolled the fallen shot up against the parapet. The bearers of the other two stood by, sweating. Anything Hornblower could say in reply was drowned for the moment by the roar of one of the guns —the men were still at the tackles, and the gun had gone off on its own volition as they ran it up. A man sat crying out with pain, for the carriage had recoiled over his foot and blood was already pouring from it onto the stone floor. The captains of the other two loaded guns made no pretence at training and aiming. The moment their guns were run up they shouted "Stand clear!" and fired.

"Carry him down to Mr. Pierce" said Hornblower, indicating the injured man. "Now let's see about these shot."

Hornblower returned to Bush with a rueful look on his face, embarrassed and self-conscious.

"What's the trouble?" asked Bush.

"Those shot are too hot" explained Hornblower. "Damn it, I didn't think of that. They're half melted in the furnace and gone out of shape so that they won't fit the bore. What a fool I was not to think of that."

As his superior officer, Bush did not admit that he had not thought of it either. He said nothing.

"And the ones that hadn't gone out of shape were too hot anyway" went on Hornblower. "I'm the damndest fool God ever made. Mad as a hatter. Did you see how that gun went off? The men'll be scared now and won't lay their guns properly—too anxious to fire it off before the recoil catches them. God, I'm a careless son of a swab."

"Easy, easy" said Bush, a prey to conflicting emotions.

Hornblower pounding his left hand with his right fist as he upbraided himself was a comic sight; Bush could not help laughing at him. And Bush knew perfectly well that Hornblower had done excellently so far, really excellently, to have mastered at a moment's notice so much of the technique of using red-hot shot. Moreover, it must be confessed that Bush had experienced, during this expedition, more than one moment of pique at Hornblower's invariable bold assumption of responsibility; and the pique may even have been roused by a stronger motive, jealousy at Hornblower's good management—an unworthy motive, which Bush would disclaim with shocked surprise if he became aware of it. Yet it made the sight of Hornblower's present discomfiture all the more amusing at the moment.

"Don't take on so" said Bush with a grin.

"But it makes me wild to be such a——"

Hornblower cut the sentence off short. Bush could actually see him calling up his self-control and mastering himself, could see his annoyance at having been self-revelatory, could see the mask of the stoical and experienced fighting man put back into place to conceal the furious passions within.

"Would you take charge here, sir?" he said; it might be another person speaking. "I'll go and take a look at the furnace, if I may. They'll have to go easy with those bellows."

"Very good, Mr. Hornblower. Send the ammunition up and I'll direct the fire on the schooner."

"Aye aye, sir. I'll send up the last shot to go into the furnace. They won't be too hot yet, sir."

Hornblower went darting down the ramp while Bush moved behind the guns to direct the fire. The fresh charges came up and were rammed home, the wet wads went in on top of the dry wads, and then the bearers began to arrive with the shot.

"Steady, all of you" said Bush. "These won't be as hot as the last batch. Take your aim carefully."

But when Bush climbed onto the parapet and trained his

telescope on the second schooner he could see that the
schooner was changing her mind. She had brailed up her
foresail and taken in her jibs; her boats were lying at an
angle to her course; and were struggling, beetle-like, off
her bows. They were pulling her round—she was going
back up the bay and deciding not to run the gauntlet of the
red-hot shot. There was the smouldering wreck of her
consort to frighten her.

"She's turning tail!" said Bush loudly. "Hit her while
you can, you men."

He saw the shot curving in the air, he saw the splashes
in the water; he remembered how yesterday he had seen
a ricochet shot from these very guns rebound from the
water and strike the *Renown's* massive side—one of the
splashes was dead true for line, and might well indicate
a hit.

"Fresh charges!" he bellowed, turning to make himself
heard down at the magazine. "Sponge out!"

But by the time the charges were in the guns the schooner
had got her head right round, had reset her foresail, and
was creeping back up the bay. Judging by the splashes of
the last salvo she would be out of range before the next
could be fired.

"Mr. Hornblower!"

"Sir!"

"'Vast sending any shot."

"Aye aye, sir."

When Hornblower came up again to the battery Bush
pointed to the retreating schooner.

"He thought better of it, did he?" commented Hornblower. "Yes, and those other two have anchored, I should
say."

His fingers were twitching for the one telescope again,
and Bush handed it over.

"The other two aren't moving either" said Hornblower, and then he swung round and trained the telescope down the bay towards the sea. "*Renown's* gone about. She's caught the wind. Six miles? Seven miles? She'll be rounding the point in an hour."

It was Bush's turn to grab for the telescope. There was no mistaking the trim of those topsails. From the *Renown* he transferred his attention to the opposite shore of the bay. There was the other battery with the Spanish flag above it—the flag was now drooping, now flapping lazily in the light wind prevailing over the shore. He could make out no sign of activity whatever, and there was some finality in his gesture as he closed the telescope and looked at his second in command.

"Everything's quiet" he said. "Nothing to be done until *Renown* comes down."

"That is so" agreed Hornblower.

It was interesting to watch Hornblower's animation ebb away. Intense weariness was obvious in his face the moment he was off his guard.

"We can feed the men" said Bush. "And I'd like to have a look at the wounded. Those damned prisoners have to be sorted out—Whiting's got 'em all herded in the casemate, men and women, captains and drum boys. God knows what provisions there are here. We've got to see about that. Then we can set a watch, dismiss the watch below, and some of us can get some rest."

"So we can" said Hornblower; reminded of the necessary activities that still remained, he resumed his stolid expression. "Shall I go down and start attending to it, sir?"

XI

THE sun at noontime was glaring down into the fort of Samaná. Within the walls the heat was pitilessly reflected inwards to a murderous concentration, so that even the corners which had shade were dreadfully hot. The sea breeze had not yet begun to blow, and from the flagstaff the White Ensign drooped spiritlessly, half covering the Spanish colours that drooped below it. Yet discipline still prevailed. On every bastion the lookouts stood in the blazing sun to guard against surprise. The marine sentries, with regular and measured step, were "walking their posts of duty in a smart and soldierly manner" in accordance with regulations, muskets sloped, scarlet tunics buttoned to the neck, crossbelts exactly in position. When one of them reached the end of his beat he would halt with a click of his heels, bring down his musket to the "order" position in three smart movements, and then, pushing his right hand forward and his left foot out, stand "at ease" until the heat and the flies drove him into motion again, when his heels would come together, the musket rise to his shoulder, and he would walk his beat once more. In the battery the guns' crew dozed on the unrelenting stone, the lucky men in the shade cast by the guns, the others in the narrow strip of shade at the foot of the parapet; but two men sat and kept themselves awake and every few minutes saw to it that the slow matches smouldering in the tubs were still alight, available to supply fire instantly if the guns had to be worked, whether to fire on ships in the bay or to beat off an attack by land. Out beyond Samaná Point H.M.S. *Renown* lay awaiting the first puffs of the sea breeze to come up the bay and get into touch with her landing party.

Beside the main storehouse Lieutenant Bush sat on a bench and tried to stay awake, cursing the heat, cursing his own kindness of heart that had led him to allow his junior officers to rest first while he assumed the responsibilities of officer on duty, envying the marines who lay asleep and snoring all about him. From time to time he stretched his legs, which were stiff and painful after all his exertions. He mopped his forehead and thought about loosening his neckcloth.

Round the corner came a hurried messenger.

"Mr. Bush, sir. Please, sir, there's a boat puttin' off from the battery across the bay."

Bush rolled a stupefied eye at the messenger.

"Heading which way?"

"Straight towards us, sir. She's got a flag—a white flag, it looks like."

"I'll come and see. No peace for the wicked" said Bush, and he pulled himself to his feet, with all his joints complaining, and walked stiffly over to the ramp and up to the battery.

The petty officer of the watch was waiting there with the telescope, having descended from the lookout tower to meet him. Bush took the glass and looked through it. A six-oared boat, black against the blue of the bay, was pulling straight towards him, as the messenger had said. From the staff in the bow hung a flag, which might be white; there was no wind to extend it. But in the boat there were no more than ten people all told, so that there could be no immediate danger to the fort in any case. It was a long row across the glittering bay. Bush watched the boat heading steadily for the fort. The low cliffs which

descended to meet the water on this side of the Samaná
peninsula sank in an easy gradient here in the neighbourhood of the fort; diagonally down the gradient ran a path
to the landing stage, which could be swept—as Bush had
already noted—by the fire of the last two guns at the
right-hand end of the battery. But there was no need to
man those guns, for this could not be an attack. And in
confirmation a puff of wind blew out the flag in the boat.
It was white.

Undeviating, the boat pulled for the landing stage and
came alongside it. There was a flash of bright metal from
the boat, and then in the heated air the notes of a trumpet
call, high and clear, rose to strike against the ears of the
garrison. Then two men climbed out of the boat onto
the landing stage. They wore uniforms of blue and white,
one of them with a sword at his side while the other carried
the twinkling trumpet, which he set to his lips and blew
again. Piercingly and sweet, the call echoed along the
cliffs; the birds which had been drowsing in the heat came
fluttering out with plaintive cries, disturbed as much by
the trumpet call as they had been by the thunder of the
artillery in the morning. The officer wearing the sword
unrolled a white flag, and then he and the trumpeter set
themselves to climb the steep path to the fort. This was a
parley in accordance with the established etiquette of war.
The pealing notes of the trumpet were proof that no surprise was intended; the white flag attested the pacific in-
tentions of the bearer.

As Bush watched the slow ascent he meditated on
what powers he had to conduct a negotiation with the
enemy, and he thought dubiously about the difficulties that
would be imposed on any negotiation by differences of
language.

"Turn out the guard" he said to the petty officer; and

then to the messenger, "My compliments to Mr. Hornblower, and ask him to come here as soon as he can."

The trumpet echoed up the path again; many of the sleepers in the fort were stirring at the sound, and it was a proof of the fatigue of the others that they went on sleeping. Down in the courtyard the tramp of feet and the sound of curt orders told how the marine guard was forming up. The white flag was almost at the edge of the ditch; the bearer halted, looking up at the parapets, while the trumpeter blew a last final call, the wild notes of the fanfare calling the last of the sleepers in the garrison to wakefulness.

"I'm here, sir" reported Hornblower.

The hat to which he raised his hand was lopsided, and he was like a scarecrow in his battered uniform. His face was clean, but it bore a plentiful growth of beard.

"Can you speak Spanish enough to deal with him?" asked Bush, indicating the Spanish officer with a jerk of his thumb.

"Well, sir—yes."

The last word was in a sense spoken against Hornblower's will. He would have liked to temporise, and then he had given the definite answer which any military situation demanded.

"Let's hear you, then."

"Aye aye, sir."

Hornblower stepped up on the parapet; the Spanish officer, looking up from the edge of the ditch, took off his hat at sight of him and bowed courteously; Hornblower did the same. There was a brief exchange of apparently polite phrases before Hornblower turned back to Bush.

"Are you going to admit him to the fort, sir?" he asked. "He says he has many negotiations to carry out."

"No" said Bush, without hesitation. "I don't want him spying round here."

Bush was not too sure about what the Spaniard could discover, but he was suspicious and cautious by temperament.

"Very good, sir."

"You'll have to go out to him, Mr. Hornblower. I'll cover you from here with the marines."

"Aye aye, sir."

With another exchange of courtesies Hornblower came down from the parapet and went down one ramp while the marine guard summoned by Bush marched up the other one. Bush, standing in an embrasure, saw the look on the Spaniard's face as the shakos and scarlet tunics and levelled muskets of the marines appeared in the other embrasures. Directly afterwards Hornblower appeared round the angle of the fort, having crossed the ditch by the narrow causeway from the main gate. Bush watched while once more hats were removed and Hornblower and the Spaniard exchanged bows, bobbing and scraping in a ludicrous Continental fashion. The Spaniard produced a paper, which he offered with a bow for Hornblower to read—his credentials, presumably. Hornblower glanced at them and handed them back. A gesture towards Bush on the parapet indicated his own credentials. Then Bush could see the Spaniard asking eager questions, and Hornblower answering them. He could tell by the way Hornblower was nodding his head that he was answering in the affirmative, and he felt dubious for a moment as to whether Hornblower might not be exceeding his authority. Yet the mere fact that he had to depend on someone else to conduct the negotiations did not irritate him; the thought that he himself might speak Spanish was utterly alien to him, and he was as reconciled to depending on an interpreter as he was to depending on cables to hoist anchors or on winds to carry him to his destination.

He changed the negotiations proceeding; observing closely he was aware when the subject under discussion changed. There was a moment when Hornblower pointed down the bay, and the Spaniard, turning, looked at the *Renown* just approaching the point. He looked long and searchingly before turning back to continue the discussion. He was a tall man, very thin, his coffee-coloured face divided by a thin black moustache. The sun beat down on tne pair of them—the trumpeter had withdrawn out of earshot—for some time before Hornblower turned and looked up at Bush.

"I'll come in to report, sir, if I may" he hailed.

"Very well, Mr. Hornblower."

Bush went down to the courtyard to meet him. Hornblower touched his hat and waited to be asked before he began his report.

"He's Colonel Ortega" said Hornblower in reply to the "Well?" that Bush addressed to him. "His credentials are from Villanueva, the Captain-General, who must be just across the bay, sir."

"What does he want?" asked Bush, trying to assimilate this first rather indigestible piece of information.

"It was the prisoners he wanted to know about first, sir" said Hornblower, "the women especially."

"And you told him they weren't hurt?"

"Yes, sir. He was very anxious about them. I told him I would ask your permission for him to take the women back with him."

"I see" said Bush.

"I thought it would make matters easier here, sir. And he had a good deal that he wanted to say, and I thought that if I appeared agreeable he would speak more freely."

"Yes" said Bush.

"Then he wanted to know about the other prisoners, sir. The men. He wanted to know if any had been killed, and when I said yes he asked which ones. I couldn't tell him that, sir—I didn't know. But I said I was sure you would supply him with a list; he said most of them had wives over there"—Hornblower pointed across the bay—"who were all anxious."

"I'll do that" said Bush.

"I thought he might take away the wounded as well as the women, sir. It would free our hands a little, and we can't give them proper treatment here."

"I must give that some thought first" said Bush.

"For that matter, sir, it might be possible to rid ourselves of all the prisoners. I fancy it would not be difficult to exact a promise from him in exchange that they would not serve again while *Renown* was in these waters."

"Sounds fishy to me" said Bush; he distrusted all foreigners.

"I think he'd keep his word, sir. He's a Spanish gentleman. Then we wouldn't have to guard them, or feed them, sir. And when we evacuate this place what are we going to do with them? Pack 'em on board *Renown*?"

A hundred prisoners in *Renown* would be an infernal nuisance, drinking twenty gallons of fresh water a day and having to be watched and guarded all the time. But Bush did not like to be rushed into making decisions, and he was not too sure that he cared to have Hornblower treating as obvious the points that he only arrived at after consideration.

"I'll have to think about that, too" said Bush.

"There was another thing that he only hinted at, sir. He wouldn't make any definite proposal, and I thought it better not to ask him."

"What was it?"

Hornblower paused before answering, and that in itself was a warning to Bush that something complicated was in the air.

"It's much more important than just a matter of prisoners, sir."

"Well?"

"It might be possible to arrange for a capitulation, sir."

"What do you mean by that?"

"A surrender, sir. An evacuation of all this end of the island by the Dons."

"My God!"

That was a startling suggestion. Bush's mind plodded along the paths it opened up. It would be an event of inter-national importance; it might be a tremendous victory. Not just a paragraph in the *Gazette*, but a whole page. Perhaps rewards, distinction—even possibly promotion. And with that Bush's mind suddenly drew back in panic, as if the path it had been following ended in a precipice. The more important the event, the more closely it would be scrutinised, the more violent would be the criticism of those who disapproved. Here in Santo Domingo there was a complicated political situation; Bush knew it to be so, although he had never attempted to find out much about it, and certainly never to analyse it. He knew vaguely that French and Spanish interests clashed in the island, and that the Negro rebellion, now almost successful, was in opposition to both. He even knew, still more vaguely, that there was an anti-slavery movement in Parliament which persistently called attention to the state of affairs here. The thought of Parliament, of the Cabinet, of the King himself scrutinising his reports actually terrified Bush. The possible rewards that he had thought about shrank to nothing in comparison with the danger he ran. If he were to enter into a negotiation that embarrassed the government he would be offered up for instant sacrifice—not a hand would be raised to help a penniless and friendless lieutenant. He remembered Buckland's frightened manner when this question had been barely hinted at; the secret orders must be drastic in this regard.

"Don't lift a finger about that" said Bush. "Don't say a word."

"Aye aye, sir. Then if he brings the subject up I'm not to listen to him?"

"Well——" That might imply flinching away from duty. "It's a matter for Buckland to deal with, if any one."

"Yes, sir. I could suggest something, sir."

"And what's that?" Bush did not know whether to be irritated or pleased that Hornblower had one more suggestion to make. But he doubted his own ability to bargain or negotiate; he knew himself to be lacking in chicane and dissimulation.

"If you made an agreement about the prisoners, sir, it would take some time to carry out. There'd be the question of the parole. I could argue about the wording of it. Then it would take some time to ferry the prisoners over. You could insist that only one boat was at the landing stage at a time—that's an obvious precaution to take. It would give time for *Renown* to work up into the bay. She can anchor down there just out of range of the other battery, sir. Then the hole'll be stopped, and at the same time we'll still be in touch with the Dons so that Mr. Buckland can take charge of the negotiations if he wishes to."

"There's something in that notion" said Bush. Certainly it would relieve him of responsibility, and it was pleasant to think of spinning out time until the *Renown* was back, ready to add her ponderous weight in the struggle.

"So you authorise me to negotiate for the return of the prisoners on parole, sir?" asked Hornblower.

"Yes" said Bush, coming to a sudden decision. "But nothing else, mark you, Mr. Hornblower. Not if you value your commission."

"Aye aye, sir. And a temporary suspension of hostilities while they are being handed over, sir?"

"Yes" said Bush, reluctantly. It was a matter necessarily arising out of the previous one, but it had a suspicious sound to it, now that Hornblower had suggested the possibility of further negotiations.

So the day proceeded to wear into afternoon. A full hour was consumed in haggling over the wording of the parole under which the captured soldiers were to be released. It was two o'clock before agreement was reached, and later than that before Bush, standing by the main gate, watched the women troop out through it, carrying their bundles of belongings. The boat could not possibly carry them all; two trips had to be made with them before the male prisoners, starting with the wounded, could begin. To rejoice Bush's heart the *Renown* appeared at last round the point; with the sea breeze beginning to blow she came nobly up the bay.

And here came Hornblower again, clearly so weary that he could hardly drag one foot after another, to touch his hat to Bush.

"*Renown* knows nothing about the suspension of hostilities, sir" he said. "She'll see the boat crossing full of Spanish soldiers, an' she'll open fire as sure as a gun."

"How are we to let her know?"

"I've been discussing it with Ortega, sir. He'll lend us a boat and we can send a message down to her."

"I suppose we can."

Sleeplessness and exhaustion had given an edge to Bush's temper. This final suggestion, when Bush came to consider it, with his mind slowed by fatigue, was the last straw.

"You're taking altogether too much on yourself, Mr. Hornblower" he said. "Damn it, I'm in command here."

"Yes, sir" said Hornblower, standing at attention, while Bush gazed at him and tried to reassemble his thoughts after this spate of ill temper. There was no denying that *Renown* had to be informed; if she were to open fire it would be in direct violation of an agreement solemnly entered into, and to which he himself was a party.

"Oh, hell and damnation!" said Bush. "Have it your own way, then. Who are you going to send?"

"I could go myself, sir. Then I could tell Mr. Buckland everything necessary."

"You mean about—about——" Bush actually did not like to mention the dangerous subject.

"About the chance of further negotiations, sir" said Hornblower stolidly. "He has to know sooner or later. And while Ortega's still here——"

The implications were obvious enough, and the suggestion was sensible.

"All right. You'd better go, I suppose. And mark my words, Mr. Hornblower, you're to make it quite clear that I've authorised no negotiations of the sort you have in mind. Not a word. I've no responsibility. You understand?"

"Aye aye, sir."

XII

THREE officers sat in what had been the commanding officer's room in Fort Samaná; in fact, seeing that Bush was now the commanding officer there, it could still be called the commanding officer's room: A bed with a mosquito net over it stood in one corner; at the other side of the room Buckland, Bush, and Hornblower sat in leather chairs. A lamp hanging from a beam overhead filled the room with its acrid smell, and lit up their sweating faces. It was hotter and stuffier even than it was in the ship, but at least here in the fort there was no brooding knowledge of a mad captain the other side of the bulkhead.

"I don't doubt for one moment" said Hornblower, "that when Villanueva sent Ortega here to open negotiations about the prisoners he also told him to put out a feeler regarding this evacuation."

"You can't be sure of that" said Buckland.

"Well, sir, put yourself in Ortega's position. Would you say a word about a subject of that importance if you weren't authorised to? If you weren't expressly ordered to, sir?"

"No, I wouldn't" said Buckland.

No one could doubt that who knew Buckland, and for himself it was the most convincing argument.

"Then Villanueva had capitulation in mind as soon as he knew that we had captured this fort and that *Renown* would be able to anchor in the bay. You can see that must be so, sir."

"I suppose so" said Buckland, reluctantly.

"And if he's prepared to negotiate for a capitulation he must either be a poltroon or in serious danger, sir."

"Well——"

"It doesn't matter which is true, sir, whether his danger is real or imaginary, from the point of view of bargaining with him."

"You talk like a sea lawyer" said Buckland. He was being forced by logic into taking a momentous decision, and he did not want to be, so that in his struggles against it he used one of the worst terms of opprobrium in his vocabulary.

"I'm sorry, sir" said Hornblower. "I meant no disrespect. I let my tongue run away with me. Of course it's for you to decide where your duty lies, sir."

Bush could see that that word "duty" had a stiffening effect on Buckland.

"Well, then, what d'you think lies behind all this?" asked Buckland. That might be intended as a temporising question, but it gave Hornblower permission to go on stating his views.

"Villanueva's been holding this end of the island against the insurgents for months now, sir. We don't know how much territory he holds, but we can guess that it's not much—only as far as the crest of those mountains across the bay, probably. Powder—lead—flints—shoes—he's probably in need of all of them."

"Judging by the prisoners we took, that's true, sir" interjected Bush. It would be hard to ascertain the motives that led him to make this contribution to the discussion; perhaps he was only interested in the truth for its own sake.

"Maybe it is" said Buckland.

"Now you've arrived, sir, and he's cut off from the sea.

He doesn't know how long we can stay here. He doesn't know what your orders are."

Hornblower did not know either, commented Bush to himself, and Buckland stirred restlessly at the allusion.

"Never mind that" he said.

"He sees himself cut off, and his supplies dwindling. If this goes on he'll have to surrender. He would rather start negotiations now, while he can still hold out, while he has something to bargain with, than wait until the last moment and have to surrender unconditionally, sir."

"I see" said Buckland.

"And he'd rather surrender to us than to the blacks, sir" concluded Hornblower.

"Yes indeed" said Bush. Everyone had heard a little about the horrors of the servile rebellion which for eight years had deluged this land with blood and scorched it with fire. The three men were silent for a space as they thought about the implications of Hornblower's last remark.

"Oh, very well then" said Buckland at length. "Let's hear what this fellow has to say."

"Shall I bring him in here, sir? He's been waiting long enough. I can blindfold him."

"Do what you like" said Buckland with resignation.

A closer view, when the handkerchief had been removed, revealed Colonel Ortega as a younger man than he might have been thought at a distance. He was very slender, and he wore his threadbare uniform with some pretence at elegance. A muscle in his left cheek twitched continually. Buckland and Bush rose slowly to their feet to acknowledge the introductions Hornblower made.

"Colonel Ortega says he speaks no English" said Hornblower.

There was only the slightest extra stress on the word "says", and only the slightest lingering in the glance that

Hornblower shot at his two superiors as he said it, but it conveyed a warning.

"Well, ask him what he wants" said Buckland.

The conversation in Spanish was formal; obviously all the opening remarks were cautious fencing as each speaker felt for the weaknesses in the other's position and sought to conceal his own. But even Bush was aware of the moment when the vague sentences ended and definite proposals began. Ortega was bearing himself as a man conferring a favour; Hornblower like someone who did not care whether a favour was conferred or not. In the end he turned to Buckland and spoke in English.

"He has terms for a capitulation pat enough" he said.

"Well?"

"Please don't let him guess what you think, sir. But he suggests a free passage for the garrison. Ships—men—civilians. Passports for the ships while on passage to a Spanish possession—Cuba or Puerto Rico, in other words, sir. In exchange he'll hand over everything intact. Military stores. The battery across the bay. Everything."

"But——" Buckland struggled wildly to keep himself from revealing his feelings.

"I haven't said anything to him worth mentioning, so far, sir" said Hornblower.

Ortega had been watching the byplay keenly enough, and now he spoke again to Hornblower, with his shoulders back and his head high. There was passion in his voice, but what was more at odds with the dignity of his bearing was a peculiar gesture with which he accentuated one of his remarks—a jerk of the hand which called up the picture of someone vomiting.

"He says otherwise he'll fight to the last" interposed Hornblower. "He says Spanish soldiers can be relied upon to die to the last man sooner than submit to dishonour.

He says we can do no more to them than we've done already—that we've reached the end of our tether, in other words, sir. And that we daren't stay longer in the island to starve him out because of the yellow fever—the *vomito negro*, sir."

In the whirl of excitement of the last few days Bush had forgotten all about the possibility of yellow fever. He found that he was looking concerned at the mention of it, and he hurriedly tried to assume an appearance of indifference. A glance at Buckland showed his face going through exactly the same transitions.

"I see" said Buckland.

It was an appalling thought. If yellow fever were to strike it might within a week leave the *Renown* without enough men to work her sails.

Ortega broke into passionate speech again, and Hornblower translated.

"He says his troops have lived here all their lives. They won't get yellow jack as easily as our men, and many of them have already had it. He has had it himself, he says, sir."

Bush remembered the emphasis with which Ortega had tapped his breast.

"And the blacks believe us to be their enemies, because of what happened in Dominica, sir, so he says. He could make an alliance with them against us. They could send an army against us here in the fort tomorrow, then. But please don't look as if you believe him, sir."

"Damn it to hell" said Buckland, exasperated. Bush wondered vaguely what it was that had happened in Dominica. History—even contemporary history—was not one of his strong points.

Again Ortega spoke.

"He says that's his last word, sir. An honourable proposal and he won't abate a jot, so he says. You could send him away now that you've heard it all and say that you'll give him an answer in the morning."

"Very well."

There were ceremonious speeches still to be made. Ortega's bows were so polite that Buckland and Bush were constrained, though reluctantly, to stand and endeavour to return them. Hornblower tied the handkerchief round Ortega's eyes again and led him out.

"What do you think about it?" said Buckland to Bush.

"I'd like to think it over, sir" replied Bush.

Hornblower came in again while they were still considering the matter. He glanced at them both before addressing himself to Buckland.

"Will you be needing me again tonight, sir?"

"Oh, damn it, you'd better stay. You know more about these Dagoes than we do. What do you think about it?"

"He made some good arguments, sir."

"I thought so too" said Buckland with apparent relief.

"Can't we turn the thumbscrews on them somehow, sir?" asked Bush.

Even if he could not make suggestions himself, he was too cautious to agree readily to a bargain offered by a foreigner, even such a tempting one as this.

"We can bring the ship up the bay" said Buckland. "But the channel's tricky. You saw that yesterday."

Good God! it was still only yesterday that the *Renown* had tried to make her way in under the fire of red-hot shot. Buckland had had a day of comparative peace, so that the mention of yesterday did not appear as strange to him.

"We'll still be under the fire of the battery across the bay, even though we hold this one" said Buckland.

"We ought to be able to run past it, sir" protested Bush. "We can keep over to this side."

"And if we do run past? They've warped their ships right up the bay again. They draw six feet less of water than we do—and if they've got any sense they'll lighten 'em so as to warp 'em farther over the shallows. Nice fools we'll look if we come in an' then find 'em out of range, an' have to run out again under fire. That might stiffen 'em so that they wouldn't agree to the terms that fellow just offered."

Buckland was in a state of actual alarm at the thought of reporting two fruitless repulses.

"I can see that" said Bush, depressed.

"If we agree" said Buckland, warming to his subject, "the blacks'll take over all this end of the island. This bay can't be used by privateers then. The blacks'll have no ships, and couldn't man 'em if they had. We'll have executed our orders. Don't you agree, Mr. Hornblower?"

Bush transferred his gaze. Hornblower had looked weary in the morning, and he had had almost no rest during the day. His face was drawn and his eyes were rimmed with red.

"We might still be able to—to put the thumbscrews on 'em, sir" he said.

"How?"

"It'd be risky to take *Renown* into the upper end of the bay. But we might get at 'em from the peninsula here, all the same, sir, if you'd give the orders."

"God bless my soul!" said Bush, the exclamation jerked out of him.

"What orders?" asked Buckland.

"If we could mount a gun on the upper end of the peninsula we'd have the far end of the bay under fire, sir. We wouldn't need hot shot—we'd have all day to knock 'em to pieces however much they shifted their anchorage."

"So we would, by George" said Buckland. There was animation in his face. "Could you get one of these guns along there?"

"I've been thinking about it, sir, an' I'm afraid we couldn't. Not quickly, at least. Twenty-four-pounders. Two an' a half tons each. Garrison carriages. We've no horses. We couldn't move 'em with a hundred men over those gullies, four miles or more."

"Then what the hell's the use of talking about it?" demanded Buckland.

"We don't have to drag a gun from here, sir" said Hornblower. "We could use one from the ship. One of those long nine-pounders we've got mounted as bow chasers. Those long guns have a range pretty nearly as good as these twenty-fours, sir."

"But how do we get it there?"

Bush had a glimmering of the answer even before Hornblower replied.

"Send it round in the launch, sir, with tackle and cables, near to where we landed yesterday. The cliff's steep there. And there are big trees to attach the cables to. We could sway the gun up easy enough. Those nine-pounders only weigh a ton."

"I know that" said Buckland, sharply.

It was one thing to make unexpected suggestions, but it was quite another to tell a veteran officer facts with which he was well acquainted.

"Yes, of course, sir. But with a nine-pounder at the top of the cliff it wouldn't be so difficult to move it across the neck of land until we had the upper bay under our fire. We wouldn't have to cross any gullies. Half a mile— uphill, but not too steep, sir—and it would be done."

"And what d'you think would happen then?"

"We'd have those ships under fire, sir. Only a nine-pounder, I know, but they're not built to take punishment. We could batter 'em into wrecks in twelve hours' steady fire. Less than that, perhaps. An' I suppose we could heat the shot if we wanted to, but we wouldn't have to. All we'd have to do would be to open fire, I think, sir."

"Why?"

"The Dons wouldn't risk those ships, sir. Ortega spoke very big about making an alliance with the blacks, but that was only talking big, sir. Give the blacks a chance an' they'll cut every white throat they can. An' I don't blame 'em—excuse me, sir."

"Well?"

"Those ships are the Dons' only way of escape. If they see they're going to be destroyed they'll be frightened. It would mean surrendering to the blacks—that or being killed to the last man. And woman, sir. They'd rather surrender to us."

"So they would, by jingo" said Bush.

"They'd climb down, d'ye think?"

"Yes—I mean I think so, sir. You could name your own terms, then. Unconditional surrender for the soldiers."

"It's what we said at the start" said Bush. "They'd rather surrender to us than to the blacks, if they have to."

"You could allow some conditions to salve their pride, sir" said Hornblower. "Agree that the women are to be conveyed to Cuba or Puerto Rico if they wish. But nothing important. Those ships would be our prizes, sir."

"Prizes, by George!" said Buckland.

Prizes meant prize money, and as commanding officer he would have the lion's share of it. Not only that—and perhaps the money was the smallest consideration—but prizes escorted triumphantly into port were much more impressive than ships sunk out of sight of the eyes of authority. And unconditional surrender had a ring of finality about it, proof that the victory gained could not be more complete.

"What do you say, Mr. Bush?" asked Buckland.

"I think it might be worth trying, sir" said Bush.

He was fatalistic now about Hornblower. Exasperation over his activity and ingenuity had died of surfeit. There was something of resignation about Bush's attitude, but there was something of admiration too. Bush was a generous soul, and there was not a mean motive in him. Hornblower's careful handling of his superior had not been lost on him, and Bush was decently envious of the tact that had been necessary. Bush realistically admitted to himself that even though he had fretted at the prospect of agreeing to Ortega's terms he had not been able to think of a way to modify them, while Hornblower had. Hornblower was a very brilliant young officer, Bush decided; he himself made no pretence at brilliance, and now he had taken the last step and had overcome his suspicions of brilliance. He made himself abandon his caution and commit himself to a definite opinion.

"I think Mr. Hornblower deserves every credit" he said.

"Of course" said Buckland—but the slight hint of surprise in his voice seemed to indicate that he did not really believe it; and he changed the subject without pursuing it further. "We'll start tomorrow—I'll get both launches out as soon as the hands've had breakfast. By noon—now what's the matter with you, Mr. Hornblower?"

"Well, sir——"

"Come on. Out with it."

"Ortega comes back tomorrow morning to hear our terms again, sir. I suppose he'll get up at dawn or not long after. He'll have a bite of breakfast. Then he'll have a few words with Villanueva. Then he'll row across the bay. He might be here at eight bells. Later than that, probably, a little——"

"Who cares when Ortega has his breakfast? What's all this rigmarole for?"

"Ortega gets here at two bells in the forenoon. If he finds we haven't wasted a minute; if I can tell him that you've rejected his terms absolutely, sir, and not only that, if we can show him the gun mounted, and say we'll open fire in an hour if they don't surrender without conditions, he'll be much more impressed."

"That's true, sir" said Bush.

"Otherwise it won't be so easy, sir. You'll either have to temporise again while the gun's being got into position, or you'll have to use threats. I'll have to say to him *if* you don't agree then we'll start hoisting a gun up. In either case you'll be allowing him time, sir. He might think of some other way out of it. The weather might turn dirty—there might even be a hurricane get up. But if he's sure we'll stand no nonsense, sir——"

"That's the way to treat 'em" said Bush.

"But even if we start at dawn——" said Buckland, and having progressed so far in his speech he realised the alternative. "You mean we can get to work now?"

"We have all night before us, sir. You could have the launches hoisted out and the gun swayed down into one of them. Slings and cables and some sort of carrying cradle prepared. Hands told off——"

"And start at dawn!"

"At dawn the boats can be round the peninsula waiting for daylight, sir. You could send some hands with a hundred fathoms of line up from the ship to here. They can start off along the path before daylight. That'd save time."

"So it would, by George!" said Bush; he had no trouble in visualising the problems of seamanship involved in hoisting a gun up the face of a cliff.

"We're shorthanded already in the ship" said Buckland. "I'll have to turn up both watches."

"That won't hurt 'em, sir" said Bush. He had already been two nights without sleep and was now contemplating a third.

"Who shall I send? I'll want a responsible officer in charge. A good seaman at that."

"I'll go if you like, sir" said Hornblower.

"No. You'll have to be here to deal with Ortega. If I send Smith I'll have no lieutenant left on board."

"Maybe you could send me, sir" said Bush. "That is, if you were to leave Mr. Hornblower in command here."

"Um——" said Buckland. "Oh well, I don't see anything else to do. Can I trust you, Mr. Hornblower?"

"I'll do my best, sir."

"Let me see——" said Buckland.

"I could go back to the ship with you in your gig, sir" said Bush. "Then there'd be no time wasted."

This prodding of a senior officer into action was something new to Bush, but he was learning the art fast. The fact that the three of them had not long ago been fellow conspirators made it easier; and once the ice was broken, as soon as Buckland had once admitted his juniors to give him counsel and advice, it became easier with repetition.

"Yes, I suppose you'd better" said Buckland, and Bush promptly rose to his feet, so that Buckland could hardly help doing the same.

Bush ran his eye over Hornblower's battered form.

"Now look you here, Mr. Hornblower" he said. "You take some sleep. You need it."

"I relieve Whiting as officer on duty at midnight, sir" said Hornblower, "and I have to go the rounds."

"Maybe that's true. You'll still have two hours before midnight. Turn in until then. And have Whiting relieve you at eight bells again."

"Aye aye, sir."

At the very thought of abandoning himself to the sleep for which he yearned Hornblower swayed with fatigue.

"You could make that an order, sir" suggested Bush to Buckland.

"What's that? Oh yes, get a rest while you can, Mr. Hornblower."

"Aye aye, sir."

Bush picked his way down the steep path to the landing stage at Buckland's heels, and took his seat beside him in the stern sheets of the gig.

"I can't make that fellow Hornblower out" said Buckland a little peevishly on one occasion as they rowed back to the anchored *Renown*.

"He's a good officer, sir" answered Bush, but he spoke a little absently. Already in his mind he was tackling the problem of hoisting a long nine-pounder up a cliff, and he was sorting out mentally the necessary equipment, and planning the necessary orders. Two heavy anchors—not merely boat grapnels—to anchor the buoy solidly. The thwarts of the launch had better be shored up to bear the weight of the gun. Travelling blocks. Slings—for the final hoist it might be safer to suspend the gun by its cascabel and trunnions.

Bush was not of the mental type that takes pleasure in theoretical exercises. To plan a campaign; to put himself mentally in the position of the enemy and think along alien lines; to devise unexpected expedients; all this was beyond his capacity. But to deal with a definite concrete problem, a simple matter of ropes and tackles and breaking strains, pure seamanship—he had a lifetime of experience to reinforce his natural bent in that direction.

XIII

"TAKE the strain" said Bush, standing on the cliff's edge and looking far, far down to where the launch floated moored to the buoy and with an anchor astern to keep her steady. Black against the Atlantic blue two ropes came down from over his head, curving slightly but almost vertical, down to the buoy. A poet might have seen something dramatic and beautiful in those spider lines cleaving the air, but Bush merely saw a couple of ropes, and the white flag down in the launch signalling that all was clear for hoisting. The blocks creaked as the men pulled in on the slack.

"Now, handsomely" said Bush. This work was too important to be delegated to Mr. Midshipman James, standing beside him. "Hoist away. Handsomely."

The creaking took on a different tone as the weight came on the blocks. The curves of the ropes altered, appeared almost deformed, as the gun began to rise from its cradle on the thwarts. The shallow, lovely catenaries changed to a harsher, more angular figure. Bush had his telescope to his eye and could see the gun stir and move, and slowly— that was what Bush meant by "handsomely" in the language of the sea—it began to upend itself, to dangle from the traveller, to rise clear of the launch; hanging, just as Bush had visualised it, from the slings through its cascabel and round its trunnions. It was safe enough— if those slings were to give way or to slip, the gun would crash through the bottom of the launch. The line about its muzzle restrained it from swinging too violently.

"Hoist away" said Bush again, and the traveller began to mount the rope with the gun pendant below it. This was the next ticklish moment, when the pull came most transversely. But everything held fast.

"Hoist away."

Now the gun was mounting up the rope. Beyond the launch's stern it dipped, with the stretching of the cable and the straightening of the curve, until its muzzle was almost in the sea. But the hoisting proceeded steadily, and it rose clear of the water, up, up, up. The sheaves hummed rhythmically in the blocks as the hands hove on the line. The sun shone on the men from its level position in the glowing east, stretching out their shadows and those of the trees to incredible lengths over the irregular plateau.

"Easy, there!" said Bush. "Belay!"

The gun had reached the cliff edge.

"Move that cat's cradle over this way a couple of feet. Now, sway in. Lower. Good. Cast off those lines."

The gun lay, eight feet of dull bronze, upon the cat's cradle that had been spread to receive it. This was a small area of stout rope-netting, from which diverged, knotted thickly to the central portion, a score or more of individual lines, each laid out separately on the ground.

"We'll get that on its way first. Take a line, each of you marines."

The thirty red-coated marines that Hornblower had sent along from the fort moved up to the cat's cradle. Their non-commissioned officers pushed them into position, and Bush checked to see that each man was there.

"Take hold."

It was better to go to a little trouble and see that everything was correctly balanced at the start rather than risk that the unwieldy lump of metal should roll off the cat's cradle and should have to be laboriously manoeuvred back into position.

"Now, all of you together when I give the word. Lift!"

The gun rose a foot from the ground as every man exerted himself.

"March! Belay that, sergeant."

The sergeant had begun to call the step, but on this irregular ground with every man supporting eighty pounds of weight it was better that they should not try to keep step.

"Halt! Lower!"

The gun had moved twenty yards towards the position Bush had selected for it.

"Carry on, sergeant. Keep 'em moving. Not too fast."

Marines were only dumb animals, not even machines, and were liable to tire. It was better to be conservative with their strength. But while they laboured at carrying the gun the necessary half-mile up to the crest the seamen could work at hauling up the rest of the stores from the launches. Nothing would be as difficult as the gun. The gun carriage was a feather-weight by comparison; even the nets, each holding twenty nine-pound cannon balls, were easy to handle. Rammers, sponges, and wad-hooks, two of each in case of accidents; wads; and now the powder charges. With only two and a half pounds of powder in each they seemed tiny compared with the eight-pound charges Bush had grown accustomed to on the lower gundeck. Last of all came the heavy timbers destined to form a smooth floor upon which the gun could be worked. They were awkward things to carry, but with each timber on the shoulders of four men they could be carried up the gentle slope fast enough, overtaking the unfortunate marines, who, streaming with sweat, were lifting and carrying, lifting and carrying, on their way up.

Bush stood for a moment at the cliff edge checking over the stores with James' assistance. Linstocks and slow match; primers and quills; barricoes of water; handspikes, hammers, and nails; everything necessary, he decided— not merely his professional reputation but his self-respect depended on his having omitted nothing. He waved his flag, and received an answer from the launches. The second launch cast off her mooring line, and then, hauling up her anchor, she went off with her consort to pull back round Samaná Point to rejoin *Renown*—in the ship they would be most desperately shorthanded until the launches' crews should come on board again. From the trees to which it was secured, over Bush's head, the rope hung down to the buoy, neglected unless it should be needed again; Bush hardly spared it a glance. Now he was free to walk up to the crest and prepare for action; a glance at the sun assured him that it was less than three hours since sunrise even now.

He organised the final carrying party and started up to the crest. When he reached it the bay opened below him. He put his glass to his eye: the three vessels were lying at anchor within easy cannon shot of where he stood, and when he swung the glass to his left he could just make out, far, far away, the two specks which were the flags flying over the fort—the swell of the land hid the body of the building from his sight. He closed the glass and applied himself to the selection of a level piece of ground on which to lay the timbers for the platform. Already the men with the lightest loads were around him, chattering and pointing excitedly until with a growl he silenced them.

The hammers thumped upon the nails as the crosspieces were nailed into position on the timbers. No sooner had they ceased than the gun carriage was swung up onto it by the lusty efforts of half a dozen men. They attached the tackles and saw to it that the gun-trucks ran easily before chocking them. The marines came staggering up, sweating and gasping under their monstrous burden. Now was the moment for the trickiest piece of work in the morning's programme. Bush distributed his steadiest men round the carrying ropes, a reliable petty officer on either side to watch that accurate balance was maintained.

"Lift and carry."

The gun lay beside the carriage on the platform.

"Lift. Lift. Higher. Not high enough. Lift, you men!"

There were gasps and grunts as the men struggled to raise the gun.

"Keep her at that! Back away, starboard side! Go with 'em, port side. Lift! Bring the bows round now. Steady!"

The gun in its cat's cradle hung precariously over the carriage as Bush lined it up.

"Now, back towards me! Steady! Lower! Slowly, damn you! Steady! For'ard a little! Now lower again!"

The gun sank down towards its position on the carriage. It rested there, the trunnions not quite in their holes, the breech not quite in position on the bed.

"Hold it! Berry! Chapman! Handspikes under those trunnions! Ease her along!"

With something of a jar the ton of metal subsided into its place on the carriage, trunnions home into their holes and breech settled upon the bed. A couple of hands set to work untying the knots that would free the cat's cradle from under the gun, but Berry, gunner's mate, had already snapped the capsquares down upon the trunnions, and the gun was now a gun, a vital fighting weapon and not an inanimate ingot of metal. The shot were being piled at the edge of the platform.

"Lay those charges out back there!" said Bush, pointing.

No one in his senses allowed unprotected explosives

nearer a gun than was necessary. Berry was kneeling on the platform, bent over the flint and steel with which he was working to catch a spark upon the tinder with which to ignite the slow match. Bush wiped away the sweat that streamed over his face and neck; even though he had not taken actual physical part in the carrying and heaving he felt the effect of his exertions. He looked at the sun again to judge the time; this was no moment for resting upon his labours.

"Gun's crew fall in!" he ordered. "Load and run up!"

He applied his eye to the telescope.

"Aim for the schooner" he said. "Take a careful aim."

The gun-trucks squealed as the handspikes trained the gun round.

"Gun laid, sir" reported the gun captain.

"Then fire!"

The gun banged out sharp and clear, a higher-pitched report than the deafening thunderous roar of the massive twenty-four-pounders. That report would resound round the bay. Even if the shot missed its mark this time, the men down in those ships would know that the next, or the next, would strike. Looking up at the high shore through hastily trained telescopes they would see the powder smoke slowly drifting along the verge of the cliff, and would recognise their doom. Over on the southern shore Villanueva would have his attention called to it, and would know that escape was finally cut off for the men under his command and the women under his protection. Yet all the same, Bush, gazing through the telescope, could mark no fall of the shot.

"Load and fire again. Make sure of your aim."

While they loaded Bush turned his telescope upon the flags over the fort, until the gun captain's cry told him that loading was completed. The gun banged out, and

Bush thought he saw the fleeting black line of the course
of the shot.

"You're firing over her. Put the quoins in and reduce the
elevation. Try again!"

He looked again at the flags. They were very slowly
descending, down out of his sight. Now they rose once
more, very slowly, fluttered for a moment at the head of the
flagstaff, and sank again. The next time they rose they
remained steady. That was the preconcerted signal. Dip-
ping the colours twice meant that the gun had been heard
in the fort and all was well. It was Bush's duty now to complete ten rounds of firing, slowly. Bush watched each round
carefully; it seemed likely that the schooner was being
hit. Those flying nine-pound balls of iron were crashing
through the frail upper works, smashing and destroying,
casting up showers of splinters.

At the eighth round something screamed through the
air like a banshee two yards over Bush's head, a whirling
irregular scream which died away abruptly behind his
back.

"What the hell was that?" demanded Bush.

"The gun's unbushed, sir" said Berry.

"God——" Bush poured out a torrent of blasphemy,
uncontrolled, almost hysterical. This was the climax of
days and nights of strain and labour, the bitterest blow
that could be imagined, with success almost within their
grasp and now snatched away. He swore frightfully, and
then came back to his senses; it would not be good for
the men to know that their officer was as disappointed as
Bush knew himself to be. His curses died away when he restrained himself, and he walked forward to look at the gun.

The damage was plain. The touchhole in the breech of a
gun, especially a bronze gun, was always a weak point.
At each round some small part of the explosion vented

itself through the hole, the blast of hot gas and unconsumed powder grains eroding the edges of the hole, enlarging it until the loss of force became severe enough to impair the efficiency of the gun. Then the gun had to be "bushed"; a tapering plug, with a hole pierced through its length and a flange round its base, had to be forced into the touchhole from the inside the gun, small end first. The hole in the plug served as the new touchhole, and the explosions of the gun served to drive the plug more and more thoroughly home, until the plug itself began to erode and to weaken, forcing itself up through the touchhole while the flange burned away in the fierce heat of the explosions until at last it would blow itself clean out, as it had done now.

Bush looked at the huge hole in the breech, a full inch wide; if the gun were to be fired in that condition half the powder charge would blow out through it. The range would be halved at best, and every subsequent round would enlarge the hole further.

"D'ye have a new vent-fitting?" he demanded.

"Well, sir——" Berry began to go slowly through his pockets, rummaging through their manifold contents while gazing absently at the sky and while Bush fumed with impatience. "Yes, sir."

Berry produced, seemingly at the eleventh hour, the cast-iron plug that meant so much.

"Lucky for you" said Bush, grimly. "Get it fitted and don't waste any more time."

"Aye aye, sir. I'll have to file it to size, sir. Then I'll have to put it in place."

"Start work and stop talking. Mr. James!"

"Sir!"

"Run to the fort." Bush took a few steps away from the gun as he spoke, so as to get out of earshot of the men.

"Tell Mr. Hornblower that the gun's unbushed. It'll be an hour before we can open fire again. Tell him I'll fire three shots when the gun's ready, and ask him to acknowledge them as before."

"Aye aye, sir."

At the last moment Bush remembered something.

"Mr. James! Don't make your report in anyone's hearing. Don't let that Spanish fellow, what's-his-name, hear about this. Not if you want to be kind to your backside."

"Aye aye, sir."

"Run!"

That would be a very long hot run for Mr. James; Bush watched him go and then turned back to the gun. Berry had selected a file from his roll of tools and was sitting on the rear step of the gun scraping away at the plug. Bush sat on the edge of the platform; the irritation at the disablement of the gun was overlaid by his satisfaction with himself as a diplomat. He was pleased at having remembered to warn James against letting Ortega into the secret. The men were chattering and beginning to skylark about; a few minutes more and they would be scattering all over the peninsula. Bush lifted his head and barked at them.

"Silence, there! Sergeant!"

"Sir?"

"Post four sentries. Give 'em beats on all four sides. No one to pass that line on any account whatever."

"Yessir."

"Let the rest of your men sit down. You gun's crew! Sit there and don't chatter like Portuguese bumboat men."

The sun was very hot, and the rásp-rasp-rasp of Berry's file was, if anything, soothing. Bush had hardly ceased speaking when fatigue and sleepliness demanded their due; his eyes closed and his chin sank on his breast. In one second he was asleep; in three he was awake again, with the world whirling round him as he recovered himself from falling over. He blinked at the unreal world; the blink prolonged itself into sleep, and again he caught himself up on the point of keeling over. Bush felt that he would give anything at all, in this world or the next, to sink quietly on to his side and allow sleep to overwhelm him. He fought down the temptation; he was the only officer present and there might be an instant emergency. Straightening his back, he glowered at the world, and then even with his back straight he went to sleep again. There was only one thing to do. He rose to his feet, with his weary joints protesting, and began to pace up and down beside the gun platform, up and down in the sunshine, with the sweat pouring off him, while the gun's crew quickly subsided into the sleep he envied them —they lay like pigs in a sty, at all angles—and while Berry's file went whit-whit-whit on the vent-fitting. The minutes dragged by and the sun mounted higher and higher. Berry paused in his work to gauge the fitting against the touchhole, and then went on filing; he paused again to clean his file, and each time Bush looked sharply at him, only to be disappointed, and to go back to thinking how much he wanted to go to sleep.

"I have it to size now, sir" said Berry at last.

"Then fit it, damn you" said Bush. "You gun's crew, wake up, there! Rise and shine! Wake up, there!"

While Bush kicked the snoring men awake Berry had produced a length of twine from his pocket. With a slowness that Bush found maddening he proceeded to tie one end into a loop and then drop the loop in through the touchhole. Then he took the wad-hook, and, walking round to the muzzle of the gun and squatting down, he proceeded to push the hook up the eight-foot length of the bore and try to catch the loop on it. Over and over again he twisted

G

the hook and withdrew it a little with no corresponding
reaction on the part of the twine hanging from the touchhole, but at last he made his catch. As he brought the
hook out the twine slid down into the hole, and when the
wad-hook was withdrawn from the muzzle the loop was
hanging on it. Still with intense deliberation Berry calmly
proceeded to undo the loop and pass the end of the twine
through the hole in the vent-fitting, and then secure the
end to a little toggle which he also took from his pocket.
He dropped the vent-fitting into the muzzle and walked
round to the breech again, and pulled in on the twine,
the vent-fitting rattling down the bore until it leaped up
to its position under the touchhole with a sharp tap that
every ear heard. Even so it was only after some minutes
of fumbling and adjustment that Berry had the vent-fitting
placed to his satisfaction with its small end in the hole,
and he gestured to the gun captain to hold it steady with
the twine. Now he took the rammer and thrust it with
infinite care up the muzzle, feeling sensitively with it and
pressing down upon the handle when he had it exactly
placed. Another gesture from Berry, and a seaman brought
a hammer and struck down upon the handle which Berry
held firm. At each blow the vent-fitting showed more
clearly down in the touchhole, rising an eighth of an inch
at a time until it was firmly jammed.

"Ready?" asked Bush as Berry waved the seaman away.

"Not quite, sir."

Berry withdrew the rammer and walked slowly round to
the breech again. He looked down at the vent-fitting with
his head first on one side and then on the other, like a
terrier at a rat-hole. He seemed to be satisfied and yet he
walked back again to the muzzle and took up the wad-
hook. Bush glared round the horizon to ease his impatience; over towards where the fort lay a tiny figure was

visible coming towards them. Bush clapped a telescope to his eye. It was a white-trousered individual, now running, now walking, and apparently waving his arm as though to attract attention. It might be Wellard; Bush was nearly sure it was. Meanwhile Berry had caught the twine again with the wad-hook and drawn it out again. He cut the toggle free from the twine with a stroke of his sheath knife and dropped it in his pocket, and then, once more as if he had all the time in the world, he returned to the breech and wound up his twine.

"Two rounds with one-third charges ought to do it now, sir" he announced. "That'll seat——"

"It can wait a few minutes longer" said Bush, interrupting him with a short-tempered delight in showing this self-satisfied skilled worker that his decisions need not all be treated like gospel.

Wellard was in clear sight of them all now, running and walking and stumbling over the irregular surface. He reached the gun gasping for breath, sweat running down his face.

"Please, sir——" he began. Bush was about to blare at him for his disrespectful approach but Wellard anticipated him. He twitched his coat into position, settled his absurd little hat on his head, and stepped forward with all the stiff precision his gasping lungs would allow.

"Mr. Hornblower's respects, sir" he said, raising his hand to his hat brim.

"Well, Mr. Wellard?"

"Please will you not reopen fire, sir."

Wellard's chest was heaving, and that was all he could say between two gasps. The sweat running down into his eyes made him blink, but he manfully stood to attention ignoring it.

"And why not, pray, Mr. Wellard?"

Even Bush could guess at the answer, but asked the question because the child deserved to be taken seriously.

"The Dons have agreed to a capitulation, sir."

"Good! Those ships there?"

"They'll be our prizes, sir."

"Hurray!" yelled Berry, his arms in the air.

Five hundred pounds for Buckland, five shillings for Berry, but prize money was something to cheer about in any case. And this was a victory, the destruction of a nest of privateers, the capture of a Spanish regiment, security for convoys going through the Mona Passage. It had only needed the mounting of the gun to search the anchorage to bring the Dons to their senses.

"Very good, Mr. Wellard, thank you" said Bush.

So Wellard could step back and wipe the sweat out of his eyes, and Bush could wonder what item in the terms of the capitulation would be likely to rob him of his next night's rest.

XIV

BUSH stood on the quarterdeck of the *Renown* at Buckland's side with his telescope trained on the fort.

"The party's leaving there now, sir" he said; and then, after an interval, "The boat's putting off from the landing stage."

The *Renown* swung at her anchor in the mouth of the Gulf of Samaná, and close beside her rode her three prizes. All four ships were jammed with the prisoners who had surrendered themselves, and sails were ready to loose the moment the *Renown* should give the signal.

"The boat's well clear now" said Bush. "I wonder—ah!"

The fort on the crest had burst into a great fountain of smoke, within which could be made out flying fragments of masonry. A moment later came the crash of the explosion. Two tons of gunpowder, ignited by the slow match left burning by the demolition party, did the work. Ramparts and bastions, tower and platform, all were dashed into ruins. Already at the foot of the steep slope to the water lay what was left of the guns, trunnions blasted off, muzzles split, and touchholes spiked; the insurgents when they came to take over the place would have no means to re-establish the defences of the bay—the other battery on the point across the water had already been blown up.

"It looks as if the damage is complete enough, sir" said Bush.

"Yes" said Buckland, his eye to his telescope observing the ruins as they began to show through the smoke and dust. "We'll get under way as soon as the boat's hoisted in, if you please."

"Aye aye, sir" said Bush.

With the boat lowered onto its chocks the hands went to the capstan and hauled the ship laboriously up to her anchor; the sails were loosed as the anchor rose clear. The main topsail aback gave her a trifle of sternway, and then, with the wheel hard over and hands at the headsail sheets, she came round. The topsails, braced up, caught the wind as the quartermaster at the wheel spun the spokes over hastily, and now she was under full command, moving easily through the water, heeling a little to the wind, the sea swinging under her cutwater, heading out close-hauled to weather Engano Point. Somebody forward began to cheer, and in a moment the entire crew was yelling lustily as the *Renown* left the scene of her victory. The prizes were getting under way at the same time, and the prize crews on board echoed the cheering. Bush's telescope could pick out Hornblower on the deck of *La Gaditana,* the big ship-rigged prize, waving his hat to the *Renown.*

"I'll see that everything is secure below, sir" said Bush.

There were marine sentries beside the midshipmen's berth, bayonets fixed and muskets loaded. From within, as Bush listened, there was a wild babble of voices. Fifty women were cramped into that space, and almost as many children. That was bad, but it was necessary to confine them while the ship got under way. Later on they could be allowed on deck, in batches perhaps, for air and exercise. The hatchways in the lower gundeck were closed by gratings, and every hatchway was guarded by a sentry. Up through the gratings rose the smell of humanity; there were four hundred Spanish soldiers confined down there in conditions not much better than prevailed in a slave ship. It was only since dawn that they had been down there, and already there was this stench. For the men, as for the women, there would have to be arrangements made to allow them to take the air in batches. It meant endless trouble and precaution; Bush had already gone to considerable trouble to organise a system by which the prisoners should be supplied with food and drink. But every water butt was full, two boat-loads of yams had been brought on board from the shore, and, given the steady breeze that could be expected, the run to Kingston would be completed in less than a week. Then their troubles would be ended and the prisoners handed over to the military authorities—probably the prisoners would be as relieved as Bush would be.

On deck again Bush looked over at the green hills of Santo Domingo out on the starboard beam as, close-hauled, the *Renown* coasted along them; on that side too, under her lee as his orders had dictated, Hornblower had the three prizes under easy sail. Even with this brisk seven-knot breeze blowing and the *Renown* with all sail set those three vessels had the heels of her if they cared to show them; privateers depended both for catching their prey and evading their enemies on the ability to work fast to the windward, and Hornblower could soon have left the *Renown* far behind if he were not under orders to keep within sight and to leeward so that the *Renown* could run down to him and protect him if an enemy should appear. The prize crews were small enough in all conscience, and just as in the *Renown* Hornblower had all the prisoners he could guard battened down below.

Bush touched his hat to Buckland as the latter came on to the quarterdeck.

"I'll start bringing the prisoners up if I may, sir" he said.

"Do as you think proper, if you please, Mr. Bush."

The quarterdeck for the women, the maindeck for the men. It was hard to make them understand that they had to take turns; those of the women who were brought on deck seemed to fancy that they were going to be permanently separated from those kept below, and there was lamentation and expostulation which accorded ill with the dignified routine which should be observed on the quarterdeck of a ship of the line. And the children knew no discipline whatever, and ran shrieking about in all directions while harassed seamen tried to bring them back to their mothers. And other seamen had to be detailed to bring the prisoners their food and water. Bush, tackling each aggravating problem as it arose, began to think that life as first lieutenant in a ship of the line (which he had once believed to be a paradise too wonderful for him to aspire to) was not worth the living.

There were thirty officers crammed into the steerage, from the elegant Villanueva down to the second mate of the *Gaditana*; they were almost as much trouble to Bush as all the other prisoners combined, for they took the air on the poop, from which point of vantage they endeavoured to hold conversations with their wives on the quarterdeck, while they had to be fed from the wardroom stores, which were rapidly depleted by the large Spanish appetites. Bush found himself looking forward more and more eagerly to their arrival at Kingston, and he had neither time nor inclination to brood over what might be their reception there, which was probably just as well, for while he could hope for commendation for the part he had played in the attack on Santo Domingo he could also fear the result of an inquiry into the circumstances which had deprived Captain Sawyer of his command.

Day by day the wind held fair; day by day the *Renown* surged along over the blue Caribbean with the prizes to leeward on the port bow; the prisoners, even the women, began to recover from their seasickness, and feeding them and guarding them became more and more matters of routine making less demand on everyone. They sighted Cape Beata to the northward and could haul their port tacks on board and lay a course direct for Kingston, but save for that they hardly had to handle a sail, for the wind blew steady and the hourly heaving of the log recorded eight knots with almost monotonous regularity. The sun rose splendidly behind them each morning; and each evening the bowsprit pointed into a flaming sunset. In the daytime the sun blazed down upon the ship save for the brief intervals when sharp rainstorms blotted out sun and sea; at night the ship rose and swooped with the following sea under a canopy of stars.

It was a dark lovely night when Bush completed his evening rounds and went in to report to Buckland. The sentries were posted; the watch below was asleep with all lights out; the watch on deck had taken in the royals as a precaution against a rain squall striking the ship without warning in the darkness; the course was east by north and Mr. Carberry had the watch, and the convoy was in sight a mile on the port bow. The guard over the captain in his cabin was at his post. All this Bush recounted to Buckland in the time-honoured fashion of the navy, and Buckland listened to it with the navy's time-honoured patience.

"Thank you, Mr. Bush."

"Thank you, sir. Good night, sir."

"Good night, Mr. Bush."

Bush's cabin opened on the half-deck; it was hot and stuffy with the heat in the tropics, but Bush did not care. He had six clear hours in which to sleep, seeing that he was going to take the morning watch, and he was not the man to waste any of that. He threw off his outer clothes, and standing in his shirt he cast a final look round his cabin before putting out the light. Shoes and trousers were on the sea-chest ready to be put on at a moment's notice in the event of an emergency. Sword and pistols were in their beckets against the bulkhead All was well. The messenger who would come to call him would bring a lamp, so, using his hand to deflect his breath, he blew out the light. Then he dropped upon the cot, lying on his back with his arms and legs spread wide so as to allow the sweat every chance to evaporate, and he closed his eyes. Thanks to his blessed stolidity of temperament he was soon asleep. At midnight he awoke long enough to hear the watch called, and to tell himself blissfully that there was no need to awake, and he had not sweated enough to make his position on the cot uncomfortable.

Later he awoke again, and looked up into the darkness with uncomprehending eyes as his ears told him all was not well. There were loud cries, there was a rush of feet overhead. Perhaps a fluky rain squall had taken the ship aback. But those were the wrong noises. Were some of those cries cries of pain? Was that the scream of a woman? Were those infernal women squabbling with each other again? Now there was another rush of feet, and wild shouting, which brought Bush off his cot in a flash. He tore open his cabin door, and as he did so he heard the bang of a musket which left him in no doubt as to what was happening. He turned back and grabbed for sword and pistol, and by the time he was outside his cabin door again the ship was full of a yelling tumult. It was as if the hatchways were the entrances to Hell, and pouring up through them were the infernal powers, screaming with triumph in the dimly lit recesses of the ship.

As he emerged the sentry under the lantern fired his musket, lantern and musket flash illuminating a wave of humanity pouring upon the sentry and instantly submerging him; Bush caught a glimpse of a woman leading the wave, a handsome mulatto woman, wife to one of the privateer officers, now screaming with open mouth and staring eyes as she led the rush. Bush levelled his pistol and fired, but they were up to him in an instant. He backed into his narrow doorway. Hands grabbed his sword blade, and he tore it through their grip; he struck wildly with his empty pistol, he kicked out with his bare feet to free himself from the hands that grabbed at him. Thrusting overhand with his sword he stabbed again and again into the mass of bodies pressing against him. Twice his head struck against the deck beams above but he did not feel the blows. Then the flood had washed past him. There were shouts and screams and blows farther along, but he himself had been passed by, saved by the groaning men who wallowed at his feet—his bare feet slipping in the hot blood that poured over them.

His first thought was for Buckland, but a single glance aft assured him that by himself he stood no chance of being of any aid to him, and in that case his post was on the quarterdeck, and he ran out, sword in hand, to make his way there. At the foot of the companion ladder there was another whirl of yelling Spaniards; above there were shouts and cries as the after guard fought it out. Forward there was other fighting going on; the stars were shining on white-shirted groups that fought and struggled with savage desperation. Unknown to himself he was yelling with the rest; a band of men turned upon him as he approached, and he felt the heavy blow of a belaying pin against his sword blade. But Bush inflamed with fighting madness was an enemy to be feared; his immense strength was allied to a lightfooted quickness. He struck and parried, leaping over the cumbered deck. He knew nothing, and during those mad minutes he thought of nothing save to fight against these enemies, to reconquer the ship by the strength of his single arm. Then he regained some of his sanity at the moment when he struck down one of the group against whom he was fighting. He must rally the crew, set an example, concentrate his men into a cohesive body. He raised his voice in a bellow.

"Renowns! Renowns! Here, Renowns! Come on!"

There was a fresh swirl in the mad confusion on the maindeck. There was a searing pain across his shoulder-blade; instinctively he turned and his left hand seized a throat and he had a moment in which to brace himself and exert all his strength, with a wrench and a heave flinging the man on to the deck.

"Renowns!" he yelled again.

There was a rush of feet as a body of men rallied round him.

"Come on!"

But the charge that he led was met by a wall of men advancing forward against him from aft. Bush and his little group were swept back, across the deck, jammed against the bulwarks. Somebody shouted something in Spanish in front of him, and there was an eddy in the ring; then a musket flashed and banged. The flash lit up the swarthy faces that ringed them round, lit up the bayonet on the muzzle of the musket, and the man beside Bush gave a sharp cry and fell to the deck; Bush could feel him flapping and struggling against his feet. Someone at least had a firearm—taken from an arms rack or from a marine—and had managed to reload it. They would be shot to pieces where they stood, if they were to stand.

"Come on!" yelled Bush again, and sprang forward.

But the disheartened little group behind him did not stir, and Bush gave back from the rigid ring. Another

musket flashed and banged, and another man fell. Someone raised his voice and called to them in Spanish. Bush
could not understand the words, but he could guess it was
a demand for surrender.

"I'll see you damned first!" he said.

He was almost weeping with rage. The thought of his
magnificent ship falling into alien hands was appalling now
that the realisation of the possibility arose in his mind. A
ship of the line captured and carried off into some Cuban
port—what would England say? What would the navy
say? He did not want to live to find out. He was a desperate man who wanted to die.

This time it was with no intelligible appeal to his men that
he sprang forward, but with a wild animal cry; he was insane
with fury, a fighting lunatic and with a lunatic's strength.
He burst through the ring of his enemies, slashing and smit-
ing, but he was the only one who succeeded; he was out on
to the clear deck while the struggle went on behind him.

But the madness ebbed away. He found himself leaning
—hiding himself, it might almost be said—beside one of
the maindeck eighteen-pounders, forgotten for the moment,
his sword still in his hand, trying with a slow brain to
take stock of his situation. Mental pictures moved slowly
across his mind's eye. He could not doubt that some
members of the ship's company had risked the ship for
the sake of their lust. There had been no bargaining; none
of the women had sold themselves in exchange for a
betrayal. But he could guess that the women had seemed
complacent, that some of the guards had neglected their
duty to take advantage of such an opportunity. Then
there would be a slow seepage of prisoners out of confine-
ment, probably the officers from out of the midshipmen's
berth, and then the sudden well-planned uprising. A torrent
of prisoners pouring up, the sentries overwhelmed, the

arms seized; the watch below, asleep in their hammocks and incapable of resistance, driven like sheep in a mass forward, herded into a crowd against the bulkhead and restrained there by an armed party while other parties secured the officers aft, and, surging on to the maindeck, captured or slew every man there. All about the ship now there must still be little groups of seamen and marines still free like himself, but weaponless and demoralised; with the coming of daylight the Spaniards would reorganise themselves and would hunt through the ship and destroy any further resistance piecemeal, group by group. It was unbelievable that such a thing could have happened, and yet it had. Four hundred disciplined and desperate men, reckless of their lives and guided by brave officers, might achieve much.

There were orders—Spanish orders—being shouted about the deck now. The ship had come up into the wind all aback when the quartermaster at the wheel had been overwhelmed, and she was wallowing in the trough of the waves, now coming up, now falling off again, with the canvas overhead all flapping and thundering. There were Spanish sea officers—those of the prizes—on board. They would be able to bring the ship under control in a few minutes. Even with a crew of landsmen they would be able to brace the yards, man the wheel, and set a course close-hauled up the Jamaica Channel. Beyond, only a long day's run, lay Santiago. Now there was the faintest, tiniest light in the sky. Morning—the awful morning—was about to break. Bush took a fresh grip of his sword hilt; his head was swimming and he passed his forearm over his face to wipe away the cobwebs that seemed to be gathering over his eyes.

And then, pale but silhouetted against the sky on the other side of the ship, he saw the topsail of another vessel moving slowly forward along the ship's side; masts, yards, rigging; another topsail slowly turning. There were wild shouts and yells from the *Renown*, a grinding crash as the two ships came together. An agonising pause, like the moment before a roller breaks upon the shore. And then up over the bulwarks of the *Renown* appeared the heads and shoulders of men; the shakos of marines, the cold glitter of bayonets and cutlasses. There was Hornblower, hatless, swinging his leg over and leaping down to the deck, sword in hand, the others leaping with him on either hand. Weak and faint as he was, Bush still could think clearly enough to realise that Hornblower must have collected the prize crews from all three vessels before running alongside in the *Gaditana*; by Bush's calculation he could have brought thirty seamen and thirty marines to this attack. But while one part of Bush's brain could think with this clarity and logic the other part of it seemed to be hampered and clogged so that what went on before his eyes moved with nightmare slowness. It might have been a slow-order drill, as the boarding party climbed down on the deck. Everything was changed and unreal. The shouts of the Spaniards might have been the shrill cries of little children at play. Bush saw the muskets levelled and fired, but the irregular volley sounded in his ears no louder than popguns. The charge was sweeping the deck; Bush tried to spring forward to join with it but his legs strangely would not move. He found himself lying on the deck and his arms had no strength when he tried to lift himself up.

He saw the ferocious bloody battle that was waged, a fight as wild and as irregular as the one that had preceded it, when little groups of men seemed to appear from nowhere and fling themselves into the struggle, sometimes on this side and sometimes on that. Now came another surge of men, nearly naked seamen with Silk at their head; Silk was swinging the rammer of a gun, a vast unwieldy weapon with which he struck out right and left at the Spaniards who broke before them. Another swirl and eddy in the fight; a Spanish soldier trying to run, limping, with a wounded thigh, and a British seaman with a boarding pike in pursuit, stabbing the wretched man under the ribs and leaving him moving feebly in the blood that poured from him.

Now the maindeck was clear save for the corpses that lay heaped upon it, although below decks he could hear the fight going on, shots and screams and crashes. It all seemed to die away. This weakness was not exactly pleasant. To allow himself to put his head down on his arm and forget his responsibilities might seem tempting, but just over the horizon of his conscious mind there were hideous nightmare things waiting to spring out on him, of which he was frightened, but it made him weaker still to struggle against them. But his head was down on his arm, and it was a tremendous effort to lift it again; later it was a worse effort still, but he tried to force himself to make it, to rise and deal with all the things that must be done. Now there was a hard voice speaking, painful to his ears.

"This 'ere's Mr. Bush, sir. 'Ere 'e is!"

Hands were lifting his head. The sunshine was agonising as it poured into his eyes, and he closed his eyelids tight to keep it out.

"Bush! Bush!" That was Hornblower's voice, pleading and tender. "Bush, please, speak to me."

Two gentle hands were holding his face between them. Bush could just separate his eyelids sufficiently to see Hornblower bending over him, but to speak called for more strength than he possessed. He could only shake his head a little, smiling because of the sense of comfort and security conveyed by Hornblower's hands.

XV

"MR. Hornblower's respects, sir" said the messenger, putting his head inside Bush's cabin after knocking on the door. "The admiral's flag is flying off Mosquito Point, an' we're just goin' to fire the salute, sir."

"Very good" said Bush.

Lying on his cot he had followed in his mind's eye all that had been going on in the ship. She was on the port tack at the moment and had clewed up all sail save topsails and jib. They must be inside Gun Key, then. He heard Hornblower's voice hailing.

"Lee braces, there! Hands wear ship."

He heard the grumble of the tiller ropes as the wheel was put over; they must be rounding Port Royal point. The *Renown* rose to a level keel—she had been heeling very slightly—and then lay over to port, so little that, lying on his cot, Bush could hardly feel it. Then came the bang of the first saluting gun. Despite the kindly warning that Hornblower had sent down Bush was taken sufficiently by surprise to start a little at the sound. He was as weak and nervous as a kitten, he told himself. At five-second intervals the salute went on, while Bush resettled himself in bed. Movement was not very easy, even allowing for his weakness, on account of all the stitches that closed the numerous cuts and gashes on his body. He was sewn together like a crazy quilt; and any movement was painful.

The ship fell oddly quiet again when the salute was over —he was nearly sure it had been fifteen guns; Lambert presumably had been promoted to vice-admiral. They must be gliding northward up Port Royal bay; Bush tried to remember how Salt Pond Hill looked, and the mountains in the background—what were they called? Liguanea, or something like that—he could never tackle these Dago names. They called it the Long Mountain behind Rock Fort.

"Tops'l sheets!" came Hornblower's voice from above. "Tops'l clew lines."

The ship must be gliding slowly to her anchorage.

"Helm-a-lee!"

Turning into the wind would take her way off her.

"Silence, there in the waist!"

Bush could imagine how the hands would be excited and chattering at coming into harbour—the old hands would be telling the new ones about the grog shops and the unholy entertainments that Kingston, just up the channel, provided for seamen.

"Let go!"

That rumble and vibration; no sailor, not even one as matter-of-fact as Bush, could hear the sound of the cable roaring through the hawsehole without a certain amount of emotion. And this was a moment of very mixed and violent emotions. This was no homecoming; it might be the end of an incident, but it would be most certainly the beginning of a new series of incidents. The immediate future held the likelihood of calamity. Not the risk of death or wounds; Bush would have welcomed that as an alternative to the ordeal that lay ahead. Even in his weak state he could still feel the tension mount in his body as his mind tried to foresee the future. He would like to move about, at least fidget and wriggle if he could not walk, in an endeavour to ease that tension, but he could not even fidget while fifty-three stitches held together the half-closed gashes on his body. There would most certainly be an inquiry into the doings on board H.M.S. *Renown,* and there was a possibility of a court-martial—of a whole series of courts-martial—as a result.

Captain Sawyer was dead. Someone among the Spaniards, drunk with blood lust, at the time when the prisoners had tried to retake the ship, had struck down the wretched lunatic when they had burst into the cabin where he was confined. Hell had no fire hot enough for the man—or woman—who could do such a thing, even though it might be looked upon as a merciful release for the poor soul which had cowered before imagined terrors for so long. It was a strange irony that at the moment a merciless hand had cut the madman's throat some among the free prisoners had spared Buckland, had taken him prisoner as he lay in his cot and bound him with his bedding so that he lay helpless while the battle for his ship was being fought out to its bloody end. Buckland would have much to explain to a court of inquiry.

Bush heard the pipes of the bosun's mates and strained his ears to hear the orders given.

"Gig's crew away! Hands to lower the gig!"

Buckland would of course be going off at once to report to the admiral, and just as Bush came to that conclusion Buckland came into the cabin. Naturally he was dressed with the utmost care, in spotless white trousers and his best uniform coat. He was smoothly shaved, and the formal regularity of his neckcloth was the best proof of the anxious attention he had given to it. He carried his cocked hat in his hand as he stooped under the deck beams, and his sword hung from his hip. But he could not speak immediately; he could only stand and stare at Bush. Usually his cheeks were somewhat pudgy, but this morning they were hollow with care; the staring eyes were glassy, and the lips were twitching. A man on his way to the gallows might look like that.

"You're going to make your report, sir?" asked Bush, after waiting for his superior to speak first.

"Yes" said Buckland.

Beside his cocked hat he held in his hand the sealed reports over which he had been labouring. Bush had been called in to help him compose the first, the anxious one regarding the displacement of Captain Sawyer from command; and his own personal report was embodied in the second one, redolent with conscious virtue, telling of the capitulation of the Spanish forces in Santo Domingo. But the third, with its account of the uprising of the prisoners on board, and its confession that Buckland had been taken prisoner asleep in bed, had been written without Bush's help.

"I wish to God I was dead" said Buckland.

"Don't say that, sir" said Bush, as cheerfully as his own apprehensions and his weak state would allow.

"I wish I was" repeated Buckland.

"Your gig's alongside, sir" said Hornblower's voice. "And the prizes are just anchoring astern of us."

Buckland turned his dead-fish eyes towards him; Hornblower was not quite as neat in appearance, but he had clearly gone to some pains with his uniform.

"Thank you" said Buckland; and then, after a pause, he asked his question explosively: "Tell me, Mr. Hornblower—this is the last chance—how did the captain come to fall down the hatchway?"

"I am quite unable to tell you, sir" said Hornblower.

There was no hint whatever to be gleaned from his expressionless face or from the words he used.

"Now, Mr. Hornblower" said Buckland, nervously tapping the reports in his hand. "I'm treating you well. You'll find I've given you all the praise I could in these reports. I've given you full credit for what you did at Santo Domingo, and for boarding the ship when the prisoners rose. Full credit, Mr. Hornblower. Won't you—won't you——?"

"I really cannot add anything to what you already know, sir" said Hornblower.

"But what am I going to say when they start asking me?" asked Buckland.

"Just say the truth, sir, that the captain was found under the hatchway and that no inquiry could establish any other indication than that he fell by accident."

"I wish I knew" said Buckland.

"You know all that will ever be known, sir. Your pardon, sir"—Hornblower extended his hand and picked a thread of oakum from off Buckland's lapel before he went on speaking—"the admiral will be overjoyed at hearing that we've wiped out the Dons at Samaná, sir. He's probably been worrying himself grey-haired over convoys in the Mona Passage. And we've brought three prizes in. He'll have his one-eighth of their value. You can't believe he'll resent that, can you, sir?"

"I suppose not" said Buckland.

"He'll have seen the prizes coming in with us—everyone in the flagship's looking at them now and wondering about them. He'll be expecting good news. He'll be in no mood to ask questions this morning, sir. Except perhaps to ask you if you'll take Madeira or sherry."

For the life of him Bush could not guess whether Hornblower's smile was natural or not, but he was a witness of the infusion of new spirits into Buckland.

"But later on——" said Buckland.

"Later on's another day, sir. We can be sure of one thing, though—admirals don't like to be kept waiting, sir."

"I suppose I'd better go" said Buckland.

Hornblower returned to Bush's cabin after having supervised the departure of the gig. This time his smile was clearly not forced; it played whimsically about the corners of his mouth.

"I don't see anything to laugh at" said Bush.

He tried to ease his position under the sheet that covered him. Now that the ship was stationary and the nearby land interfered with the free course of the wind the ship was much warmer already; the sun was shining down mercilessly, almost vertically over the deck that lay hardly more than a yard above Bush's upturned face.

"You're quite right, sir" said Hornblower, stooping over him and adjusting the sheet. "There's nothing to laugh at."

"Then take that damned grin off your face" said Bush, petulantly. Excitement and the heat were working on his weakness to make his head swim again.

"Aye aye, sir. Is there anything else I can do?"

"No" said Bush.

"Very good, sir. I'll attend to my other duties, then."

Alone in his cabin Bush rather regretted Hornblower's absence. As far as his weakness would permit, he would have liked to discuss the immediate future; he lay and thought about it, muzzy-mindedly, while the sweat soaked the bandages that swathed him. But there could be no logical order in his thoughts. He swore feebly to himself. Listening, he tried to guess what was going on in the ship with hardly more success than when he had tried to guess the future. He closed his eyes to sleep, and he opened them again when he started wondering about how Buckland was progressing in his interview with Admiral Lambert.

A lob-lolly boy—sick-berth attendant—came in with a tray that bore a jug and a glass. He poured out a glassful of liquid and with an arm supporting Bush's neck he held it to Bush's lips. At the touch of the cool liquid, and as its refreshing scent reached his nose, Bush suddenly realised he was horribly thirsty, and he drank eagerly, draining the glass.

"What's that?" he asked.

"Lemonade, sir, with Mr. Hornblower's respects."

"Mr. Hornblower?"

"Yes, sir. There's a bumboat alongside an' Mr. Hornblower bought some lemons an' told me to squeeze 'em for you."

"My thanks to Mr. Hornblower."

"Aye aye, sir. Another glass, sir?"

"Yes."

That was better. Later on there were a whole succession of noises which he found hard to explain to himself: the tramp of booted feet on the deck, shouted órders, oars and more oars rowing alongside. Then there were steps outside his cabin door and Clive, the surgeon, entered, ushering in a stranger, a skinny, white-haired man with twinkling blue eyes.

"I'm Sankey, surgeon of the naval hospital ashore" he announced. "I've come to take you where you'll be more comfortable."

"I don't want to leave the ship" said Bush.

"In the service" said Sankey with professional cheerfulness "you should have learned that it is the rule always to have to do what you don't want to do."

He turned back the sheet and contemplated Bush's bandaged form.

"Pardon this liberty" he said, still hatefully cheerful, "but I have to sign a receipt for you—I trust you've never signed a receipt for ship's stores without examining into their condition, lieutenant."

"Damn you to hell!" said Bush.

"A nasty temper" said Sankey with a glance at Clive. "I fear you have not prescribed a sufficiency of opening medicine."

He laid hands on Bush, and with Clive's assistance dexterously twitched him over so that he lay face downward.

"The Dagoes seem to have done a crude job of carving you, sir" went on Sankey, addressing Bush's defenceless back. "Nine wounds, I understand."

"And fifty-three stitches" added Clive.

"That will look well in the *Gazette*" said Sankey with a giggle; and proceeded to extemporise a quotation: "Lieutenant—ah—Bush received no fewer than nine wounds in the course of his heroic defence, but I am happy to state that he is rapidly recovering from them."

Bush tried to turn his head so as to snarl out an appropriate reply, but his neck was one of the sorest parts of him and he could only growl unintelligibly, and he was not turned on to his back again until his growls had died down.

"And now we'll whisk our little cupid away" said Sankey. "Come in, you stretcher men."

Carried out on to the maindeck Bush found the sunlight blinding, and Sankey stooped to draw the sheet over his eyes.

"Belay that!" said Bush, as he realised his intention, and there was enough of the old bellow in his voice to cause Sankey to pause. "I want to see!"

The explanation of the trampling and bustle on the deck was plain now. Across the waist was drawn up a guard of one of the West Indian regiments, bayonets fixed and every man at attention. The Spanish prisoners were being brought up through the hatchways for despatch to the shore in the lighters alongside. Bush recognised Ortega, limping along with a man on either side to support him; one trouser leg had been cut off and his thigh was bandaged, and the bandage and the other trouser leg were black with dried blood.

"A cut-throat crew, to be sure" said Sankey. "And now, if you have feasted your eyes on them long enough, we can sway you down into the boat."

Hornblower came hurrying down from the quarterdeck and went down on his knee beside the stretcher.

"Are you all right, sir?" he asked anxiously.

"Yes, thank'ee" said Bush.

"I'll have your gear packed and sent ashore after you, sir."

"Thank you."

"Careful with those slings" snapped Hornblower, as the tackles were being attached to the stretcher.

"Sir! Sir!" Midshipman James was dancing about at Hornblower's elbow, anxious for his attention. "Boat's heading for us with a captain aboard."

That was news demanding instant consideration.

"Good-bye, sir" said Hornblower. "Best of luck, sir. See you soon."

He turned away and Bush felt no ill will at this brief farewell, for a captain coming on board had to be received with the correct compliments. Moreover, Bush himself was desperately anxious to know the business that brought this captain on board.

"Hoist away!" ordered Sankey.

"Avast!" said Bush; and in reply to Sankey's look of inquiry, "Let's wait a minute."

"I have no objection myself to knowing what's going on" said Sankey.

The calls of the bosun's mates shrilled along the deck. The sideboys came running; the military guard wheeled to face the entry port; the marines formed up beside them. Up through the entry port came the captain, his gold lace flaming in the sunshine. Hornblower touched his hat.

"You are Mr. Hornblower, at present the senior lieutenant on board this ship?"

"Yes, sir. Lieutenant Horatio Hornblower, at your service."

"My name is Cogshill" said the captain, and he produced a paper which he proceeded to unfold and read aloud. "Orders from Sir Richard Lambert, Vice Admiral of the Blue, Knight of the Bath, Commanding His Majesty's ships and vessels on the Jamaica station, to Captain James Edward Cogshill, of His Majesty's ship *Buckler*. You are hereby requested and required to repair immediately on board of His Majesty's ship *Renown* now lying in Port Royal bay and to take command pro tempore of the aforesaid ship *Renown*."

Cogshill folded his paper again. The assumption of command, even temporarily, of a king's ship was a solemn act, only to be performed with the correct ceremonial. No orders that Cogshill might give on board would be legal until he had read aloud the authority by which he gave them. Now he had "read himself in", and now he held the enormous powers of a captain on board—he could make and unmake warrant officers, he could order imprisonment or the lash, by virtue of the delegation of power from the King in Council down through the Lords of the Admiralty and Sir Richard Lambert.

"Welcome on board, sir" said Hornblower, touching his hat again.

"Very interesting" said Sankey, when Bush had been swayed down into the hospital boat alongside and Sankey had taken his seat beside the stretcher. "Take charge, cox'n. I knew Cogshill was a favourite of the admiral's. Promotion to a ship of the line from a twenty-eight-gun frigate is a long step for our friend James Edward. Sir Richard has wasted no time."

"The orders said it was only—only temporary" said Bush, not quite able to bring out the words "pro tempore" with any aplomb.

"Time enough to make out the permanent orders in due form" said Sankey. "It is from this moment that Cogshill's pay is increased from ten shillings to two pounds a day."

The Negro oarsmen of the hospital boat were bending to their work, sending the launch skimming over the glittering water, and Sankey turned his head to look at the squadron lying at anchor in the distance—a three-decker and a couple of frigates.

"That's the *Buckler*" he said, pointing. "Lucky for Cogshill his ship was in here at this moment. There'll be plenty of promotion in the admiral's gift now. You lost two lieutenants in the *Renown*?"

"Yes" said Bush. Roberts had been cut in two by a shot from Samaná during the first attack, and Smith had been killed at the post of duty defending the quarterdeck when the prisoners rose.

"A captain and two lieutenants" said Sankey meditatively. "Sawyer had been insane for some time, I understand?"

"Yes."

"And yet they killed him?"

"Yes."

"A chapter of accidents. It might have been better for your first lieutenant if he had met the same fate."

Bush did not make any reply to that remark, even though the same thought had occurred to him. Buckland had been taken prisoner in his bed, and he would never be able to live that down.

"I think" said Sankey, judicially, "he will never be able to look for promotion. Unfortunate for him, seeing that he could otherwise have expected it as a result of your successes in Santo Domingo, on which so far I have not congratulated you, sir. My felicitations."

"Thank you" said Bush.

"A resounding success. Now it will be interesting to see what use Sir Richard—may his name be ever revered—will make of all these vacancies. Cogshill to the *Renown*. That seems certain. Then a commander must be promoted to the *Buckler*. The ineffable joy of post rank! There are four commanders on this station—I wonder which of them will enter through the pearly gates? You have been on this station before, I believe, sir?"

"Not for three years" said Bush.

"Then you can hardly be expected to be up to date regarding the relative standing of the officers here in Sir Richard's esteem. Then a lieutenant will be made commander. No doubt about who that will be."

Sankey spared Bush a glance, and Bush asked the question which was expected of him.

"Who?"

"Dutton. First lieutenant of the flagship. Are you acquainted with him?"

"I think so. Lanky fellow with a scar on his cheek?"

"Yes. Sir Richard believes that the sun rises and sets on him. And I believe that Lieutenant Dutton—Commander as he soon will be—is of the same opinion."

Bush had no comment to make, and he would not have made one if he had. Surgeon Sankey was quite obviously a scatter-brained old gossip, and quite capable of repeating any remarks made to him. He merely nodded—as much of a nod as his sore neck and his recumbent position allowed—and waited for Sankey to continue his monologue.

"So Dutton will be a commander. That'll mean vacancies for three lieutenants. Sir Richard will be able to gladden

the hearts of three of his friends by promoting their sons
from midshipmen. Assuming, that is to say, that Sir Richard
has as many as three friends."

"Oars! Bowman!" said the coxswain of the launch;
they were rounding the tip of the jetty. The boat ran
gently alongside and was secured; Sankey climbed out
and supervised the lifting of the stretcher. With steady
steps the Negro bearers began to carry the stretcher up the
road towards the hospital, while the heat of the island
closed round Bush like the warm water in a bath.

"Let me see" said Sankey, falling into step beside the
stretcher. "We had just promoted three midshipmen to
lieutenant. So among the warrant ranks there will be three
vacancies. But let me see—I fancy you had casualties in
the *Renown*?"

"Plenty" said Bush.

Midshipmen and master's mates had given their lives in
defence of their ship.

"Of course. That was only to be expected. So there will
be many more than three vacancies. So the hearts of the
supernumeraries, of the volunteers, of all those unfortunates
serving without pay in the hope of eventual preferment,
will be gladdened by numerous appointments. From the
limbo of nothingness to the inferno of warrant rank. The
path of glory—I do not have to asperse your knowledge of
literature by reminding you of what the poet said."

Bush had no idea what the poet said, but he was not
going to admit it.

"And now we are arrived" said Sankey. "I will attend
you to your cabin."

Inside the building the darkness left Bush almost blind
for a space after the dazzling sunshine. There were whitewashed corridors; there was a long twilit ward divided by
screens into minute rooms. He suddenly realised that he

was quite exhausted, that all he wanted to do was to close
his eyes and rest. The final lifting of him from the stretcher
to the bed and the settling of him there seemed almost
more than he could bear. He had no attention to spare for
Sankey's final chatter. When the mosquito net was at last
drawn round his bed and he was left alone he felt as if
he were at the summit of a long sleek green wave, down
which he went gliding, gliding, endlessly gliding. It was
almost a pleasant sensation, but not quite.

When he reached the foot of the wave he had to struggle
up it again, recovering his strength, through a night and
a day and another night, and during that time he came to
learn about the life in the hospital—the sounds, the groans
that came from other patients behind other screens, the
not-quite-muffled howls of lunatic patients at the far end
of the whitewashed corridor; morning and evening rounds;
by the end of his second day there he had begun to listen
with appetite for the noises that presaged the bringing in
of his meals.

"You are a fortunate man" remarked Sankey, examining
his stitched-up body. "These are all incised wounds. Not
a single deep puncture. It's contrary to all my professional
experience. Usually the Dagoes can be relied upon to use
their knives in a more effective manner. Just look at this
cut here."

The cut in question ran from Bush's shoulder to his
spine, so that Sankey could not literally mean what he had
just said.

"Eight inches long at least" went on Sankey. "Yet not
more than two inches deep, even though, as I suspect, the
scapula is notched. Four inches with the point would have
been far more effective. This other cut here seems to be
the only one that indicates any ambition to plumb the
arterial depths. Clearly the man who wielded the knife

here intended to stab. But it was a stab from above downwards, and the jagged beginning of it shows how the point was turned by the ribs down which the knife slid, severing a few fibres of latissimus dorsi but tailing off at the end into a mere superficial laceration. The effort of a tyro. Turn over, please. Remember, Mr. Bush, if ever you use a knife, to give an upward inclination to the point. The human ribs lie open to welcome an upward thrust; before a downward thrust they overlap and forbid all entrance, and the descending knife, as in this case, bounds in vain from one rib to the next, knocking for admission at each in turn and being refused."

"I'm glad of that" said Bush. "Ouch!"

"And every cut is healing well" said Sankey. "No sign of mortification."

Bush suddenly realised that Sankey was moving his nose about close to his body; it was by its smell that gangrene first became apparent.

"A good clean cut" said Sankey, "rapidly sutured and bound up in its own blood, can be expected to heal by first intention more often than not. Many times more often than not. And these are mostly clean cuts, haggled, as I said, only a little here and there. Bend this knee if you please. Your honourable scars, Mr. Bush, will in the course of a few years become almost unnoticeable. Thin lines of white whose crisscross pattern will be hardly a blemish on your classic torso."

"Good" said Bush; he was not quite sure what his torso was, but he was not going to ask Sankey to explain all these anatomical terms.

This morning Sankey had hardly left him before he returned with a visitor.

"Captain Cogshill to inspect you" he said. "Here he is, sir."

Cogshill looked down at Bush upon the bed.

"Doctor Sankey gives me the good news that you are recovering rapidly" he said.

"I think I am, sir."

"The admiral has ordered a court of inquiry, and I am nominated a member of the court. Naturally your evidence will be required, Mr. Bush, and it is my duty to ascertain how soon you will be able to give it."

Bush felt a little wave of apprehension ripple over him. A court of inquiry was only a shade less terrifying than the court-martial to which it might lead. Even with a conscience absolutely clear Bush would rather—far rather —handle a ship on a lee shore in a gale than face questions and have to give answers, submit his motives to analysis and misconstruction, and struggle against the entanglements of legal forms. But it was medicine that had to be swallowed, and the sensible thing was to hold his nose and gulp it down however nauseating.

"I'm ready at any time, sir."

"Tomorrow I shall take out the sutures, sir" interposed Sankey. "You will observe that Mr. Bush is still weak. He was entirely exsanguinated by his wounds."

"What do you mean by that?"

"I mean he was drained of his blood. And the ordeal of taking out the sutures——"

"The stitches, do you mean?"

"The stitches, sir. The ordeal of removing them may momentarily retard Mr. Bush's recovery of his strength. But if the court will indulge him with a chair when he gives his evidence——"

"That can certainly be granted."

"Then in three days from now he can answer any necessary questions."

"Next Friday, then?"

"Yes, sir. That is the earliest. I could wish it would be later."

"To assemble a court on this station" explained Cogshill with his cold courtesy, "is not easy, when every ship is away on necessary duty so much of the time. Next Friday will be convenient."

"Yes, sir" said Sankey.

It was some sort of gratification to Bush, who had endured so much of Sankey's chatter, to see him almost subdued in his manner when addressing someone as eminent as a captain.

"Very well, then" said Cogshill. He bowed to Bush. "I wish you the quickest of recoveries."

"Thank you, sir" said Bush.

Even lying on his back he could not check the instinctive attempt to return the bow, but his wounds hurt him when he started to double up in the middle and prevented him from appearing ridiculous. With Cogshill gone Bush had time to worry about the future; the fear of it haunted him a little even while he ate his dinner, but the lob-lolly boy who came to take away the remains ushered in another visitor, the sight of whom drove away the black thoughts. It was Hornblower, standing at the door with a basket in his hand, and Bush's face lit up at the sight of him.

"How are you, sir?" asked Hornblower.

They shook hands, each reflecting the pleasure of the other's greeting.

"All the better for seeing you" said Bush, and meant it.

"This is my first chance of coming ashore" said Hornblower. "You can guess that I've been kept busy."

Bush could guess easily enough; it was no trouble to him to visualise all the duties that had been heaped on Hornblower, the necessity to complete *Renown* again with powder and shot, food and water, to clean up the ship

H

after the prisoners had been removed, to eradicate the traces of the recent fighting, to attend to the formalities connected with the disposal of the prizes, the wounded, the sick, and the effects of the dead. And Bush was eager to hear the details, as a housewife might be when illness had removed her from the supervision of her household. He plied Hornblower with questions, and the technical discussion that ensued prevented Hornblower for some time from indicating the basket he had brought.

"Pawpaws" he said. "Mangoes. A pineapple. That's only the second pineapple I've ever seen."

"Thank you. Very kind of you" said Bush. But it was utterly beyond possibility that he could give the least hint of the feeling that the gift evoked in him, that after lying lonely for these days in the hospital he should find that someone cared about him—that in any case someone should give him so much as a thought. The words he spoke were limping and quite inadequate, and only a sensitive and sympathetic mind could guess at the feelings which the words concealed rather than expressed. But he was saved from further embarrassment by Hornblower abruptly introducing a new subject.

"The admiral's taking the *Gaditana* into the navy" he announced.

"Is he, by George!"

"Yes. Eighteen guns—six-pounders and nines. She'll rate as a sloop of war."

"So he'll have to promote a commander for her."

"Yes."

"By George!" said Bush again.

Some lucky lieutenant would get that important step. It might have been Buckland—it still might be, if no weight were given to the consideration that he had been captured asleep in bed.

"Lambert's renaming her the *Retribution*" said Hornblower.

"Not a bad name, either."

"No."

There was silence for a moment; each of them was reliving, from his own point of view, those awful minutes while the *Renown* was being recaptured, while the Spaniards who tried to fight it out were slaughtered without mercy.

"You know about the court of inquiry, I suppose?" asked Bush; it was a logical step from his last train of thought.

"Yes. How did you know about it?"

"Cogshill's just been in here to warn me that I'll have to give evidence."

"I see."

There followed silence more pregnant than the last as they thought about the ordeal ahead. Hornblower deliberately broke it.

"I was going to tell you" he said, "that I had to reeve new tiller lines in *Renown*. Both of them were frayed—there's too much wear there. I think they're led round too sharp an angle."

That provoked a technical discussion which Hornblower encouraged until it was time for him to leave.

XVI

THE court of inquiry was not nearly as awe-inspiring as a court-martial. There was no gun fired, no court-martial flag hoisted; the captains who constituted the board wore their everyday uniforms, and the witnesses were not required to give their evidence under oath; Bush had forgotten about this last fact until he was called into the court.

"Please take a seat, Mr. Bush" said the president. "I understand you are still weak from your wounds."

Bush hobbled across to the chair indicated and was just able to reach it in time to sit down. The great cabin of the *Renown*—here, where Captain Sawyer had lain quivering and weeping with fear—was sweltering hot. The president had the logbook and journal in front of him, and he held in his hand what Bush recognised to be his own report regarding the attack on Samaná, which he had addressed to Buckland.

"This report of yours does you credit, Mr. Bush" said the president. "It appears that you stormed this fort with no more than six casualties, although it was constructed with a ditch, parapets, and ramparts in regular style, and defended by a garrison of seventy men, and armed with twenty-four-pounders."

"We took them by surprise, sir" said Bush.

"It is that which is to your credit."

The surprise of the garrison of Samaná could not have been greater than Bush's own surprise at this reception; he was expecting something far more unpleasant and inquisitorial. A glance across at Buckland, who had been called in before him, was not quite so reassuring; Buckland was pale and unhappy. But there was something he must say before the thought of Buckland should distract him.

"The credit should be given to Lieutenant Hornblower, sir" he said. "It was his plan."

"So you very handsomely say in your report. I may as well say at once that it is the opinion of this court that all the circumstances regarding the attack on Samaná and the subsequent capitulation are in accordance with the best traditions of the service."

"Thank you, sir."

"Now we come to the next matter. The attempt of the prisoners to capture the *Renown*. You were by this time acting as first lieutenant of the ship, Mr. Bush?"

"Yes, sir."

Step by step Bush was taken through the events of that night. He was responsible under Buckland for the arrangements made for guarding and feeding the prisoners. There were fifty women, wives of the prisoners, under guard in the midshipmen's berth. Yes, it was difficult to supervise them as closely as the men. Yes, he had gone his rounds after pipedown. Yes, he had heard a disturbance. And so on.

"And you were found lying among the dead, unconscious from your wounds?"

"Yes, sir."

"Thank you, Mr. Bush."

A fresh-faced young captain at the end of the table asked a question.

"And all this time Captain Sawyer was confined to his cabin, until he was murdered?"

The president interposed.

"Captain Hibbert, Mr. Buckland has already enlightened us regarding Captain Sawyer's indisposition."

There was annoyance in the glance that the president of the court turned upon Captain Hibbert, and light suddenly dawned upon Bush. Sawyer had a wife, children, friends, who would not desire that any attention should be called to the fact that he had died insane. The president of the court was probably acting under explicit orders to hush that part of the business up. He would welcome questions about it no more than Bush himself would, now that Sawyer was dead in his country's cause. Buckland could not have been very closely examined about it, either. His unhappy look must be due to having to describe his inglorious part in the attempt on the *Renown*.

"I don't expect any of you gentlemen wish to ask Mr. Bush any more questions?" asked the president of the court in such a way that questions could not possibly have been asked. "Call Lieutenant Hornblower."

Hornblower made his bow to the court; he was wearing that impassive expression which Bush knew by now to conceal an internal turbulence. He was asked as few questions on Samana as Bush had been.

"It has been suggested" said the president, "that this attack on the fort, and the hoisting up of the gun to search the bay, were on your initiative?"

"I can't think why that suggestion was made, sir. Mr. Buckland bore the entire responsibility."

"I won't press you further about that, Mr. Hornblower, then. I think we all understand. Now, let us hear about your recapture of the *Renown*. What first attracted your attention?"

It called for steady questioning to get the story out of Hornblower. He had heard a couple of musket shots, which had worried him, and then he saw the *Renown* come up into the wind, which made him certain something was seriously wrong. So he had collected his prize crews together and laid the *Renown* on board.

"Were you not afraid of losing the prizes, Mr. Hornblower?"

"Better to lose the prizes than the ship, sir. Besides——"

"Besides what, Mr. Hornblower?"

"I had every sheet and halliard cut in the prizes before we left them, sir. It took them some time to reeve new ones, so it was easy to recapture them."

"You seem to have thought of everything, Mr. Hornblower" said the president, and there was a buzz of approval through the court. "And you seem to have made a very prompt counter-attack on the *Renown*. You did not wait to ascertain the extent of the danger? Yet for all you knew the attempt to take the ship might have already failed."

"In that case no harm was done except the disabling of the rigging of the prizes, sir. But if the ship had actually fallen into the hands of the prisoners it was essential that an attack should be directed on her before any defence could be organised."

"We understand. Thank you, Mr. Hornblower."

The inquiry was nearly over. Carberry was still too ill with his wounds to be able to give evidence; Whiting of the marines was dead. The court conferred only a moment before announcing its findings.

"It is the opinion of this court" announced the president, "that strict inquiry should be made among the Spanish prisoners to determine who it was that murdered Captain Sawyer, and that the murderer, if still alive, should be brought to justice. And as the result of our examination of the surviving officers of H.M.S. *Renown* it is our opinion that no further action is necessary."

That meant there would be no court-martial. Bush found himself grinning with relief as he sought to meet Hornblower's eye, but when he succeeded his smile met with a cold reception. Bush tried to shut off his smile and look like a man of such clear conscience that it was no relief to be told that he would not be court-martialled. And a glance at Buckland changed his elation to a feeling of pity. The man was desperately unhappy; his professional ambitions had come to an abrupt end. After the capitulation of Samaná he must have cherished hope, for with that considerable achievement to his credit, and his captain unfit for service, there was every possibility that he would receive the vital promotion to commander at least, possibly even to captain. The fact that he had been surprised in bed meant an end to all that. He would always be remembered for it, and the fact would remain in people's minds when the circumstances were forgotten. He was doomed to remain an ageing lieutenant.

Bush remembered guiltily that it was only by good fortune that he himself had awakened in time. His wounds might be painful, but they had served an invaluable purpose in diverting attention from his own responsibility; he had fought until he had fallen unconscious, and perhaps that was to his credit, but Buckland would have done the same had the opportunity been granted him. But Buckland was damned, while he himself had come through the ordeal at least no worse off than he had been before. Bush felt the illogicality of it all, although he would have been hard pressed if he had to put it into words. And in any case logical thinking on the subject of reputation and promotion was not easy, because during all these years Bush had become more and more imbued with the knowledge that the service was a hard and ungrateful one, in which fortune was even more capricious than in other walks of life. Good luck came and went in the navy as unpredictably as death chose its victims when a broadside swept a crowded deck. Bush was fatalistic and resigned about that, and it was not a state of mind conducive to penetrating thought.

"Ah, Mr. Bush" said Captain Cogshill, "it's a pleasure to see you on your feet. I hope you will remain on board to dine with me. I hope to secure the presence of the other lieutenants."

"With much pleasure, sir" said Bush. Every lieutenant said that in reply to his captain's invitation.

"In fifteen minutes' time, then? Excellent."

The captains who had constituted the court of inquiry were leaving the ship, in strict order of seniority, and the calls of the bosun's mates echoed along the deck as each one left, a careless hand to a hat brim in acknowledgment of the compliments bestowed. Down from the entry port went each in turn, gold lace, epaulettes, and all, these blessed individuals who had achieved the ultimate beatitude of post rank, and the smart gigs pulled away towards the anchored ships.

"You're dining on board, sir?" said Hornblower to Bush.

"Yes."

On the deck of their own ship the "sir" came quite naturally, as naturally as it had been dropped when Hornblower had been visiting his friend in the hospital ashore. Hornblower turned to touch his hat to Buckland.

"May I leave the deck to Hart, sir? I'm invited to dine in the cabin."

"Very well, Mr. Hornblower." Buckland forced a smile. "We'll have two new lieutenants soon, and you'll cease to be the junior."

"I shan't be sorry, sir."

These men who had been through so much together

were grasping eagerly at trivialities to keep the conversation going for fear lest more serious matters should lift their ugly heads.

"Time for us to go along" said Buckland.

Captain Cogshill was a courtly host. There were flowers in the great cabin now; they must have been kept hidden away in his sleeping cabin while the inquiry was being held so as not to detract from the formality of the proceedings. And the cabin windows were wide open, and a wind scoop brought into the cabin what little air was moving.

"That is a land-crab salad before you, Mr. Hornblower. Coconut-fed land crab. Some prefer it to dairy-fed pork. Perhaps you will serve it to those who would care for some?"

The steward brought in a vast smoking joint which he put on the table.

"A saddle of fresh lamb" said the captain. "Sheep do badly in these islands and I fear this may not be fit to eat. But perhaps you will at least try it. Mr. Buckland, will you carve? You see, gentlemen, I still have some real potatoes left—one grows weary of yams. Mr. Hornblower, will you take wine?"

"With pleasure, sir."

"And Mr. Bush—to your speedy recovery, sir."

Bush drained his glass thirstily. Sankey had warned him, when he left the hospital, that over indulgence in spirituous liquors might result in inflammation of his wounds, but there was pleasure in pouring the wine down his throat and feeling the grateful warmth it brought to his stomach. The dinner proceeded.

"You gentlemen who have served on this station before must be acquainted with this" said the captain, contemplating a steaming dish that had been laid before him. "A West Indian pepper pot—not as good as one finds in

Trinidad, I fear. Mr. Hornblower, will you make your first essay? Come in!"

The last words were in response to a knock on the cabin door. A smartly dressed midshipman entered. His beautiful uniform, his elegant bearing, marked him as one of that class of naval officer in receipt of a comfortable allowance from home, or even of substantial means of his own. Some sprig of the nobility, doubtless, serving his legal time until favouritism and interest should whisk him up the ladder of promotion.

"I'm sent by the admiral, sir" he announced.

Of course. Bush, his perceptions comfortably sensitised with wine, could see at once that with those clothes and that manner he must be on the admiral's staff.

"And what's your message?" asked Cogshill.

"The admiral's compliments, sir, and he'd like Mr. Hornblower's presence on board the flagship as soon as is convenient."

"And dinner not half-way finished" commented Cogshill, looking at Hornblower. But an admiral's request for something as soon as convenient meant immediately, convenient or not. Very likely it was a matter of no importance, either.

"I'd better leave, sir, if I may" said Hornblower. He glanced at Buckland. "May I have a boat, sir?"

"Pardon me, sir" interposed the midshipman. "The admiral said that the boat which brought me would serve to convey you to the flagship."

"That settles it" said Cogshill. "You'd better go, Mr. Hornblower. We'll save some of this pepper pot for you against your return."

"Thank you, sir" said Hornblower, rising.

As soon as he had left, the captain asked the inevitable question.

"What in the world does the admiral want with Hornblower?"

He looked round the table and received no verbal reply. There was a strained look on Buckland's face, however, as Bush saw. It seemed as if in his misery Buckland was clairvoyant.

"Well, we'll know in time" said Cogshill. "The wine's beside you, Mr. Buckland. Don't let it stagnate."

Dinner went on. The pepper pot rasped on Bush's palate and inflamed his stomach, making the wine doubly grateful when he drank it. When the cheese was removed, and the cloth with it, the steward brought in fruit and nuts in silver dishes.

"Port" said Captain Cogshill. " '79. A good year. About this brandy I know little, as one might expect in these times."

Brandy could only come from France, smuggled, presumably, and as a result of trading with the enemy.

"But here" went on the captain, "is some excellent Dutch geneva—I bought it at the prize sale after we took St. Eustatius. And here is another Dutch liquor—it comes from Curaçao, and if the orange flavour is not too sickly for your palates you might find it pleasant. Swedish schnapps, fiery but excellent, I fancy—that was after we captured Saba. The wise man does not mix grain and grape, so they say, but I understand schnapps is made from potatoes, and so does not come under the ban. Mr. Buckland?"

"Schnapps for me" said Buckland a little thickly.

"Mr. Bush?"

"I'll drink along with you, sir."

That was the easiest way of deciding.

"Then let us make it brandy. Gentlemen, may Boney grow bonier than ever."

They drank the toast, and the brandy went down to warm Bush's interior to a really comfortable pitch. He was feeling happy and relaxed, and two toasts later he was feeling better than he had felt since the *Renown* left Plymouth.

"Come in!" said the captain.

The door opened slowly, and Hornblower stood framed in the opening. There was the old look of strain in his face; Bush could see it even though Hornblower's figure seemed to waver a little before his eyes—the way objects appeared over the rack of red-hot cannon balls at Samaná—and although Hornblower's countenance seemed to be a little fuzzy round the edges.

"Come in, come in, man" said the captain. "The toasts are just beginning. Sit in your old place. Brandy for heroes, as Johnson said in his wisdom. Mr. Bush!"

"V–victorious war. O–oceans of gore. P–prizes galore. B–b–beauty ashore. Hic" said Bush, inordinately proud of himself that he had remembered that toast and had it ready when called upon.

"Drink fair, Mr. Hornblower" said the captain, "we have a start of you already. A stern chase is a long chase."

Hornblower put his glass to his lips again.

"Mr. Buckland!"

"Jollity and—jollity and—jollity and—and—and—mirth" said Buckland, managing to get the last word out at last. His face was as red as a beetroot and seemed to Bush's heated imagination to fill the entire cabin like the setting sun; most amusing.

"You've come back from the admiral, Mr. Hornblower" said the captain with sudden recollection.

"Yes, sir."

The curt reply seemed out of place in the general atmosphere of good-will; Bush was distinctly conscious of it, and of the pause which followed.

"Is all well?" asked the captain at length, apologetic about prying into someone else's business and yet led to do so by the silence.

"Yes, sir." Hornblower was turning his glass round and round on the table between long nervous fingers, every finger a foot long, it seemed to Bush. "He has made me commander into *Retribution*."

The words were spoken quietly, but they had the impact of pistol shots in the silence of the room.

"God bless my soul!" said the captain. "Then that's our new toast. To the new commander, and a cheer for him too!"

Bush cheered lustily and downed his brandy.

"Good old Hornblower!" he said. "Good old Hornblower!"

To him it was really excellent news; he leaned over and patted Hornblower's shoulder. He knew his face was one big smile, and he put his head on one side and his shoulder on the table so that Hornblower should get the full benefit of it.

Buckland put his glass down on the table with a sharp tap.

"Damn you!" he said. "Damn you! Damn you to Hell!"

"Easy there!" said the captain hastily. "Let's fill the glasses. A brimmer there, Mr. Buckland. Now, our country! Noble England! Queen of the waves!"

Buckland's anger was drowned in the fresh flood of liquor, yet later in the session his sorrows overcame him and he sat at the table weeping quietly, with the tears running down his cheeks; but Bush was too happy to allow Buckland's misery to affect him. He always remembered that afternoon as one of the most successful dinners he had ever attended. He could also remember Hornblower's smile at the end of dinner.

"We can't send you back to the hospital today" said Hornblower. "You'd better sleep in your own cot tonight. Let me take you there."

That was very agreeable. Bush put both arms round Hornblower's shoulders and walked with dragging feet. It did not matter that his feet dragged and his legs would not function while he had this support; Hornblower was the best man in the world and Bush could announce it by singing "For He's a Jolly Good Fellow" while lurching along the alleyway. And Hornblower lowered him onto the heaving cot and grinned down at him as he clung to the edges of the cot; Bush was a little astonished that the ship should sway like this while at anchor.

XVII

THAT was how Hornblower came to leave the *Renown*. The coveted promotion was in his grasp, and he was busy enough commissioning the *Retribution*, making her ready for sea, and organising the scratch crew which was drafted into her. Bush saw something of him during this time, and could congratulate him soberly on the epaulette which, worn on the left shoulder, marked him as a commander, one of those gilded individuals for whom bosuns' mates piped the side and who could look forward with confidence to eventual promotion to captain. Bush called him "sir", and even when he said it for the first time the expression did not seem unnatural.

Bush had learned something during the past few weeks which his service during the years had not called to his attention. Those years had been passed at sea, among the perils of the sea, amid the ever-changing conditions of wind and weather, deep water and shoal. In the ships of the line in which he had served there had only been minutes of battle for every week at sea, and he had gradually become fixed in the idea that seamanship was the one requisite for a naval officer. To be master of the countless details of managing a wooden sailing ship; not only to be able to handle her under sail, but to be conversant with all the petty but important trifles regarding cordage and cables, pumps and salt pork, dry rot and the Articles of War; that was what was necessary. But he knew now of other qualities equally necessary: a bold and yet thoughtful initiative, moral as well as physical courage, tactful handling both of superiors and of subordinates, ingenuity and quickness of thought. A fighting navy needed to fight, and needed fighting men to lead it.

Yet even though this realisation reconciled him to Hornblower's promotion, there was irony in the fact that he was plunged back immediately into petty detail of the most undignified sort. For now he had to wage war on the insect world and not on mankind; the Spanish prisoners in the six days they had been on board had infested the ship with all the parasites they had brought with them. Fleas, lice, and bedbugs swarmed everywhere, and in the congenial environment of a wooden ship in the tropics full of men they flourished exceedingly. Heads had to be cropped and bedding baked; and in a desperate attempt to wall in the bedbugs woodwork had to be repainted—a success of a day or two flattered only to deceive, for after each interval the pests showed up again. Even the cockroaches and the rats that had always been in the ship seemed to multiply and become omnipresent.

It was perhaps an unfortunate coincidence that the height of his exasperation with this state of affairs coincided with the payment of prize money for the captures at Samaná. A hundred pounds to spend, a couple of days' leave granted by Captain Cogshill, and Hornblower at a loose end at the same time—those two days were a lurid period, during which Hornblower and Bush contrived to spend each of them a hundred pounds in the dubious delights of Kingston. Two wild days and two wild nights, and then Bush went back on board the *Renown*, shaken and limp, only too glad to get out to sea and recover. And when he returned from his first cruise under Cogshill's command Hornblower came to say goodbye.

"I'm sailing with the land breeze tomorrow morning" he said.

"Whither bound, sir?"

"England" said Hornblower.

Bush could not restrain a whistle at the news. There were men in the squadron who had not seen England for ten years.

"I'll be back again" said Hornblower. "A convoy to the Downs. Despatches for the Commissioners. Pick up the replies and a convoy out again. The usual round."

For a sloop of war it was indeed the usual round. The *Retribution* with her eighteen guns and disciplined crew could fight almost any privateer afloat; with her speed and handiness she could cover a convoy more effectively than the ship of the line or even the frigates that accompanied the larger convoys to give solid protection.

"You'll get your commission confirmed, sir" said Bush, with a glance at Hornblower's epaulette.

"I hope so" said Hornblower.

Confirmation of a commission bestowed by a commander-in-chief on a foreign station was a mere formality.

"That is" said Hornblower, "if they don't make peace."

"No chance of that, sir" said Bush; and it was clear from Hornblower's grin that he, too, thought there was no possibility of peace either, despite the hints in the two-months-old newspapers that came out from England to the effect that negotiations were possible. With Bonaparte in supreme power in France, restless, ambitious, and unscrupulous, and with none of the points settled that were in dispute between the two countries, no fighting man could believe that the negotiations could result even in an armistice, and certainly not in a permanent peace.

"Good luck in any case, sir" said Bush, and there was no mere formality about those words.

They shook hands and parted; it says much for Bush's feelings towards Hornblower that in the grey dawn next morning he rolled out of his cot and went up on deck to watch the *Retribution*, ghost-like under her topsails, and with the lead going in the chains, steal out round the point, wafted along by the land breeze. Bush watched her go; life in the service meant many partings. Meanwhile there was war to be waged against bedbugs.

Eleven weeks later the squadron was in the Mona Passage, beating against the trade winds. Lambert had brought them out here with the usual double objective of every admiral, to exercise his ships and to see an important convoy through the most dangerous part of its voyage. The hills of Santo Domingo were out of sight at the moment over the westerly horizon, but Mona was in sight ahead, table-topped and, from this point of view, an unrelieved oblong in outline; over on the port bow lay Mona's little sister Monita, exhibiting a strong family resemblance.

The lookout frigate ahead sent up a signal.

"You're too slow, Mr. Truscott" bellowed Bush at the signal midshipman, as was right and proper.

"Sail in sight, bearing northeast" read the signal midshipman, glass to eye.

That might be anything, from the advanced guard of a French squadron broken out from Brest to a wandering trader.

The signal came down and was almost instantly replaced.

"Friendly sail in sight bearing northeast" read Truscott.

A squall came down and blotted out the horizon. The *Renown* had to pay off momentarily before its impact. The rain rattled on the deck as the ship lay over, and then the wind abruptly moderated, the sun came out again, and the squall was past. Bush busied himself with the task of regaining station, of laying the *Renown* her exact two cables' length astern of her next ahead. She was last in the line of three, and the flagship was the first. Now the strange

sail was well over the horizon. She was a sloop of war as
the telescope showed at once; Bush thought for a moment
that she might be the *Retribution*, returned after a very
quick double passage, but it only took a second glance to
make sure she was not. Truscott read her number and
referred to the list.

"*Clara*, sloop of war: Captain Ford" he announced.

The *Clara* had sailed for England with despatches three
weeks before the *Retribution*, Bush knew.

"*Clara* to Flag" went on Truscott. "Have despatches."

She was nearing fast. Up the flagship's halliards soared
a string of black balls which broke into flags at the top.

"All ships" read Truscott, with excitement evident in
his voice, for this meant that the *Renown* would have
orders to obey. "Heave-to."

"Main tops'l braces!" yelled Bush. "Mr. Abbott! My
respects to the captain and the squadron's heaving-to."

The squadron came to the wind and lay heaving easily
over the rollers. Bush watched the *Clara's* boat dancing
over the waves towards the flagship.

"Keep the hands at the braces, Mr. Bush" said Captain
Cogshill. "I expect we'll fill again as soon as the despatches are delivered."

But Cogshill was wrong. Bush watched through his
glass the officer from the *Clara* go up the flagship's side,
but the minutes passed and the flagship still lay hove-to,
the squadron still pitched on the waves. Now a new string
of black balls went up the flagship's halliards.

"All ships" read Truscott. "Captains repair on board
the flagship."

"Gig's crew away!" roared Bush.

It must be important, or at least unusual, news for the
admiral to wish to communicate it to the captains immediately and in person. Bush walked the quarterdeck with

Buckland while they waited. The French fleet might be out; the Northern Alliance might be growing restive again. The King's illness might have returned. It might be anything; they could be only certain that it was not nothing. The minutes passed and lengthened into half-hours; it could hardly be bad news—if it were, Lambert would not be wasting precious time like this, with the whole squadron going off slowly to leeward. Then at last the wind brought to their ears, over the blue water, the high-pitched sound of the pipes of the bosun's mates in the flagship. Bush clapped his glass to his eye.

"First one's coming off" he said.

Gig after gig left the flagship's side, and now they could see the *Renown's* gig with her captain in the sternsheets. Buckland went to meet him as he came up the side. Cogshill touched his hat; he was looking a little dazed.

"It's peace" he said.

The wind brought them the sound of cheering from the flagship—the announcement must have been made to the ship's company on board, and it was the sound of that cheering that gave any reality at all to the news the captain brought.

"Peace, sir?" asked Buckland.

"Yes, peace. Preliminaries are signed. The ambassadors meet in France next month to settle the terms, but it's peace. All hostilities are at an end—they are to cease in every part of the world on arrival of this news."

"Peace!" said Bush.

For nine years the world had been convulsed with war; ships had burned and men had bled from Manila to Panama, west about and east about. It was hard to believe that he was living now in a world where men did not fire cannons at each other on sight. Cogshill's next remark had a bearing on this last thought.

"National ships of the French, Batavian, and Italian
Republics will be saluted with the honours due to foreign
ships of war" he said.

Buckland whistled at that, as well he might. It meant
that England had recognised the existence of the red
republics against which she had fought for so long. Yesterday it had been almost treason to speak the word "republic". Now a captain could use it casually in an official
statement.

"And what happens to us, sir?" asked Buckland.

"That's what we must wait to hear" said Cogshill. "But
the navy is to be reduced to peacetime establishment. That
means that nine ships out of ten will be paid off."

"Holy Moses!" said Bush.

Now the next ship ahead was cheering, the sound coming
shrilly through the air.

"Call the hands" said Cogshill. "They must be told."

The ship's company of the *Renown* rejoiced to hear the
news. They cheered as wildly as did the crews of the other
ships. For them it meant the approaching end of savage
discipline and incredible hardship. Freedom, liberty, a
return to their homes. Bush looked down at the sea of
ecstatic faces and wondered what the news implied for him.
Freedom and liberty, possibly; but they meant life on a
lieutenant's half pay. That was something he had never
experienced; in his earliest youth he had entered the navy
as a midshipman—the peacetime navy which he could
hardly remember—and during the nine years of the war he
had only known two short intervals of leave. He was not
too sure that he cared for the novel prospects that the
future held out to him.

He glanced up at the flagship and turned to bellow at
the signal midshipman.

"Mr. Truscott! Don't you see that signal? Attend to

your duties, or it will be the worse for you, peace or no peace."

The wretched Truscott put his glass to his eye.

"All ships" he read. "Form line on the larboard tack."

Bush glanced at the captain for permission to proceed.

"Hands to the braces, there!" yelled Bush. "Fill that main tops'l. Smarter than that, you lubbers! Full and by, quartermaster. Mr. Cope, haven't you eyes in your head? Take another pull at that weather-brace! God bless my soul! Easy there! Belay!"

"All ships" read Truscott with his telescope, as the *Renown* gathered way and settled in the wake of her next ahead. "Tack in succession."

"Stand by to go about!" yelled Bush.

He noted the progress of the next ahead, and then spared time to rate the watch for its dilatoriness in going to its stations for tacking ship.

"You slow-footed slobs! I'll have some of you dancing at the gratings before long!"

The next ahead had tacked by now, and the *Renown* was advancing into the white water she had left behind.

"Ready about!" shouted Bush. "Headsail sheets! Helm-a-lee!"

The *Renown* came ponderously about and filled on the starboard tack.

"Course sou'west by west" said Truscott, reading the next signal.

Southwest by west. The admiral must be heading back for Port Royal. He could guess that was the first step towards the reduction of the fleet to its peacetime establishment. The sun was warm and delightful, and the *Renown*, steadying before the wind, was roaring along over the blue Caribbean. She was keeping her station well; there was no need to shiver the mizzen topsail yet. This was a good life. He could not make himself believe that it was coming to an end. He tried to think of a winter's day in England, with nothing to do. No ship to handle. Half pay—his sisters had half his pay as it was, which would mean there would be nothing for him, as well as nothing to do. A cold winter's day. No, he simply could not imagine it, and he left off trying.

XVIII

IT was a cold winter's day in Portsmouth; a black frost, and there was a penetrating east wind blowing down the street as Bush came out of the dockyard gates. He turned up the collar of his pea-jacket over his muffler and crammed his hands into his pockets, and he bowed his head into the wind as he strode forward into it, his eyes watering, his nose running, while that east wind seemed to find its way between his ribs, making the scars that covered them ache anew. He would not allow himself to look up at the Keppel's Head as he went past it. In there, he knew, there would be warmth and good company. The fortunate officers with prize money to spend; the incredibly fortunate officers who had found themselves appointments in the peacetime navy—they would be in there yarning and taking wine with each other. He could not afford wine. He thought longingly for a moment about a tankard of beer, but he rejected the idea immediately, although the temptation was strong. He had a month's half pay in his pocket —he was on his way back from the Clerk of the Cheque from whom he had drawn it—but that had to last four and a half weeks and he knew he could not afford it.

He had tried of course for a billet in the merchant service, as mate, but that was as hopeless a prospect at present as obtaining an appointment as lieutenant. Having started life as a midshipman and spent all his adult life in the fighting service he did not know enough about bills of lading or cargo stowage. The merchant service looked on the navy with genial contempt, and said the latter always had a hundred men available to do a job the merchantman had to do with six. And with every ship that was paid off a fresh batch of master's mates, trained for the merchant service and pressed from it, sought jobs in their old profession, heightening the competition every month.

Someone came out from a side street just in front of him and turned into the wind ahead of him—a naval officer. That gangling walk; those shoulders bent into the wind; he could not help but recognise Hornblower.

"Sir! Sir!" he called, and Hornblower turned.

There was a momentary irritation in his expression but it vanished the moment he recognised Bush.

"It's good to see you" he said, his hand held out.

"Good to see *you*, sir" said Bush.

"Don't call me 'sir'" said Hornblower.

"No, sir? What—why——?"

Hornblower had no greatcoat on; and his left shoulder was bare of the epaulette he should have worn as a commander. Bush's eyes went to it automatically. He could see the old pin-holes in the material which showed where the epaulette had once been fastened.

"I'm not a commander" said Hornblower. "They didn't confirm my appointment."

"Good God!"

Hornblower's face was unnaturally white—Bush was accustomed to seeing it deeply tanned—and his cheeks were hollow, but his expression was set in the old unrevealing cast that Bush remembered so well.

"Preliminaries of peace were signed the day I took *Retribution* into Plymouth" said Hornblower.

"What infernal luck!" said Bush.

Lieutenants waited all their lives for the fortunate combination of circumstances that might bring them promotion, and most of them waited in vain. It was more than likely now Hornblower would wait in vain for the rest of his life.

"Have you applied for an appointment as lieutenant?" asked Bush.

"Yes. And I suppose you have?" replied Hornblower.

"Yes."

There was no need to say more than that on that subject. The peacetime navy employed one-tenth of the lieutenants who were employed in wartime; to receive an appointment one had to be of vast seniority or else have powerful friends.

"I spent a month in London," said Hornblower. "There was always a crowd round the Admiralty and the Navy Office."

"I expect so" said Bush.

The wind came shrieking round the corner.

"God, but it's cold!" said Bush.

His mind toyed with the thought of various ways to continue the conversation in shelter. If they went to the Keppel's Head now it would mean paying for two pints of beer, and Hornblower would have to pay for the same.

"I'm going into the Long Rooms just here" said Hornblower. "Come in with me—or are you busy?"

"No, I'm not busy" said Bush, doubtfully "but——"

"Oh, it's all right" said Hornblower. "Come on."

There was reassurance in the confident way in which Hornblower spoke about the Long Rooms. Bush only knew of them by reputation. They were frequented by officers of the navy and the army with money to spare. Bush had heard much about the high stakes that were indulged in at play there, and about the elegance of the refreshments offered by the proprietor. If Hornblower could speak thus casually about the Long Rooms he could not be as desperately hard up as he seemed to be. They crossed the street and Hornblower held open the door and ushered him through. It was a long oak-panelled room: the gloom of the outer day was made cheerful here by the light of candles, and a magnificent fire flamed on the hearth. In the centre several card tables with chairs round them stood ready for play; the ends of the room were furnished as comfortable lounges. A servant in a green baize apron was making the room tidy, and came to take their hats and Bush's coat as they entered.

"Good morning, sir" he said.

"Good morning, Jenkins" said Hornblower.

He walked with unconcealed haste over to the fire and stood before it warming himself. Bush saw that his teeth were chattering.

"A bad day to be out without your pea-jacket" he said.

"Yes" said Hornblower.

He clipped that affirmative a little short, so that in a minute degree it failed to be an indifferent, flat agreement. It was that which caused Bush to realise that it was not eccentricity or absent-mindedness that had brought Hornblower out into a black frost without his greatcoat. Bush looked at Hornblower sharply, and he might even have asked a tactless question if he had not been forestalled by the opening of an inner door beside them. A short, plump, but exceedingly elegant gentleman came in; he was dressed in the height of fashion, save that he wore his hair long, tied back and with powder in the style of the last generation. This made his age hard to guess. He looked at the pair of them with keen dark eyes.

"Good morning, Marquis" said Hornblower. "It is a pleasure to present—M. le Marquis de Sainte-Croix—Lieutenant Bush."

The Marquis bowed gracefully, and Bush endeavoured to imitate him. But for all that graceful bow, Bush was quite unaware of the considering eyes running over him.

A lieutenant looking over a likely hand, or a farmer looking at a pig at a fair, might have worn the same expression. Bush guessed that the Marquis was making a mental estimate as to how much Bush might be good for at the card tables, and suddenly became acutely conscious of his shabby uniform. Apparently the Marquis reached the same conclusion as Bush did, but he began a conversation nevertheless.

"A bitter wind" he said.

"Yes" said Bush.

"It will be rough in the Channel" went on the Marquis, politely raising a professional topic.

"Indeed it will" agreed Bush.

"And no ships will come in from the westward."

"You can be sure of that."

The Marquis spoke excellent English. He turned to Hornblower.

"Have you seen Mr. Truelove lately?" he asked.

"No" said Hornblower. "But I met Mr. Wilson."

Truelove and Wilson were names familiar to Bush; they were the most famous prize agents in England—a quarter of the navy at least employed that firm to dispose of their captures for them. The Marquis turned back to Bush.

"I hope you have been fortunate in the matter of prize money, Mr. Bush?" he said.

"No such luck" said Bush. His hundred pounds had gone in a two days' debauch at Kingston.

"The sums they handle are fabulous, nothing less than fabulous. I understand the ship's company of the *Caradoc* will share seventy thousand pounds when they come in."

"Very likely" said Bush. He had heard of the captures the *Caradoc* had made in the Bay of Biscay.

"But while this wind persists they must wait before enjoying their good fortune, poor fellows. They were not paid off on the conclusion of peace, but were ordered to

Malta to assist in relieving the garrison. Now they are expected back daily."

For an immigrant civilian the Marquis displayed a laudable interest in the affairs of the service. And he was consistently polite, as his next speech showed.

"I trust you will consider yourself at home here, Mr. Bush" he said. "Now I hope you will pardon me, as I have much business to attend to."

He withdrew through the curtained door, leaving Bush and Hornblower looking at each other.

"A queer customer" said Bush.

"Not so queer when you come to know him" said Hornblower.

The fire had warmed him by now, and there was a little colour in his cheeks.

"What do you *do* here?" asked Bush, curiosity finally overcoming his politeness.

"I play whist" said Hornblower.

"Whist?"

All that Bush knew about whist was that it was a slow game favoured by intellectuals. When Bush gambled he preferred something with a greater element of chance and which did not make any demand on his thoughts.

"A good many men from the services drop in here for whist" said Hornblower. "I'm always glad to make a fourth."

"But I'd heard——"

Bush had heard of all sorts of other games being played in the Long Rooms: hazard, vingt-et-un, even roulette.

"The games for high stakes are played in there" said Hornblower, pointing to the curtained door. "I stay here."

"Wise man" said Bush. But he was quite sure there was some further information that was being withheld from him. And he was not actuated by simple curiosity. The affection and the interest that he felt towards Hornblower drove him into further questioning.

"Do you win?" he asked.

"Frequently" said Hornblower. "Enough to live."

"But you have your half pay?" went on Bush.

Hornblower yielded in face of this persistence.

"No" he said. "I'm not entitled."

"Not entitled?" Bush's voice rose a semitone. "But you're a permanent lieutenant."

"Yes. But I was a temporary commander. I drew three months' full pay for that rank before the Admiralty refused to confirm."

"And then they put you under stoppages?"

"Yes. Until I've repaid the excess." Hornblower smiled; a nearly natural smile. "I've lived through two months of it. Only five more and I'll be back on half pay."

"Holy Peter!" said Bush.

Half pay was bad enough; it meant a life of constant care and economy, but one could live. Hornblower had nothing at all. Bush knew now why Hornblower had no greatcoat. He felt a sudden wave of anger. A recollection rose in his mind, as clear to his inward eye as this pleasant room was to his outward one. He remembered Hornblower swinging himself down, sword in hand, on to the deck of the *Renown*, plunging into a battle against odds which could only result in either death or victory. Hornblower, who had planned and worked endlessly to ensure success—and then had flung his life upon the board as a final stake; and today Hornblower was standing with chattering teeth trying to warm himself beside a fire by the charity of a frog-eating gambling-hall keeper with the look of a dancing master.

"It's a hellish outrage" said Bush, and then he made his offer. He offered his money, even though he knew as he offered it that it meant most certainly that he would go hungry, and that his sisters, if not exactly hungry, would hardly have enough to eat. But Hornblower shook his head.

"Thank you" he said. "I'll never forget that. But I can't accept it. You know that I couldn't. But I'll never cease to be grateful to you. I'm grateful in another way, too. You've brightened the world for me by saying that."

Even in the face of Hornblower's refusal Bush repeated his offer, and tried to press it, but Hornblower was firm in his refusal. Perhaps it was because Bush looked so downcast that Hornblower gave him some further information in the hope of cheering him up.

"Things aren't as bad as they seem" he said. "You don't understand that I'm in receipt of regular pay—a permanent salarium from our friend the Marquis."

"I didn't know that" said Bush.

"Half a guinea a week" explained Hornblower. "Ten shillings and sixpence every Saturday morning, rain or shine."

"And what do you have to do for it?" Bush's half pay was more than twice that sum.

"I only have to play whist" explained Hornblower. "Only that. From twelve midday until two in the morning I'm here to play whist with any three that need a fourth."

"I see" said Bush.

"The Marquis in his generosity also makes me free of these rooms. I have no subscription to pay. No table money. And I can keep my winnings."

"And pay your losses?"

Hornblower shrugged.

"Naturally. But the losses do not come as often as one might think. The reason's simple enough. The whist players who find it hard to obtain partners, and who are cold-shouldered by the others, are naturally the bad players. Strangely anxious to play, even so. And when the Marquis happens to be in here and Major Jones and Admiral Smith and Mr. Robinson are seeking a fourth while everyone seems strangely preoccupied he catches my eye—the sort of reproving look a wife might throw at a husband talking too loud at a dinner party—and I rise to my feet and offer to be the fourth. It is odd they are flattered to play with Hornblower, as often it costs them money."

"I see" said Bush again, and he remembered Hornblower standing by the furnace in Fort Samaná organising the firing of red-hot shot at the Spanish privateers.

"The life is not entirely one of beer and skittles, naturally" went on Hornblower; with the dam once broken he could not restrain his loquacity. "After the fourth hour or so it becomes irksome to play with bad players. When I go to Hell I don't doubt that my punishment will be always to partner players who pay no attention to my discards. But then on the other hand I frequently play a rubber or two with the good players. There are moments when I would rather lose to a good player than win from a bad one."

"That's just the point" said Bush, harking back to an old theme. "How about the losses?"

Bush's experiences of gambling had mostly been of losses, and in this hard-headed moment he could remember the times when he had been weak.

"I can deal with them" said Hornblower. He touched his breast pocket. "I keep ten pounds here. My *corps de réserve*, you understand. I can always endure a run of losses in consequence. Should that reserve be depleted, then sacrifices have to be made to build it up again."

The sacrifices being skipped meals, thought Bush grimly. He looked so woebegone that Hornblower offered further comfort.

"But five more months" he said "and I'll be on half pay again. And before that—who knows? Some captain may take me off the beach."

I

"That's true" said Bush.

It was true insofar as the possibility existed. Sometimes ships were recommissioned. A captain might be in need of a lieutenant; a captain might invite Hornblower to fill the vacancy. But every captain was besieged by friends seeking appointments, and in any event the Admiralty was also besieged by lieutenants of great seniority—or lieutenants with powerful friends—and captains were most likely to listen to recommendations of high authority.

The door opened and a group of men came in.

"It's high time for customers to arrive" said Hornblower, with a grin at Bush. "Stay and meet my friends."

The red coats of the army, the blue coats of the navy, the bottle-green and snuff-coloured coats of civilians; Bush and Hornblower made room for them before the fire after the introductions were made, and the coat-tails were parted as their wearers lined up before the flames. But the exclamations about the cold, and the polite conversation, died away rapidly.

"Whist?" asked one of the newcomers tentatively.

"Not for me. Not for us" said another, the leader of the red-coats. "The Twenty-Ninth Foot has other fish to fry. We've a permanent engagement with our friend the Marquis in the next room. Come on, Major, let's see if we can call a main right this time."

"Then will you make a four, Mr. Hornblower? How about your friend Mr. Bush?"

"I don't play" said Bush.

"With pleasure" said Hornblower. "You will excuse me, Mr. Bush, I know. There is the new number of the *Naval Chronicle* on the table there. There's a *Gazette* letter on the last page which might perhaps hold your interest for a while. And there is another item you might think important, too."

Bush could guess what the letter was even before he picked the periodical up, but when he found the place there was the same feeling of pleased shock to see his name in print there, as keen as the first time he saw it: "I have the honour to be, etc., WM. BUSH."

The *Naval Chronicle* in these days of peace found it hard, apparently, to obtain sufficient matter to fill its pages, and gave much space to the reprinting of these despatches. "Copy of a letter from Vice-Admiral Sir Richard Lambert to Evan Nepean, Esq., Secretary to the Lords Commissioners of the Admiralty." That was only Lambert's covering letter enclosing the reports. Here was the first one—it was with a strange internal sensation that he remembered helping Buckland with the writing of it, as the *Renown* ran westerly along the coast of Santo Domingo the day before the prisoners broke out. It was Buckland's report on the fighting at Samaná. To Bush the most important line was "in the handsomest manner—under the direction of Lieutenant William Bush, the senior officer, whose report I enclose". And here was his very own literary work, as enclosed by Buckland.

H.M.S. Renown, *off Santo Domingo. January 9th, 1802*
SIR,
    I have the honour to inform you . . .

Bush relived those days of a year ago as he reread his own words; those words which he had composed with so much labour even though he had referred, during the writing of them, to other reports written by other men so as to get the phrasing right.

    . . . I cannot end this report without a reference to the gallant conduct and most helpful suggestions of Lieutenant Horatio Hornblower, who was my second in command on this occasion, and to whom in great part the success of the expedition is due.

There was Hornblower now, playing cards with a post captain and two contractors.

Bush turned back through the pages of the *Naval Chronicle*. Here was the Plymouth letter, a daily account of the doings in the port during the last month.

"Orders came down this day for the following ships to be paid off. . . ." "Came in from Gibraltar *La Diana*, 44, and the *Tamar*, 38, to be paid off as soon as they go up the harbour and to be laid up." "Sailed the *Caesar*, 80, for Portsmouth, to be paid off." And here was an item just as significant, or even more so: "Yesterday there was a large sale of serviceable stores landed from different men of war." The navy was growing smaller every day and with every ship that was paid off another batch of lieutenants would be looking for billets. And here was an item—"This afternoon a fishing boat turning out of atwater jibed and overset, by which accident two industrious fishermen with large families were drowned." This was the *Naval Chronicle*, whose pages had once bulged with the news of the Nile and of Camperdown; now it told of accidents to industrious fishermen. Bush was too interested in his own concerns to feel any sympathy towards their large families.

There was another drowning as a final item; a name— a combination of names—caught Bush's attention so that he read the paragraph with a quickened pulse.

Last night the jolly boat of His Majesty's cutter *Rapid*, in the Revenue service, while returning in the fog from delivering a message on shore, was swept by the ebb tide athwart the hawse of a merchantman anchored off Fisher's Nose, and capsized. Two seamen and Mr. Henry Wellard, Midshipman, were drowned. Mr. Wellard was a most promising young man recently appointed to the *Rapid*, having served as a volunteer in His Majesty's ship *Renown*.

Bush read the passage and pondered over it. He thought it important to the extent that he read the remainder of the *Naval Chronicle* without taking in any of it; and it was with surprise that he realised he would have to leave quickly in order to catch the carrier's waggon back to Chichester.

A good many people were coming into the Rooms now; the door was continually opening to admit them. Some of them were naval officers with whom he had a nodding acquaintance. All of them made straight for the fire for warmth before beginning to play. And Hornblower was on his feet now; apparently the rubber was finished, and Bush took the opportunity to catch his eye and give an indication that he wished to leave. Hornblower came over to him. It was with regret that they shook hands.

"When do we meet again?" asked Hornblower.

"I come in each month to draw my half pay" said Bush. "I usually spend the night because of the carrier's waggon. Perhaps we could dine——?"

"You can always find me here" said Hornblower. "But —do you have a regular place to stay?"

"I stay where it's convenient" replied Bush.

They both of them knew that meant that he stayed where it was cheap.

"I lodge in Highbury Street. I'll write the address down." Hornblower turned to a desk in the corner and wrote on a sheet of paper which he handed to Bush. "Would you care to share my room when next you come? My land-lady is a sharp one. No doubt she will make a charge for a cot for you, but even so——"

"It'll save money" said Bush, putting the paper in his pocket; his grin as he spoke masked the sentiment in his next words. "And I'll see more of you."

"By George, yes" said Hornblower. Words were not adequate.

Jenkins had come sidling up and was holding Bush's greatcoat for him to put on. There was that in Jenkins' manner which told Bush that gentlemen when helped into their coats at the Long Rooms presented Jenkins with a shilling. Bush decided at first that he would be eternally damned before he parted with a shilling, and then he changed his mind. Maybe Hornblower would give Jenkins a shilling if he did not. He felt in his pocket and handed the coin over.

"Thank you, sir" said Jenkins.

With Jenkins out of earshot again Bush lingered, wondering how to frame his question.

"That was hard luck on young Wellard" he said, tentatively.

"Yes" said Hornblower.

"D'you think" went on Bush, plunging desperately "he had anything to do with the captain's falling down the hatchway?"

"I couldn't give an opinion" answered Hornblower. "I didn't know enough about it."

"But——" began Bush, and checked himself again; he knew by the look on Hornblower's face that it was no use asking further questions.

The Marquis had come into the room and was looking round in unobtrusive inspection. Bush saw him take note of the several men who were not playing, and of Hornblower standing in idle gossip by the door. Bush saw the meaning glance which he directed at Hornblower, and fell into sudden panic.

"Good-bye" he said, hastily.

The black northeast wind that greeted him in the street was no more cruel than the rest of the world.

XIX

IT was a short, hard-faced woman who opened the door in reply to Bush's knock, and she looked at Bush even harder when he asked for Lieutenant Hornblower. "Top of the house" she said, at last, and left Bush to find his way up.

There could be no doubt about Hornblower's pleasure at seeing him. His face was lit with a smile and he drew Bush into the room while shaking his hand. It was an attic, with a steeply sloping ceiling; it contained a bed and a night table and a single wooden chair, but, as far as Bush's cursory glance could discover, nothing else at all.

"And how is it with you?" asked Bush, seating himself in the proffered chair, while Hornblower sat on the bed.

"Well enough" replied Hornblower—but was there, or was there not, a guilty pause before that answer? In any case the pause was covered up by the quick counter-question. "And with you?"

"So-so" said Bush.

They talked indifferently for a space, with Hornblower asking questions about the Chichester cottage that Bush lived in with his sisters.

"We must see about your bed for tonight" said Hornblower at the first pause. "I'll go down and give Mrs. Mason a hail."

"I'd better come too" said Bush.

Mrs. Mason lived in a hard world, quite obviously; she turned the proposition over in her mind for several seconds before she agreed to it.

"A shilling for the bed" she said. "Can't wash the sheets for less than that with soap as it is."

"Very good" said Bush.

He saw Mrs. Mason's hand held out, and he put the shilling into it; no one could be in any doubt about Mrs. Mason's determination to be paid in advance by any friend of Hornblower's. Hornblower had dived for his pocket when he caught sight of the gesture, but Bush was too quick for him.

"And you'll be talking till all hours" said Mrs. Mason. "Mind you don't disturb my other gentlemen. And douse the light while you talk, too, or you'll be burning a shilling's worth of tallow."

"Of course" said Hornblower.

"Maria! Maria!" called Mrs. Mason.

A young woman—no, a woman not quite young—came up the stairs from the depths of the house at the call.

"Yes, Mother?"

Maria listened to Mrs. Mason's instructions for making up a truckle bed in Mr. Hornblower's room.

"Yes, Mother" she said.

"Not teaching today, Maria?" asked Hornblower pleasantly.

"No, sir." The smile that lit her plain face showed her keen pleasure at being addressed.

"Oak-Apple Day? No, not yet. It's not the King's Birthday. Then why this holiday?"

"Mumps, sir" said Maria. "They all have mumps, except Johnnie Bristow."

"That agrees with everything I've heard about Johnnie Bristow" said Hornblower.

"Yes, sir" said Maria. She smiled again, clearly pleased not only that Hornblower should jest with her but also because he remembered what she had told him about the school.

Back in the attic again Hornblower and Bush resumed their conversation, this time on a more serious plane. The state of Europe occupied their attention.

"This man Bonaparte" said Bush. "He's a restless cove."

"That's the right word for him" agreed Hornblower.

"Isn't he satisfied? Back in '96 when I was in the old *Superb* in the Mediterranean—that was when I was commissioned lieutenant—he was just a general. I can remember hearing his name for the first time, when we were blockading Toulon. Then he went to Egypt. Now he's First Consul—isn't that what he calls himself?"

"Yes. But he's Napoleon now, not Bonaparte any more. First Consul for life."

"Funny sort of name. Not what I'd choose for myself."

"Lieutenant Napoleon Bush" said Hornblower. "It wouldn't sound well."

They laughed together at the ridiculous combination.

"The *Morning Chronicle* says he's going a step farther" went on Hornblower. "There's talk that he's going to call himself Emperor."

"Emperor!"

Even Bush could catch the connotations of that title, with its claims to universal pre-eminence.

"I suppose he's mad?" asked Bush.

"If he is, he's the most dangerous madman in Europe."

"I don't trust him over this Malta business. I don't trust him an inch" said Bush, emphatically. "You mark my words, we'll have to fight him again in the end. Teach him a lesson he won't forget. It'll come sooner or later— we can't go on like this."

"I think you're quite right" said Hornblower. "And sooner rather than later."

"Then——" said Bush.

He could not talk and think at the same time, not when his thoughts were as tumultuous as the ones this conclusion called up; war with France meant the re-expansion of the navy; the threat of invasion and the needs of convoy would mean the commissioning of every small craft that could float and carry a gun. It would mean the end of half pay for him; it would mean walking a deck again and handling a ship under sail. And it would mean hardship again, danger, anxiety, monotony—all the concomitants of war. These thoughts rushed into his brain with so much velocity, and in such a continuous stream, that they made a sort of whirlpool of his mind, in which the good and the bad circled after each other, each in turn chasing the other out of his attention.

"War's a foul business" said Hornblower, solemnly. "Remember the things you've seen."

"I suppose you're right" said Bush; there was no need to particularise. But it was an unexpected remark, all the same. Hornblower grinned and relieved the tension.

"Well" he said, "Boney can call himself Emperor if he likes. I have to earn my half guinea at the Long Rooms."

Bush was about to take this opportunity to ask Hornblower how he was profiting there, but he was interrupted by a rumble outside the door and a knock.

"Here comes your bed" said Hornblower, walking over to open the door.

Maria came trundling the thing in. She smiled at them.

"Over here or over there?" she asked.

Hornblower looked at Bush.

"It doesn't matter" said Bush.

"I'll put it against the wall, then."

"Let me help" said Hornblower.

"Oh no, sir. Please sir, I can do it."

The attention fluttered her—and Bush could see that

with her sturdy figure she was in no need of help. To cover her confusion she began to thump at the bedding, putting the pillows into the pillowslips.

"I trust you have already had the mumps, Maria?" said Hornblower.

"Oh yes, sir. I had them as a child, on both sides."

The exercise and her agitation between them had brought the colour into her cheeks. With blunt but capable hands she spread the sheet. Then she paused as another implication of Hornblower's inquiry occurred to her.

"You've no need to worry, sir. I shan't give them to you if you haven't had them."

"I wasn't thinking about that" said Hornblower.

"Oh, sir" said Maria, twitching the sheet into mathematical smoothness. She spread the blankets before she looked up again. "Are you going out directly, sir?"

"Yes. I ought to have left already."

"Let me take that coat of yours for a minute, sir. I can sponge it and freshen it up."

"Oh, I wouldn't have you go to that trouble, Maria."

"It wouldn't be any trouble, sir. Of course not. Please let me, sir. It looks——"

"It looks the worse for wear" said Hornblower, glancing down at it. "There's no cure for old age that's yet been discovered."

"Please let me take it, sir. There's some spirits of hartshorn downstairs. It will make quite a difference. Really it will."

"But——"

"Oh, please, sir."

Hornblower reluctantly put up his hand and undid a button.

"I'll only be a minute with it" said Maria, hastening to him. Her hands were extended to the other buttons, but a sweep of Hornblower's quick nervous fingers had antici-pated her. He pulled off his coat and she took it out of his hands.

"You've mended that shirt yourself" she said, accusingly.

"Yes, I have."

Hornblower was a little embarrassed at the revelation of the worn garment. Maria studied the patch.

"I would have done that for you if you'd asked me, sir."

"And a good deal better, no doubt."

"Oh, I wasn't saying that, sir. But it isn't fit that you should patch your own shirts."

"Whose should I patch, then?"

Maria giggled.

"You're too quick with your tongue for me" she said. "Now, just wait here and talk to the lieutenant while I sponge this."

She darted out of the room and they heard her footsteps hurrying down the stairs, while Hornblower looked half-ruefully at Bush.

"There's a strange pleasure" he said, "in knowing that there's a human being who cares whether I'm alive or dead. Why that should give pleasure is a question to be debated by the philosophic mind."

"I suppose so" said Bush.

He had sisters who devoted all their attention to him whenever it was possible, and he was used to it. At home he took their ministrations for granted. He heard the church clock strike the half-hour, and it recalled his thoughts to the further business of the day.

"You're going to the Long Rooms now?" he asked.

"Yes. And you, I suppose, want to go to the dockyard? The monthly visit to the Clerk of the Cheque?"

"Yes."

"We can walk together as far as the Rooms, if you care to. As soon as our friend Maria returns my coat to me."

"That's what I was thinking" said Bush.

It was not long before Maria came knocking at the door again.

"It's done" she said, holding out the coat. "It's nice and fresh now."

But something seemed to have gone out of her. She seemed a little frightened, a little apprehensive.

"What's the matter, Maria?" asked Hornblower, quick to feel the change of attitude.

"Nothing. Of course there's nothing the matter with me" said Maria, defensively, and then she changed the subject. "Put your coat on now, or you'll be late."

Walking along Highbury Street Bush asked the question he had had in mind for some time, regarding whether Hornblower had experienced good fortune lately at the Rooms. Hornblower looked at him oddly.

"Not as good as it might be" he said.

"Bad?"

"Bad enough. My opponents' aces lie behind my kings, ready for instant regicide. And my opponents' kings lie behind my aces, so that when they venture out from the security of the hand they survive all perils and take the trick. In the long run the chances right themselves mathematically. But the periods when they are unbalanced in the wrong direction can be distressing."

"I see" said Bush, although he was not too sure that he did; but one thing he did know, and that was that Hornblower had been losing. And he knew Hornblower well enough by now to know that when he talked in an airy fashion as he was doing now he was more anxious than he cared to admit.

They had reached the Long Rooms. and paused at the door.

"You'll call in for me on your way back?" asked Hornblower. "There's an eating house in Broad Street with a fourpenny ordinary. Sixpence with pudding. Would you care to try it?"

"Yes, indeed. Thank you. Good luck" said Bush, and he paused before continuing. "Be careful."

"I shall be careful" said Hornblower, and went in through the door.

The weather was in marked contrast with what had prevailed during Bush's last visit. Then there had been a black frost and an east wind; today there was a hint of spring in the air. As Bush walked along the Hard the harbour entrance revealed itself to him on his left, its muddy water sparkling in the clear light. A flush-decked sloop was coming out with the ebb, the gentle puffs of wind from the northwest just giving her steerage way. Despatches for Halifax, perhaps. Money to pay the Gibraltar garrison. Or maybe a reinforcement for the revenue cutters that were finding so much difficulty in dealing with the peacetime wave of smuggling. Whatever it was, there were fortunate officers on board, with an appointment, with three years' employment ahead of them, with a deck under their feet and a wardroom in which to dine. Lucky devils. Bush acknowledged the salute of the porter at the gate and went into the yard.

He emerged into the late afternoon and made his way back to the Long Rooms. Hornblower was at a table near the corner and looked up to smile at him, the candlelight illuminating his face. Bush found himself the latest *Naval Chronicle* and settled himself to read it. Beside him a group of army and navy officers argued in low tones regarding the difficulties of living in the same world as Bonaparte.

Malta and Genoa, Santo Domingo and Miquelet, came up in the conversation.

"Mark my words" said one of them, thumping his hand with his fist, "we'll be at war with him again soon enough."

There was a murmur of agreement.

"It'll be war to the knife" supplemented another. "If once he drives us to extremity, we shall never rest until Mr. Napoleon Bonaparte is hanging to the nearest tree."

The others agreed to that with a fierce roar, like wild beasts.

"Gentlemen" said one of the players at Hornblower's table, looking round over his shoulder. "Could you find it convenient to continue your discussion at the far end of the room? This end is dedicated to the most scientific and difficult of all games."

The words were uttered in a pleasant high tenor, but it was obvious that the speaker had every expectation of being instantly obeyed.

"Very good, my lord" said one of the naval officers.

That made Bush look more closely, and he recognised the speaker, although it was six years since he had seen him last. It was Admiral Lord Parry, who had been made a lord after Camperdown; now he was one of the commissioners of the navy, one of the people who could make or break a naval officer. The mop of snow-white curls that ringed the bald spot on the top of his head, his smooth old-man's face, his mild speech, accorded ill with the nickname of "Old Bloody bones" which had been given him by the lower-deck far back in the American War. Hornblower was moving in very high society. Bush watched Lord Parry extend a skinny white hand and cut the cards to Hornblower. It was obvious from his colouring that Parry, like Hornblower, had not been to sea for a long time. Hornblower dealt and the game proceeded in its paralysing stillness; the cards made hardly a sound as they fell on the green cloth, and each trick was picked up and laid down almost silently, with only the slightest click. The line of tricks in front of Parry grew like a snake, silent as a snake gliding over a rock, like a snake it closed on itself and then lengthened again, and then the hand was finished and the cards swept together.

"Small slam" said Parry as the players attended to their markers, and that was all that was said. The two tiny words sounded as clearly and as briefly in the silence as two bells in the middle watch. Hornblower cut the cards and the next deal began in the same mystic silence. Bush could not see the fascination of it. He would prefer a game in which he could roar at his losses and exult over his winnings; and preferably one in which the turn of a single card, and not of the whole fifty-two, would decide who had won and who had lost. No, he was wrong. There was undoubtedly a fascination about it, a poisonous fascination. Opium? No. This silent game was like the quiet interplay of duelling swords as compared with the crash of cutlass blades, and it was as deadly. A small-sword through the lungs killed as effectively as—more effectively than—the sweep of a cutlass.

"A short rubber" commented Parry; the silence was over, and the cards lay in disorder on the table.

"Yes, my lord" said Hornblower.

Bush, taking note of everything with the keen observation of anxiety, saw Hornblower put his hand to his breast pocket—the pocket that he had indicated as holding his reserve—and take out a little fold of one-pound notes. When he had made his payment Bush could see that what he returned to his pocket was only a single note.

"You encountered the worst of good fortune" said Parry, pocketing his winnings. "On the two occasions when you dealt, the trump that you turned up proved to be the only one that you held. I cannot remember another occasion when the dealer has held a singleton trump twice running."

"In a long enough period of play, my lord" said Hornblower, "every possible combination of cards can be expected."

He spoke with a polite indifference that for a moment almost gave Bush heart to believe his losses were not serious, until he remembered the single note that had been put back into Hornblower's breast pocket.

"But it is rare to see such a run of ill luck" said Parry. "And yet you play an excellent game, Mr.—Mr.—please forgive me, but your name escaped me at the moment of introduction."

"Hornblower" said Hornblower.

"Ah, yes, of course. For some reason the name is familiar to me."

Bush glanced quickly at Hornblower. There never was such a perfect moment for reminding a Lord Commissioner about the fact that his promotion to commander had not been confirmed.

"When I was a midshipman, my lord" said Hornblower, "I was seasick while at anchor in Spithead on board the *Justinian*. I believe the story is told."

"That doesn't seem to be the connection I remember" answered Parry. "But we have been diverted from what I was going to say. I was about to express regret that I cannot give you your immediate revenge, although I should be most glad to have the opportunity of studying your play of the cards again."

"You are very kind, my lord" said Hornblower, and Bush writhed—he had been writhing ever since Hornblower had given the go-by to that golden opportunity. This last speech had a flavour of amused bitterness that

K

Bush feared would be evident to the admiral. But fortunately Parry did not know Hornblower as well as Bush did.

"Most unfortunately" said Parry, "I am due to dine with Admiral Lambert."

This time the coincidence startled Hornblower into being human.

"Admiral Lambert, my lord?"

"Yes. You know him?"

"I had the honour of serving under him on the Jamaica station. This is Mr. Bush, who commanded the storming party from the *Renown* that compelled the capitulation of Santo Domingo."

"Glad to see you, Mr. Bush" said Parry, and it was only just evident that if he was glad he was not overjoyed. A commissioner might well find embarrassment at an encounter with an unemployed lieutenant with a distinguished record. Parry lost no time in turning back to Hornblower.

"It was in my mind" he said, "to try to persuade Admiral Lambert to return here with me after dinner so that I could offer you your revenge. Would we find you here if we did?"

"I am most honoured, my lord" said Hornblower with a bow, but Bush noted the uncontrollable flutter of his fingers towards his almost empty breast pocket.

"Then would you be kind enough to accept a semi-engagement? On account of Admiral Lambert I can make no promise, except that I will do my best to persuade him."

"I'm dining with Mr. Bush, my lord. But I would be the last to stand in the way."

"Then we may take it as being settled as near as may be?"

"Yes, my lord."

Parry withdrew then, ushered out by his flag lieutenant who had been one of the whist four, with all the dignity and pomp that might be expected of a peer, an admiral, and a commissioner, and he left Hornblower grinning at Bush.

"D'you think it's time for us to dine too?" he asked.

"I think so" said Bush.

The eating house in Broad Street was run, as might almost have been expected, by a wooden-legged sailor. He had a pert son to assist him, who stood by when they sat at a scrubbed oaken table on oak benches, their feet in the sawdust, and ordered their dinner.

"Ale?" asked the boy.

"No. No ale" said Hornblower.

The pert boy's manner gave some indication of what he thought about gentlemen of the navy who ate the four-penny ordinary and drank nothing with it. He dumped the loaded plates in front of them: boiled mutton—not very much mutton—potatoes and carrots and parsnips and barley and a dab of pease pudding, all swimming in pale gravy.

"It keeps away hunger" said Hornblower.

It might indeed do that, but apparently Hornblower had not kept hunger away lately. He began to eat his food with elaborate unconcern, but with each mouthful his appetite increased and his restraint decreased. In an extra-ordinarily short time his plate was empty; he mopped it clean with his bread and ate the bread. Bush was not a slow eater, but he was taken a little aback when he looked up and saw that Hornblower had finished every mouthful while his own plate was still half full. Hornblower laughed nervously.

"Eating alone gives one bad habits" he said—and the best proof of his embarrassment was the lameness of his explanation.

He was aware of that, as soon as he had spoken, and he tried to carry it off by leaning back on his bench in a superior fashion; and to show how much at ease he was he thrust his hands into the side pockets of his coat. As he did so his whole expression changed. He lost some of the little colour there was in his cheeks. There was utter consternation in his expression—there was even fear. Bush took instant alarm; he thought Hornblower must have had a seizure, and it was only after that first thought that he connected Hornblower's changed appearance with his gesture of putting his hands in his pockets. But a man who had found a snake in his pocket would hardly wear that look of horror.

"What's the matter?" asked Bush. "What in God's name——?"

Hornblower slowly drew his right hand out of his pocket. He kept it closed for a moment round what it held, and then he opened it, slowly, reluctantly, like a man fearful of his destiny. Harmless enough; it was a silver coin—a half-crown.

"That's nothing to take on about" said Bush, quite puzzled. "I wouldn't even mind finding a half-crown in my pocket."

"But—but——" stammered Hornblower, and Bush began to realise some of the implications.

"It wasn't there this morning" said Hornblower, and then he smiled the old bitter smile. "I know too well what money I have in my pockets."

"I suppose you do" agreed Bush; but even now, with his mind going back through the events of the morning, and making the obvious deductions, he could not understand quite why Hornblower should be so worried. "That wench put it there?"

"Yes. Maria" said Hornblower. "It must have been her. That's why she took my coat to sponge it."

"She's a good soul" said Bush.

"Oh God!" said Hornblower. "But I can't—I can't——"

"Why not?" asked Bush, and he really thought that question unanswerable.

"No" said Hornblower. "It's—it's—I wish she hadn't done it. The poor girl——"

"'Poor girl' be blowed!" said Bush. "She's only trying to do you a good turn."

Hornblower looked at him for a long time without speaking, and then he made a little hopeless gesture, as though despairing of ever making Bush see the matter from his point of view.

"You can look like that if you like" said Bush, steadily, determined to stick to his guns, "but there's no need to act as if the French had landed just because a girl slips half a crown into your pocket."

"But don't you see——" began Hornblower, and then he finally abandoned all attempt at explanation. Under Bush's puzzled gaze he mastered himself. The unhappiness left his face, and he assumed his old inscrutable look—it was as if he had shut down the vizor of a helmet over his face.

"Very well" he said. "We'll make the most of it, by God!"

Then he rapped on the table.

"Boy!"

"Yessir."

"We'll have a pint of wine. Let someone run and fetch it at once. A pint of wine—port wine."

"Yessir."

"And what's the pudding today?"

"Currant duff, sir."

"Good. We'll have some. Both of us. And let's have a saucer of jam to spread on it."

"Yessir."

"And we'll need cheese before our wine. Is there any cheese in the house, or must you send out for some?"

"There's some in the house, sir."

"Then put it on the table."

"Yessir."

Now was it not, thought Bush, exactly what might be expected of Hornblower that he should push away the half of his huge slice of currant duff unfinished? And he only had a nibble of cheese, hardly enough to clear his palate. He raised his glass, and Bush followed his example.

"To a lovely lady" said Hornblower.

They drank, and now there was an irresponsible twinkle in Hornblower's eyes that worried Bush even while he told himself that he was tired of Hornblower's tantrums. He decided to change the subject, and he prided himself on the tactful way in which he did so.

"To a fortunate evening" he said, raising his glass in his turn.

"A timely toast" said Hornblower.

"You can afford to play?" asked Bush.

"Naturally."

"You can stand another run of bad luck?"

"I can afford to lose one rubber" answered Hornblower.

"Oh."

"But on the other hand if I win the first I can afford to lose the next two. And if I win the first and second I can afford to lose the next three. And so on."

"Oh."

That did not sound too hopeful; and Hornblower's gleaming eyes looking at him from his wooden countenance were positively disturbing. Bush shifted uneasily in his seat and changed the conversation again.

"They're putting the *Hastings* into commission again" he said. "Had you heard?"

"Yes. Peacetime establishment—three lieutenants, and all three selected two months back."

"I was afraid that was so."

"But our chance will come" said Hornblower. "Here's to it."

"D'you think Parry will bring Lambert to the Long Rooms?" asked Bush when he took the glass from his lips.

"I have no doubt about it" said Hornblower.

Now he was restless again.

"I must be back there soon" he said. "Parry might hurry Lambert through his dinner."

"My guess is that he would" said Bush, preparing to rise.

"There's no necessity for you to come back with me if you don't care to" said Hornblower. "You might find it wearisome to sit idle there."

"I wouldn't miss it for worlds" said Bush.

XX

THE Long Rooms were full with the evening crowd. At nearly every table in the outer room there were earnest parties playing serious games, while through the curtained door that opened into the inner room came a continuous murmur that indicated that play in there was exciting and noisy. But for Bush standing restlessly by the fire, occasionally exchanging absent-minded remarks with the people who came and went, there was only one point of interest, and that was the candle-lit table near the wall where Hornblower was playing in very exalted society. His companions were the two admirals and a colonel of infantry, the latter a bulky man with a face almost as red as his coat, whom Parry had brought with him along with Admiral Lambert. The flag lieutenant who had previously partnered Parry was now relegated to the role of onlooker, and stood beside Bush, and occasionally made incomprehensible remarks about the play. The Marquis had looked in more than once. Bush had observed his glance to rest upon the table with something of approval. No matter if there were others who wanted to play; no matter if the rules of the room gave any visitor the right to join a table at the conclusion of a rubber; a party that included two flag officers and a field officer could do as it pleased.

Hornblower had won the first rubber to Bush's enormous relief, although actually he had not been able to follow the details of the play and the score well enough to know that such was the case until the cards were swept up and payments made. He saw Hornblower tuck away some money into that breast pocket.

"It would be pleasant" said Admiral Parry, "if we could restore the old currency, would it not? If the country could dispense with these dirty notes and go back again to our good old golden guineas?"

"Indeed it would" said the colonel.

"The longshore sharks" said Lambert, "meet every ship that comes in from abroad. Twenty-three and sixpence they offer for every guinea, so you can be sure they are worth more than that."

Parry took something from his pocket and laid it on the table.

"Boney has restored the French currency, you see" he said. "They call this a napoleon, now that he is First Consul for life. A twenty-franc piece—a louis d'or, as we used to say."

"Napoleon, First Consul" said the colonel, looking at the coin with curiosity, and then he turned it over. "French Republic."

"The 'republic' is mere hypocrisy, of course" said Parry. "There never was a worse tyranny since the days of Nero."

"We'll show him up" said Lambert.

"Amen to that" said Parry, and then he put the coin away again. "But we are delaying the business of the evening. I fear that is my fault. Let us cut again. Ah, I partner you this time, colonel. Would you care to sit opposite me? I omitted to thank you, Mr. Hornblower, for your excellent partnership."

"You are too kind, my lord" said Hornblower, taking the chair at the admiral's right.

The next rubber began and progressed silently to its close.

"I am glad to see that the cards have decided to be kind

to you, Mr. Hornblower" said Parry, "even though our honours have reduced your winnings. Fifteen shillings, I believe?"

"Thank you" said Hornblower, taking the money.

Bush remembered what Hornblower had said about being able to afford to lose three rubbers if he won the first two.

"Damned small stakes in my opinion, my lord" said the colonel. "Must we play as low as this?"

"That is for the company to decide" replied Parry. "I myself have no objection. Half a crown instead of a shilling? Let us ask Mr. Hornblower."

Bush turned to look at Hornblower with renewed anxiety.

"As you will, my lord" said Hornblower, with the most elaborate indifference.

"Sir Richard?"

"I don't mind at all" said Lambert.

"Half a crown a trick, then" said Parry. "Waiter, fresh cards, if you please."

Bush had hurriedly to revise his estimate of the amount of losses Hornblower could endure. With the stakes nearly trebled it would be bad if he lost a single rubber.

"You and I again, Mr. Hornblower" said Parry, observing the cut. "You wish to retain your present seat?"

"I am indifferent, my lord."

"I am not" said Parry. "Nor am I yet so old as to decline to change my seat in accordance with the run of the cards. Our philosophers have not yet decided that it is a mere vulgar superstition."

He heaved himself out of his chair and moved opposite Hornblower, and play began again, with Bush watching more anxiously even than at the start. He watched each side in turn take the odd trick, and then three times running he saw Hornblower lay the majority of tricks in front of him. During the next couple of hands he lost count of the score, but finally he was relieved to see only two tricks before the colonel when the rubber ended.

"Excellent" said Parry, "a profitable rubber, Mr. Hornblower. I'm glad you decided to trump my knave of hearts. It must have been a difficult decision for you, but it was undoubtedly the right one."

"It deprived me of a lead I could well have used" said Lambert. "The opposition was indeed formidable, colonel."

"Yes" agreed the colonel, not quite as good-temperedly. "And twice I held hands with neither an ace nor a king, which helped the opposition to be formidable. Can you give me change, Mr. Hornblower?"

There was a five-pound note among the money that the colonel handed over to Hornblower, and it went into the breast pocket of his coat.

"At least, colonel" said Parry, when they cut again, "you have Mr. Hornblower as your partner this time."

As the rubber proceeded Bush was aware that the flag-lieutenant beside him was watching with greater and greater interest.

"By the odd trick, by George!" said he when the last cards were played.

"That was a close shave, partner" said the colonel, his good humour clearly restored. "I hoped you held that queen, but I couldn't be sure."

"Fortune was with us, sir" said Hornblower.

The flag lieutenant glanced at Bush; it seemed as if the flag lieutenant was of opinion that the colonel should have been in no doubt, from the previous play, that Hornblower held the queen. Now that Bush's attention was drawn to it, he decided that Hornblower must have thought just the same—the slightest inflection in his voice implied it—but was sensibly not saying so.

"I lose a rubber at five pounds ten and win one at fifteen shillings" said the colonel, receiving his winnings from Lambert. "Who'd like to increase the stakes again?"

To the credit of the two admirals they both glanced at Hornblower without replying.

"As you gentlemen wish" said Hornblower.

"In that case I'm quite agreeable" said Parry.

"Five shillings a trick, then" said the colonel. "That makes the game worth playing."

"The game is always worth playing" protested Parry.

"Of course, my lord" said the colonel, but without suggesting that they should revert to the previous stakes.

Now the stakes were really serious; by Bush's calculation a really disastrous rubber might cost Hornblower twenty pounds, and his further calculation told him that Hornblower could hardly have more than twenty pounds tucked away in his breast pocket. It was a relief to him when Hornblower and Lambert won the next rubber easily.

"This is a most enjoyable evening" said Lambert, and he smiled with a glance down at the fistful of the colonel's money he was holding; "nor am I referring to any monetary gains."

"Instructive as well as amusing" said Parry, paying out to Hornblower.

Play proceeded, silently as ever, the silence only broken by the brief interchanges of remarks between rubbers. Now that he could afford it, fortunately, Hornblower lost a rubber, but it was a cheap one, and he immediately won another profitable one. His gains mounted steadily with hardly a setback. It was growing late, and Bush was feeling weary, but the players showed few signs of fatigue, and the flag lieutenant stayed on with the limitless patience he must have acquired during his present appointment, philosophic and fatalistic since he could not possibly do anything to accelerate his admiral's decision to go to bed. The other players drifted away from the room; later still the curtained door opened and the gamblers from the inner room came streaming out, some noisy, some silent, and the Marquis made his appearance, silent and unruffled, to watch the final rubbers with unobtrusive interest, seeing to it that the candles were snuffed and fresh ones brought, and new cards ready on demand. It was Parry who first glanced at the clock.

"Half-past three" he said. "Perhaps you gentlemen——?"

"Too late to go to bed now, my lord" said the colonel. "Sir Richard and I have to be up early, as you know."

"My orders are all given" said Lambert.

"So are mine" said the colonel.

Bush was stupid with long late hours spent in a stuffy atmosphere, but he thought he noticed an admonitory glance from Parry, directed at the two speakers. He wondered idly what orders Lambert and the colonel would have given, and still more idly why they should be orders that Parry did not wish to be mentioned. There seemed to be just the slightest trace of hurry, just the slightest hint of a desire to change the subject, in Parry's manner when he spoke.

"Very well, then, we can play another rubber, if Mr. Hornblower has no objection?"

"None at all, my lord."

Hornblower was imperturbable; if he had noticed anything remarkable about the recent interchange he gave no sign of it. Probably he was weary, though—Bush was led to suspect that by his very imperturbability. Bush knew by now that Hornblower worked as hard to conceal his human weaknesses as some men worked to conceal ignoble birth.

Hornblower had the colonel as partner, and no one could be in the room without being aware that this final rubber was being played in an atmosphere of even fiercer competition than its predecessors. Not a word was spoken between the hands; the score was marked, the tricks swept up, the other pack proffered and cut in deadly silence. Each hand was desperately close, too. In nearly every case it was only a single trick that divided the victors and the vanquished, so that the rubber dragged on and on with painful slowness. Then a hand finished amid a climax of tension. The flag lieutenant and the Marquis had kept count of the score, and when Lambert took the last trick they uttered audible sighs, and the colonel was so moved that he broke the silence at last.

"Neck and neck, by God!" he said. "This next hand must settle it."

But he was properly rebuked by the stony silence with which his remark was received. Parry merely took the cards from the colonel's right side and passed them over to Hornblower to cut. Then Parry dealt, and turned up the king of diamonds as trump, and the colonel led. Trick succeeded trick. For a space, after losing a single trick, Lambert and Parry carried all before them. Six tricks lay before Parry, and only one before Hornblower. The colonel's remark about being neck and neck was fresh in Bush's ears. One more trick out of the next six would give the rubber to the two admirals. Five to one was long odds, and Bush uncomfortably resigned himself to his friend losing this final rubber. Then the colonel took a trick and the game was still alive. Hornblower took the next trick, so that there was still hope. Hornblower led the ace of diamonds, and before it could be played to he laid down his other three cards to claim the rest of the tricks; the queen and knave of diamonds lay conspicuously on the table.

"Rubber!" exclaimed the colonel, "we've won it, partner! I thought all was lost."

Parry was ruefully contemplating his fallen king.

"I agree that you had to lead your ace, Mr. Hornblower" he said, "but I would be enchanted to know why you were so certain that my king was unguarded. There were two other diamonds unaccounted for. Would it be asking too much of you to reveal the secret?"

Hornblower raised his eyebrows in some slight surprise at a question whose answer was so obvious.

"You were marked with the king, my lord" he said, "but it was the rest of your hand which was significant, for you were also marked with holding three clubs. With only four cards in your hand the king could not be guarded."

"A perfect explanation" said Parry; "it only goes to confirm me in my conviction that you are an excellent whist player, Mr. Hornblower."

"Thank you, my lord."

Parry's quizzical smile had a great deal of friendship in it. If Hornblower's previous behaviour had not already won Parry's regard, this last coup certainly had.

"I'll bear your name in mind, Mr. Hornblower" he said. "Sir Richard has already told me the reason why it was familiar to me. It was regrettable that the policy of immediate economy imposed on the Admiralty by the Cabinet should have resulted in your commission as commander not being confirmed."

"I thought I was the only one who regretted it, my lord."

Bush winced again when he heard the words; this was the time for Hornblower to ingratiate himself with those in authority, not to offend them with unconcealed bitterness. This meeting with Parry was a stroke of good fortune that any half-pay naval officer would give two fingers for. Bush was reassured, however, by a glance at the speakers. Hornblower was smiling with infectious lightheartedness, and Parry was smiling back at him. Either the implied bitterness had escaped Parry's notice or it had only existed in Bush's mind.

"I was actually forgetting that I owe you a further thirty-five shillings" said Parry, with a start of recollection. "Forgive me. There, I think that settles my monied indebtedness; I am still in your debt for a valuable experience."

It was a thick wad of money that Hornblower put back in his pocket.

"I trust you will keep a sharp lookout for footpads on your way back, Mr. Hornblower" said Parry with a glance.

"Mr. Bush will be walking home with me, my lord. It would be a valiant footpad that would face him."

"No need to worry about footpads tonight" interposed the colonel. "Not tonight."

The colonel wore a significant grin; the others displayed a momentary disapproval of what apparently was an indiscretion, but the disapproval faded out again when the colonel waved a hand at the clock.

"Our orders go into force at four, my lord" said Lambert.

"And now it is half-past. Excellent."

The flag lieutenant came in at that moment; he had slipped out when the last card was played.

"The carriage is at the door, my lord" he said.

"Thank you. I wish you gentlemen a good evening, then."

They all walked to the door together; there was the carriage in the street, and the two admirals, the colonel, and the flag lieutenant mounted into it. Hornblower and Bush watched it drive away.

"Now what the devil are those orders that come into force at four?" asked Bush. The earliest dawn was showing over the rooftops.

"God knows" said Hornblower.

They headed for the corner of Highbury Street.

"How much did you win?"

"It was over forty pounds—it must be about forty-five pounds" said Hornblower.

"A good night's work."

"Yes. The chances usually right themselves in time.' There was something flat and listless in Hornblower's tone as he spoke. He took several more strides before he burst out into speech again with a vigour that was in odd contrast. "I wish to God it had happened last week. Yesterday, even."

"But why?"

"That girl. That poor girl."

"God bless my soul!" said Bush. He had forgotten all about the fact that Maria had slipped half a crown into Hornblower's pocket and he was surprised that Hornblower had not forgotten as well. "Why trouble your head about her?"

"I don't know" said Hornblower, and then he took two more strides. "But I do."

Bush had no time to meditate over this curious avowal, for he heard a sound that made him grasp Hornblower's elbow with sudden excitement.

"Listen!"

Ahead of them, along the silent street, a heavy military tread could be heard. It was approaching. The faint light shone on white crossbelts and brass buttons. It was a military patrol, muskets at the slope, a sergeant marching beside it, his chevrons and his half-pike revealing his rank.

"Now, what the deuce——?" said Bush.

"Halt!" said the sergeant to his men; and then to the other two, "May I ask you two gentlemen who you are?"

"We are naval officers" said Bush.

The lantern the sergeant carried was not really necessary to reveal them. The sergeant came to attention.

"Thank you, sir" he said.

"What are you doing with this patrol, sergeant?" asked Bush.

"I have my orders, sir" replied the sergeant. "Begging your pardon, sir. By the left, quick—march!"

The patrol strode forward, and the sergeant clapped his hand to his half-pike in salute as he passed on.

"What in the name of all that's holy?" wondered Bush. "Boney can't have made a surprise landing. Every bell would be ringing if that were so. You'd think the press gang was out, a real hot press. But it can't be."

"Look there!" said Hornblower.

Another party of men was marching along the street, but not in red coats, not with the military stiffness of the soldiers. Checked shirts and blue trousers; a midshipman marching at the head, white patches on his collar and his dirk at his side.

"The press gang for certain!" exclaimed Bush. "Look at the bludgeons!"

Every seaman carried a club in his hand.

"Midshipman!" said Hornblower, sharply. "What's all this?"

The midshipman halted at the tone of command and the sight of the uniforms.

"Orders, sir" he began, and then, realising that with the growing daylight he need no longer preserve secrecy, especially to naval men, he went on. "Press gang, sir. We've orders to press every seaman we find. The patrols are out on every road."

"So I believe. But what's the press for?"

"Dunno, sir. Orders, sir."

That was sufficient answer, maybe.

"Very good. Carry on."

"The press, by jingo!" said Bush. "Something's happening."

"I expect you're right" said Hornblower.

They had turned into Highbury Street now, and were making their way along to Mrs. Mason's house.

"There's the first results" said Hornblower.

They stood on the doorstep to watch them go by, a hundred men at least, escorted along by a score of seamen with staves, a midshipman in command. Some of the pressed men were bewildered and silent; some were talking volubly—the noise they were making was rousing the street. Every man among them had at least one hand in a trouser pocket; those who were not gesticulating had both hands in their pockets.

"It's like old times" said Bush with a grin. "They've cut their waistbands."

With their waistbands cut it was necessary for them to keep a hand in a trouser pocket, as otherwise their trousers would fall down. No one could run away when handicapped in this fashion.

"A likely looking lot of prime seamen" said Bush, running a professional eye over them.

"Hard luck on them, all the same" said Hornblower.

"Hard luck?" said Bush in surprise.

Was the ox unlucky when it was turned into beef? Or for that matter was the guinea unlucky when it changed hands? This was life; for a merchant seaman to find himself a sailor of the King was as natural a thing as for his hair to turn grey if he should live so long. And the only way to secure him was to surprise him in the night, rouse him out of bed, snatch him from the grog shop and the brothel, converting him in a single second from a free man earning his livelihood in his own way into a pressed man who could not take a step on shore of his own free will without risking being flogged round the fleet. Bush could no more sympathise with the pressed man than he could sympathise with the night being replaced by day.

Hornblower was still looking at the press gang and the recruits.

"It may be war" he said, slowly.

"War!" said Bush.

"We'll know when the mail comes in" said Hornblower. "Parry could have told us last night, I fancy."

"But—war!" said Bush.

The crowd went on down the street towards the dock-yard, its noise dwindling with the increasing distance, and Hornblower turned towards the street door, taking the ponderous key out of his pocket. When they entered the house they saw Maria standing at the foot of the staircase, a candlestick with an unlighted candle in her hand. She wore a long coat over her nightclothes; she had put on her mobcap hastily, for a couple of curling papers showed under its edge.

"You're safe!" she said.

"Of course we're safe, Maria" said Hornblower. "What do you think could happen to us?".

"There was all that noise in the street" said Maria. "I looked out. Was it the press gang?"

"That's just what it was" said Bush.

"Is it—is it war?"

"That's what it may be."

"Oh!" Maria's face revealed her distress. "Oh!"

Her eyes searched their faces.

"No need to worry, Miss Maria" said Bush. "It'll be many a long year before Boney brings his flat-bottoms up Spithead."

"It's not that" said Maria. Now she was looking only at Hornblower. In a flash she had forgotten Bush's existence.

"You'll be going away!" she said.

"I shall have my duty to do if I am called upon, Maria" said Hornblower.

Now a grim figure appeared climbing the stairs from the basement—Mrs. Mason; she had no mobcap on so that her curl papers were all visible.

"You'll disturb my other gentlemen with all this noise" she said.

"Mother, they think it's going to be war" said Maria.

"And not a bad thing perhaps if it means some people will pay what they owe."

"I'll do that this minute" said Hornblower hotly. "What's my reckoning, Mrs. Mason?"

"Oh, please, please——" said Maria interposing.

"You just shut your mouth, miss" snapped Mrs. Mason. "It's only because of you that I've let this young spark run on."

"Mother!"

" 'I'll pay my reckoning' he says, like a lord. And not a shirt in his chest. His chest'd be at the pawnbroker's too if I hadn't nobbled it."

"I said I'd pay my reckoning and I mean it, Mrs. Mason" said Hornblower with enormous dignity.

"Let's see the colour of your money, then" stipulated Mrs. Mason, not in the least convinced. "Twenty-seven and six."

Hornblower brought a fistful of silver out of his trouser pocket. But there was not enough there, and he had to extract a note from his breast pocket, revealing as he did so that there were many more.

"So!" said Mrs. Mason. She looked down at the money

in her hand as if it were fairy gold, and opposing emotions waged war in her expression.

"I think I might give you a week's warning, too" said Hornblower, harshly.

"Oh no!" said Maria.

"That's a nice room you have upstairs" said Mrs. Mason. "You wouldn't be leaving me just on account of a few words."

"Don't leave us, Mr. Hornblower" said Maria.

If ever there was a man completely at a loss it was Hornblower. After a glance at him Bush found it hard not to grin. The man who could keep a cool head when playing for high stakes with admirals—the man who fired the broadside that shook the *Renown* off the mud when under the fire of red-hot shot—was helpless when confronted by a couple of women. It would be a picturesque gesture to pay his reckoning—if necessary to pay an extra week's rent in lieu of warning—and to shake the dust of the place from his feet. But on the other hand he had been allowed credit here, and it would be a poor return for that consideration to leave the moment he could pay. But to stay on in a house that knew his secrets was an irksome prospect too. The dignified Hornblower who was ashamed of ever appearing human would hardly feel at home among people who knew that he had been human enough to be in debt. Bush was aware of all these problems as they confronted Hornblower, of the kindly feelings and the embittered ones. And Bush could be fond of him even while he laughed at him, and could respect him even while he knew of his weaknesses.

"When did you gennelmen have supper?" asked Mrs. Mason.

"I don't think we did" answered Hornblower, with a side glance at Bush.

"You must be hungry, then, if you was up all night. Let me cook you a nice breakfast. A couple of thick chops for each of you. Now how. about that?"

"By George!" said Hornblower.

"You go on up" said Mrs. Mason. "I'll send the girl up with hot water an' you can shave. Then when you come down there'll be a nice breakfast ready for you. Maria, run and make the fire up."

Up in the attic Hornblower looked whimsically at Bush.

"That bed you paid a shilling for is still virgin" he said. "You haven't had a wink of sleep all night and it's my fault. Please forgive me."

"It's not the first night I haven't slept" said Bush. He had not slept on the night they stormed Samaná; many were the occasions in foul weather when he had kept the deck for twenty-four hours continuously. And after a month of living with his sisters in the Chichester cottage, of nothing to do except to weed the garden, of trying to sleep for twelve hours a night for that very reason, the variety of excitement he had gone through had been actually pleasant. He sat down on the bed while Hornblower paced the floor.

"You'll have plenty more if it's war" Hornblower said; and Bush shrugged his shoulders.

A thump on the door announced the arrival of the maid of all work of the house, a can of hot water in each hand. Her ragged dress was too large for her—handed down presumably from Mrs. Mason or from Maria—and her hair was tousled, but she, too, turned wide eyes on Hornblower as she brought in the hot water. Those wide eyes were too big for her skinny face, and they followed Hornblower as he moved about the room, and never had a glance for Bush. It was plain that Hornblower was as much the hero of this fourteen-year-old foundling as he was of Maria.

"Thank you, Susie" said Hornblower; and Susie dropped an angular curtsey before she scuttled from the room with one last glance round the door as she left.

Hornblower waved a hand at the wash-hand stand and the hot water.

"You first" said Bush.

Hornblower peeled off his coat and his shirt and addressed himself to the business of shaving. The razor blade rasped on his bristly cheeks; he turned his face this way and that so as to apply the edge. Neither of them felt any need for conversation, and it was practically in silence that Hornblower washed himself, poured the wash water into the slop pail, and stood aside for Bush to shave himself.

"Make the most of it" said Hornblower. "A pint of fresh water twice a week for shaving'll be all you'll get if you have your wish."

"Who cares?" said Bush.

He shaved, restropped his razor with care, and put it back into his roll of toilet articles. The scars that seamed his ribs gleamed pale as he moved. When he had finished dressing he glanced at Hornblower.

"Chops" said Hornblower. "Thick chops. Come on."

There were several places laid at the table in the dining-room opening out of the hall, but nobody else was present; apparently it was not the breakfast hour of Mrs. Mason's other gentlemen.

"Only a minute, sir" said Susie, showing up in the door-way for a moment before hurrying down into the kitchen.

She came staggering back laden with a tray; Hornblower pushed back his chair and was about to help her, but she checked him with a scandalised squeak and managed to put the tray safely on the side table without accident.

"I can serve you, sir" she said.

She scuttled back and forward between the two tables like the boys running with the nippers when the cable was being hove in. Coffee-pot and toast, butter and jam, sugar and milk, cruet and hot plates and finally a wide dish which she laid before Hornblower; she took off the cover and there was a noble dish of chops whose delightful scent, hitherto pent up, filled the room.

"Ah!" said Hornblower, taking up a spoon and fork to serve. "Have you had your breakfast, Susie?"

"Me, sir? No, sir. Not yet, sir."

Hornblower paused, spoon and fork in hand, looking from the chops to Susie and back again. Then he put down the spoon and thrust his right hand into his trouser pocket.

"There's no way in which you can have one of these chops?" he said.

"Me, sir? Of course not, sir."

"Now here's half a crown."

"Half a crown, sir!"

That was more than a day's wages for a labourer.

"I want a promise from you, Susie."

"Sir—sir——!"

Susie's hands were behind her.

"Take this, and promise me that the first chance that comes your way, the moment Mrs. Mason lets you out, you'll buy yourself something to eat. Fill that wretched little belly of yours. Faggots and pease pudding, pig's trotters, all the things you like. Promise me."

"But sir——"

Half a crown, the prospect of unlimited food, were things that could not be real.

"Oh, take it" said Hornblower testily.

"Yes, sir."

Susie clasped the coin in her skinny hand.

"Don't forget I have your promise."

"Yes, sir, please sir, thank you, sir."

"Now put it away and clear out quick."

"Yes, sir."

She fled out of the room and Hornblower began once more to serve the chops.

"I'll be able to enjoy my breakfast now" said Hornblower self-consciously.

"No doubt" said Bush; he buttered himself a piece of toast, dabbed mustard on his plate—to eat mustard with mutton marked him as a sailor, but he did it without a thought. With good food in front of him there was no need for thought, and he ate in silence. It was only when Hornblower spoke again that Bush realised that Hornblower had been construing the silence as accusatory of something.

"Half a crown" said Hornblower, defensively "may mean many things to many people. Yesterday——"

"You're quite right" said Bush, filling in the gap as politeness dictated, and then he looked up and realised that it was not because he had no more to say that Hornblower had left the sentence uncompleted.

Maria was standing framed in the dining-room door; her bonnet, gloves, and shawl indicated that she was about to go out, presumably to early marketing since the school where she taught was temporarily closed.

"I—I looked in to see that you had everything you wanted" she said. The hesitation in her speech seemed to indicate that she had heard Hornblower's last words, but it was not certain.

"Thank you. Delightful" mumbled Hornblower.

"Please don't get up" said Maria, hastily and with a hint of hostility, as Hornblower and Bush began to rise. Her eyes were wet.

A knocking on the street door relieved the tension, and Maria fled to answer it. From the dining-room they heard a masculine voice, and Maria reappeared, a corporal of marines towering behind her dumpy form.

"Lieutenant Hornblower?" he asked.

"That's me."

"From the admiral, sir."

The corporal held out a letter and a folded newspaper. There was a maddening delay while a pencil was found for Hornblower to sign the receipt. Then the corporal took his leave with a clicking of heels and Hornblower stood with the letter in one hand and the newspaper in the other.

"Oh, open it—please open it" said Maria.

Hornblower tore the wafer and unfolded the sheet. He read the note, and then reread it, nodding his head as if the note confirmed some preconceived theory.

"You see that sometimes it is profitable to play whist" he said, "in more ways than one."

He handed the note over to Bush; his smile was a little lopsided.

SIR [read Bush]

It is with pleasure that I take this opportunity of informing you in advance of any official notification that your promotion to Commander is now confirmed and that you will be shortly appointed to the Command of a Sloop of War.

"By God, sir!" said Bush. "Congratulations. For the second time, sir. It's only what you deserve, as I said before."

"Thank you" said Hornblower. "Finish reading it."

The arrival at this moment of the Mail Coach with the London newspapers [said the second paragraph] enables me to send you the information regarding the changed situation without being unnecessarily prolix in this letter. You will gather from what you read in the accompanying copy of the

Sun the reasons why conditions of military secrecy should prevail during our very pleasant evening so that I need not apologise for not having enlightened you, while I remain,

Your obedient servant,

PARRY

By the time Bush had finished the letter Hornblower had opened the newspaper at the relevant passage, which he pointed out to Bush.

Message from HIS MAJESTY

House of Commons, March 8, 1803

The CHANCELLOR OF THE EXCHEQUER brought down the following message from HIS MAJESTY:

"His Majesty thinks it necessary to acquaint the House of Commons, that, as very considerable military preparations are carrying on in the ports of France and Holland, he has judged it expedient to adopt additional measures of precaution for the security of his dominions.

GEORGE R."

That was all Bush needed to read. Boney's fleet of flat-bottomed boats, and his army of invasion mustered along the Channel coast, were being met by the appropriate and necessary countermove. Last night's press-gang measures, planned and carried out with a secrecy for which Bush could feel nothing except wholehearted approval (he had led too many press gangs not to know how completely seamen made themselves scarce at the first hint of a press) would provide the crews for the ships necessary to secure England's safety. There were ships in plenty, laid up in every harbour in England; and officers—Bush knew very well how many officers were available. With the fleet manned and at sea England could laugh at the treacherous attack Boney had planned.

"They've done the right thing for once, by God!" said Bush, slapping the newspaper.

"But what is it?" asked Maria.

She had been standing silent, watching the two men, her glance shifting from one to the other in an endeavour to read their expressions. Bush remembered that she had winced at his outburst of congratulation.

"It'll be war next week" said Hornblower. "Boney won't endure a bold answer."

"Oh" said Maria. "But you—what about you?"

"I'm made commander" said Hornblower. "I'm going to be appointed to a sloop of war."

"Oh" said Maria again.

There was a second or two of agonised effort at self-control, and then she broke down. Her head drooped farther and farther, until she put her gloved hands to her face, turning away from the two men so that they only saw her shoulders with the shawl across them, shaking with sobs.

"Maria" said Hornblower gently. "Please, Maria, please don't."

Maria turned and presented a slobbered face to him, unevenly framed in the bonnet which had been pushed askew.

"I'll n-n-never see you again" sobbed Maria. "I've been so happy with the m-m-mumps at school, I thought I'd m-m-make your bed and do your room. And n-now this happens!"

"But, Maria" said Hornblower—his hands flapped helplessly—"I've my duty to do."

"I wish I was d-dead! Indeed I wish I was dead!" said Maria, and the tears poured down her cheeks to drip upon her shawl; they streamed from eyes which had a fixed look of despair, while the wide mouth was shapeless.

This was something Bush could not endure. He liked pretty, saucy women. What he was looking at now jarred on him unbearably—perhaps it rasped his aesthetic sensibility, unlikely though it might seem that Bush should have such a thing. Perhaps he was merely irritated by the spectacle of uncontrolled hysteria, but if that was the case he was irritated beyond all bearing. He felt that if he had to put up with Maria's water-works for another minute he would break a blood vessel.

"Let's get out of here" he said to Hornblower.

In reply he received a look of surprise. It had not occurred to Hornblower that he might run away from a situation for which his temperament necessarily made him feel responsible. Bush knew perfectly well that, given time, Maria would recover. He knew that women who wished themselves dead one day could be as lively as crickets the next day after another man had chucked them under the chin. In any case he did not see why he and Hornblower should concern themselves about something which was entirely Maria's fault.

"Oh!" said Maria; she stumbled forward and supported herself with her hands upon the table with its cooling coffee-pot and its congealing half-consumed chops. She lifted her head and wailed again.

"Oh, for God's sake——" said Bush in disgust. He turned to Hornblower. "Come along."

By the time Bush was on the staircase he realised that Hornblower had not followed him, would not follow him. And Bush did not go back to fetch him. Even though Bush was not the man to desert a comrade in peril; even though he would gladly take his place in a boat launching out through the most dreadful surf to rescue men in danger; even though he would stand shoulder to shoulder with Hornblower and be hewn to pieces with him by an overwhelming enemy; for all this he would not go back to save Hornblower. If Hornblower was going to be foolish Bush felt he could not stop him. And he salved his conscience by telling himself that perhaps Hornblower would not be foolish.

Up in the attic Bush set about rolling up his nightshirt with his toilet things. The methodical checking over of his razor and comb and brushes, seeing that nothing was left behind, soothed his irritated nerves. The prospect of immediate employment and immediate action revealed itself to him in all its delightful certainty, breaking through the evaporating clouds of his irritation. He began to hum to himself tunelessly. It would be sensible to call in again at the dockyard—he might even look in at the Keppel's Head to discuss the morning's amazing news; both courses would be advisable if he wanted to secure for himself quickly a new appointment. Hat in hand he tucked his neat package under his arm and cast a final glance round the room to make sure that he had left nothing, and he was still humming as he closed the attic door behind him. On the staircase, about to step down into the hall, he stood for a moment with one foot suspended, not in doubt as to whether he should go into the dining-room, but arranging in his mind what he should say when he went in.

Maria had dried her tears. She was standing there smiling, although her bonnet was still askew. Hornblower was smiling too; it might be with relief that Maria had left off weeping. He looked round at Bush's entrance, and his face revealed surprise at the sight of Bush's hat and bundle.

"I'm getting under way" said Bush. "I have to thank you for your hospitality, sir."

"But—" said Hornblower "you don't have to go just yet."

There was that "sir" again in Bush's speech. They had been through so much together, and they knew so much about each other. Now war was coming again, and Hornblower was Bush's superior officer. Bush explained what he wanted to do before taking the carrier's cart back to Chichester, and Hornblower nodded.

"Pack your chest" he said. "It won't be long before you need it."

Bush cleared his throat in preparation for the formal words he was going to use.

"I didn't express my congratulations properly" he said portentously. "I wanted to say that I don't believe the Admiralty could have made a better choice out of the whole list of lieutenants when they selected you for promotion, sir."

"You're too kind" said Hornblower.

"I'm sure Mr. Bush is quite right" said Maria.

She gazed up at Hornblower with adoration shining in her face, and he looked down at her with infinite kindness. And already there was something a little proprietorial about the adoration, and perhaps there was something wistful about the kindness.